Sicilian Nights

Zara Fitch

To Lydia
Memories of Taormina!
Thank you
Zara

Published in 2013 by FeedARead.com Publishing –
Arts Council funded

A CIP catalogue record for this title is available from the British Library.

Chapter One

Hadn't she thought it would be so easy loving Tony when she first met him that summer in Taormina?

"You've got to come over here, Sarah, I keep telling you, it's paradise." Her friend Ruth was a holiday rep working the season in Sicily.

"I know, but…"

"Come on, love, you need a break from that stuffy old museum, doesn't that dreadful boss of yours ever let you have holidays?"

"Of course she does, Meredith isn't that bad," Sarah replied, ever the loyal employee.

"Well, then, what are you waiting for, it will do you good to get away. You've had a rotten time, love, I know that, what with your dad dying and then that bastard Michael walking out on you. You're still not over him, are you? It's been months now and you're still pining away. You can't go on fretting for him forever, you know, you've got to get on with your life."

Sarah sighed, knowing it was true, yet still feeling raw from her losses. After what she had thought were two happy years together, Michael had suddenly disappeared from her life. Coming home from work one day she had found all evidence of him gone. No note, nothing. Not even a dirty sock. She'd never really got over the shock of him walking out like that. Happening so soon after the death of her dad, it came as a double blow.

"Come on, love, come over here as soon as you can," Ruth said. "I promise you we'll have fun."

Although she didn't feel like going on a jolly holiday, the following week, as she was walking back from Tesco, she found herself booking a flight at the local travel agents who assured her Sicily was an increasingly popular destination. What the hell, she thought, maybe Ruth was right, it would do her good.

Flying alone was a thrilling experience, her tummy turned over on take-off and three hours later the hot air hit her as she stepped down from the plane, a feeling of excitement bubbling within her. Emerging at the arrivals at Catania, she could feel the foreignness surrounding her. A language that sounded like gibberish. Men in dark glasses standing around, sun-tanned arrogance in their stance. Taxi drivers, coach drivers, leering and waiting, looking her up and down, making her feel self-conscious as she scanned the chaos for a sign of Ruth. No one was smiling. She spotted Ruth outside jabbering on her mobile. Feeling relief, she dragged her case out into the hot sunshine and suddenly Ruth was hugging her.

"*Benvenuto*! Welcome to Sicilia. I'm so pleased to see you again, Sarah, it's been ages!" They laughed and hugged. "God, you do look white, love, but don't worry, you'll soon get a tan here."

"I certainly hope so, it's boiling!" Sarah felt pasty and sweaty, her long sleeve t-shirt sticking to her armpits, her jeans thick and tight, her long hair hanging heavy around her face.

"Come on, let's get to the bus quickly, the air con is on full blast." Ruth's blonde curls bounced as she tottered in her high heels across the road, dressed in her short blue skirt and white shirt, the uniform of SunStops

Travel. “About time you came out to see me, don’t you think, it is my second year here, after all.”

“I wanted to see what you are raving about.”

“Oh, you’ll soon see, love, I promise you.”

Sarah looked out at the horizon, the volcano rising above the city in the haze of the heated afternoon.

Ruth pulled her suitcase onto the bus. “Jesus, love, what on earth have you got in here, bricks?”

“Well, you warned me how glamorous it is here, so I want to look my best, don’t I?” Sarah smiled.

“I’m sure you will. I can see you’ve kept that perfect figure of yours. Unlike me, I’m always battling with the bulges.” Ruth had always worried about her weight, Sarah remembered. When they had worked together at Fosters, the publishing house, Ruth was constantly on a diet, oscillating between extreme denial and excessive indulgence.

Ruth didn’t stop talking all the way back to the hotel. Sarah would rather have contemplated the views skimming past, the run-down streets of the city of Catania, the highway running along the coast, and finally the dramatic drive up the mountain to Taormina, a medieval town built on a cliff overlooking the sea. As the bus climbed higher and higher, the drive became breathtaking. Sarah gasped. “It’s magical, like something out of a fairy tale,” she said, gazing out at the cypress trees, cerise and orange bougainvillea, the deep blue sky and flat azure sea, Mount Etna smoking in the distance.

“Oh love, I’m so used to it, I don’t even bother to look any more,” Ruth replied, waving her hand, dismissing Sarah’s rapture.

Ruth had booked Sarah into a charming hotel near the centre of town, her own apartment being too small to accommodate any guests. Everything was chintzy and kitsch, clean and tidy. Long shuttered windows opened to a small balcony facing the bay below and the volcano in the distance.

"It's amazing." Sarah stood on the balcony, transfixed by the view.

"I thought you'd say that. Happens to us all, this enchantment. Course it can become a fatal attraction, this place." Ruth sighed.

"What do you mean? It's paradise, isn't it?"

"Yes, it is and that's why I wanted you to come. Let's take a wander into town, I've got the rest of the afternoon off."

Everything was up hill and down. Cobbled stone sloping steep streets and steps. Views of the mountains and sea. Narrow streets, crooked quaint apartments, small balconies crammed with flowers in pots, cascading colour. Palm trees and bougainvillea. And jasmine everywhere, delicate white flowers, gathered in masses. Secret steps leading somewhere, hidden narrow passageways and turnings, unsuspected layers of life, siestas behind shutters. Smells and shouts, children skipping on the street, scooters roaring heedless and fearless, no pavements to separate safety from danger. The charming decay of the district. Ancient walls, churches and squares. Old fashioned faces, glamorous girls, men and boys staring boldly. The long wide Corso Umberto lined with cafés and bars, designer shops, touristic gifts, pizzas, snacks, gelato.

Ruth led them to a small café where they sat outside sipping chilled white wine. "Cheers, love, here's to your arrival."

"And here's to us," Sarah replied, the sun warm on her back, the wine dry yet fruity. The prospect of a whole week ahead here in this enchanting place filled her with a sense of anticipation and excitement.

Back at the hotel having sat on the balcony contemplating the peace and beauty laid out before her she tore herself away to get ready for her first night out on the town as Ruth called it. She unpacked all her clothes, hoping the creases would fall out with the heat. Dressing carefully in a frothy layered skirt, silk strappy top and high-heeled sandals, her chestnut-coloured hair piled up attractively, displaying her long delicate neck, she looked at her reflection as she applied her make-up, her grey eyes wide and innocent. She felt suddenly as if she was someone else, as if being here she was getting away from herself. She felt liberated somehow. She could be who she wanted, do what she wanted.

Ruth met her in the small reception of the hotel. "Get a look at you! All glammed up and dressed to kill!"

Sarah laughed. "Let's hit the town then!"

They ate at one of Ruth's favourite restaurants, sitting outside in the small garden, trees and shrubs surrounding them, blocking out the road outside. Crisp white napkins were shaken out and placed on their laps by the handsome smiling young waiters. Ruth flirted and ordered for them. "Leave it all to me, love, they know me here."

Sarah was impressed and drank back the complimentary welcome glass of prosecco. They ate an *antipasto* plate of mixed raw fish to share, followed by spaghetti *alla Norma*. "It's traditional here, this dish, any pasta, but always with *melanzana*, that's aubergine to you, ricotta cheese and tomatoes. Delicious." Ruth tucked in before Sarah had managed to get any onto her fork, needing the spoon to help her. Between them they drank a bottle of good white wine, though as Ruth explained all the wines were good in Sicily. After that came tiramisu, espresso and limoncello.

"I'm full to the brim, Ruth. Not to mention drunk." Sarah felt unsteady as they left the restaurant and started to walk up the street leading to the Corso, her high heels, the cobbled streets and uneven steps impeding her progress even further.

"The night's young yet, love. Let's go and have a drink."

The Corso was busy, people walking leisurely, after-dinner strolls. Ruth stopped outside a small bar entitled Stella Luna, the signs of the moon and stars hanging with tiny lanterns. Inside it looked dark. "Look, I've never been in here, love. Don't know why. Want to give it a try, your first night and a first time for both of us?"

Sarah shrugged. "Yes, anywhere will do so long as I can sit down."

Inside it was dimly lit and the air seemed heavy and intimate. The theme continued with lights in the shape of stars, small wooden tables each with a star candle and small wooden chairs lining the walls.

"These shoes are killing me," Sarah said, plonking herself down at a table, leaving Ruth to go up to the bar and order their drinks.

"Hey, have you seen that dish?" Ruth returned, putting the shots of sambuca on the table.

"What?" Sarah had slipped off one of her sandals and was rubbing her foot.

"Him. Look. He's staring right at you. Singing his heart out to you he is, listen to him." Ruth grinned at him, showing her white teeth and pink gums, and raised her glass.

Sarah looked up and giggled, feeling rather dizzy, not accustomed to all the drinking or male attention they seemed to receive wherever they went. She slipped her sandal on quickly.

"He's gorgeous, isn't he, look at him, all that dark hair and those blue eyes. But a lot older than you, I'd say. More my type," she said, nudging Sarah.

"Oh, stop it," Sarah said, returning his stare, secretly flattered.

Everyone was clapping. The singer stood up from the piano and bowed. He lingered at the bar. Suddenly more drinks arrived at their table and there he was standing in front of them.

"May I join you?" he asked, sitting down before waiting for a reply.

"Of course, please do. You play and sing so beautifully," Ruth enthused, shaking her hair and leaning forward to show her tanned cleavage. He shrugged and thanked her, looking at Sarah. She sipped her sambuca, smiling sedately over the top of her sticky glass, feeling too tipsy to speak.

"Do you sing?" he asked, looking at her as he lit a cigarette, tossing the packet on the table. Philip Morris.

"What? Me?" Sarah asked, shaking her head, feeling herself going hot as he stared at her with his brilliant blue eyes. "Only sometimes."

"Only in the shower," Ruth laughed.

"But you can sing, no?" he asked, smiling at her.

"Karaoke nights there have been many, but not too many of them were sober," Sarah said, referring to memorable nights at the Pickwick Papers pub with her friends from the museum.

He shook his head and smiled, obviously not understanding.

"Course I'd like to," she continued, rephrasing things after another sip of sambuca. "I love all those mellow tunes, you know. I go to Brighton and listen to live jazz in the streets, it's great."

"You do? So why don't you sing with me now?"

"What?"

"Why not, come on, I have to go back for a few more songs. Tell me, what do you know. How about *The Girl from Ipanema*?"

"What? You must be joking." She laughed.

"You know it, surely, it's a famous song. Come on." He stood up, stubbed out his cigarette and took her hand, pulling her up. Finding herself standing beside his piano, still holding the glass of sambuca, she knocked back the remains, suddenly feeling far too sober.

"I don't think I'm up to it, sorry." She was about to turn away when the spotlight appeared to be on them.

He put his hand on her shoulder. "Don't worry, I count you in, one, two, then you sing with me, okay."

It wasn't okay but she did it, as drunk as she was, as wobbly as her voice sounded, she did it. He sang with her, supporting her voice and she kept looking at him, not knowing whether she wanted to laugh or scream, piss her knickers or run out of the bar. Then it was over as suddenly as it began.

"God, Sarah, I must be completely pissed but that sounded quite good. Since when did you have a voice like that?" Ruth looked at her in amazement as Sarah sat back down at the table, her legs about to give way.

Sarah laughed, feeling exhilarated and relieved. "We are both drunk, silly, that's why I sounded half decent. God knows I wouldn't have had the guts to do it sober. In fact I need another drink, I'm shaking."

"You're not bad," he said, sitting down with them as a bottle of prosecco arrived.

Sarah laughed again. "Just a fluke."

"A what?"

"It doesn't matter. It won't happen again."

"Why not? Did you not enjoy it? Singing with me, I mean?" He looked at her.

"Sure I did." She smiled at him, feeling her heart flip over.

"Okay, then." He poured the sparkling wine into the flutes and raised his to Sarah. "Here's to success." He looked at her, his blue eyes insistent. "Come and have lunch with me tomorrow and we can talk more about your singing," he said, handing her his card. "Call me."

"What a smoothie he is," Ruth said as they walked back to the hotel, the smell of jasmine scenting the night air. "You didn't waste your time either, did you?"

Sarah giggled, "He's lovely, isn't he?"

"Yeah, but be careful, Sarah, you can't just go out to lunch with him, you know."

"Why not?" Sarah was still wobbling, her heart still thumping.

"Well, I mean, he'll want more than that, won't he? How many lunches do you think you'll manage before he gets tired of you?"

"Give me a chance, I haven't had one yet."
"Well, it's up to you."
"You're the one who told me to come out here and have fun."
"All I'm saying is, be careful. You don't know what these men are like, I do. I've been here long enough and I can tell you they are trouble."
"Okay, I won't go then."
"No, you go, but don't say I didn't warn you. Don't come crying to me."
"Alright, I won't."

Sarah went back to her hotel room, annoyed with Ruth and smitten with Tony. She couldn't believe she had stood up and sung with a handsome stranger in a bar in Sicily. Who would have thought it possible? She looked down at the card still clutched in her hand. Antonio Pagano, gold italic script on midnight blue.

Lying in bed she went over and over the scene, cringing at her performance, wondering what Tony must have thought of her. She felt weak just remembering how he looked at her. She got up and drank some water, feeling dehydrated after all the alcohol, not wanting a headache in the morning.

Standing on the terrace after breakfast she called his number with a shaking hand. On the street below there were people shouting, cars beeping and motorbikes roaring, while Etna stood majestic and silent above them all. Ruth sat waiting inside, having come to see Sarah to make up, suggesting she call him on her mobile.

"Sorry I was stern with you last night, love, it's only because I care about you and I don't want you to be hurt again."

"But it was you who told me to come here to forget about Michael, remember?"

"I know, I just didn't think it would happen on the night you arrived, that's all. And what a night it was. Anyway, come on, tell me, what did he say?"

"We are having lunch today at the beach."

"Where?"

"Somewhere called Spisone, the Dolce Vita?"

"Yes, I know it, very nice."

"So, do I have your blessing?"

"Yes, of course you have, love. I have to go to work anyway, so I can't be with you all the time. Go for it girl." She kissed Sarah's cheek. "See you later, I want to hear all about it."

He collected her on his shiny silver Vespa. He wore jeans and a blue t-shirt, his dark hair blown back by the breeze, his blue eyes covered by dark glasses. If he was hoping to impress her, it was working. Looking down at her pale legs in her shorts she wished she had applied some fake tan before she had flown out here. She struggled to get on the back of the scooter and clutched onto him, her arms around his waist, as they drove down to the beach. She closed her eyes, too afraid to look at the road ahead, though once she got used to it there was something exhilarating about driving so fast, dodging the cars.

At the Dolce Vita, a small café on the beach, he ordered them a plate of bruschetta and a bottle of white wine, Corvo Glicine. Sarah drank her first glass almost in one gulp, hoping it would calm her nerves but it made her giggly.

"I am serious, you know. About the singing. Do you sing in England?" he asked, pouring more wine into her glass.

Sarah laughed. "Course not. I work in a museum."

"Oh. But singing is better, I think, no? Would you like to try it again? Tonight?"

"You're not serious, surely?" She found his deep blue eyes rather disarming.

"Of course I am. I am serious about everything."

Ruth was right, he did want more than lunch. It was a week in paradise: lying on the rocks in the hot sticky sunshine, listening to the waves rolling in; speeding on the scooter up to the mountains, eating figs from the trees; walking round the Byzantine church, crumbling in isolation; climbing up broken steps to castles, exploring old palaces and the ruins of tiny hillside towns. He picked her wild flowers and fed her ice cream, peeled her blood-red oranges and told her stories of the ancient island once called Trinacria, the three-cornered isle, now the symbol of Sicily, the face of Medusa with three legs.

Every evening she would go to the Stella Luna and listen to him play the piano, sitting up at the bar on a high stool, her bare knees and shoulders polished and shiny by the sun, sipping a glass of chilled prosecco. His dark hair shining in the low lights, his blue eyes beaming on her, she felt he was singing only for her and she thrilled to the glamorous hours she was spending with him. Each night he would ask her to sing with him and she was surprised at how confident she began to feel, singing beside him, all those jazz numbers she loved and knew so well. *Satin Doll. Someone to Watch Over Me. I'm Thru With Love.*

Afterwards they would walk the winding way home to her hotel, his arm around her shoulder. He would stop and kiss her under the jasmine tree, his kiss as soft and sweet and heady as the smell of the jasmine growing up the walls of the old hotel, climbing high above her. The tiny white flowers were like stars in the sky, there were so many of them. "Jasmine belongs to the night. It's the smell of Sicily," he whispered to her. "The smell of love."

He came up to her room every night. It was so easy and natural. For Sarah the intimacy was as instant and unexpected as the singing.

"I worship your body, Sarah," he said, sighing as he ran his hand over the smooth skin of her flat tummy, up to the roundedness of her breast. He kissed the tip. She laughed and looked down at herself, almost objectively, seeing how her body excited him. Creamy and soft, she was blessed with good skin, almost unblemished, and a fat free figure, no matter how many cream cakes she consumed. "I adore you, Sarah," he continued as he kissed her thigh down to her toes, looking at her as he did so.

She had always played down her rather unusual, striking looks, was always more modest than she should be, shy even. Michael had never made much fuss about her, ever practical as he was. Hardly erotic, he had even been known to keep his socks on, since his feet were always cold. But Tony made her feel glorious, his goddess, as he called her. She couldn't have imagined feeling like this. Tony was an expert lover. She ventured to tell him. It was their last night together and they lay in bed trying to stretch out the hours they had left to share.

"And so I should be," he replied, laughing. "I am over forty, you know, though I don't look it. You are much younger, I can tell. And not so experienced, but that is what I like," he said, kissing her neck.

"But how old do you think I am?" she asked.

He studied her face, taking in her clear grey eyes, her soft smooth skin, her long dark chestnut hair. "I think you are something like twenty years old. Too young."

"For what? For you? Anyway, you're wrong, I'm much older than that, so there."

He stroked her cheek and sighed, becoming serious. "The problem is, Sarah, I don't want you to go home. I know this is your little adventure and so it must end. But..."

"What?" She sat up looking at him.

"I want you to stay here. We could sing together at the bar."

"But I have to go home. I have a job to go back to, my family."

"I am offering you a job here."

"But I'm not really a singer. As much as I would love to be."

"I am offering you the chance, don't you see that?"

Sarah shook her head. "It's not that easy. I have to go back home, Tony."

"Why? Don't you want to stay here with me?"

She looked at him, feeling sad. This was just a holiday romance wasn't it, good while it lasted. She couldn't expect anything more. Could she?

Ruth took her to the airport on her minibus. It was an early flight. Sarah felt sick.

"Oh love, what on earth has happened to you, I thought this would do you good, but you look terrible. I've hardly seen you all week. You've got it bad, I can see."

Tears were rolling down Sarah's cheeks. "I wouldn't even let him come to the airport. I've rejected him, Ruth, but I think I love him."

"Sarah, the idea was to have a good time, not to fall in love."

Sarah tried to smile through her tears, dabbing at her eyes with an already soggy tissue.

"I'm sorry, love, you know this is all my fault."

Sarah shook her head. "I'm glad it happened. I'm glad I came." She watched the scenery roll by, the beauty of it breaking her heart.

"Look, we've got time, let's have a coffee now that you are all checked in," Ruth said, leading the way to the small crowded café bar.

They stood with plastic cups of cappuccino and Sarah watched the brown sugar slowly sink through the foamy milk.

"I've met someone too," Ruth said, looking at Sarah.

"Who?"

"Just some married guy. You met him at the Stella Luna, he was there one night. He's a lifeguard. Tall. Called Saro, remember?"

Sarah couldn't, not immediately. Then she remembered. His teeth. Black at the tops. Bad caps. "Oh Ruth, really? Are you sure?"

"What do you mean?"

"Well, especially if he is married."

"That's got nothing to do with it. Anyway, I like him."

"And you were the one telling me to be careful."

"Come to that, how much do you know about your precious Tony?"

"Not everything, obviously."

"Well then."

"Well then what?"

"Who knows what he is hiding."

"He isn't hiding anything. In fact he wants me to stay here and sing with him full time at the bar."

"Bloody hell, and you said no?"

"Of course I did. It's a crazy idea. And he's a lot older than me."

"But you could give it a try, why not? It would be great for me if you were here. And if it doesn't work out you can always just go home."

Sarah sighed. "We'll see."

Back at Gatwick, Sarah told herself the best thing she could do would be to forget all about that week in another world. She returned to her job at the Museum of East London, sitting at the computer entering numbers and information, cataloguing collections of ceramics and pieces of stone unearthed from ancient civilisations. Her eyes were blurry and sometimes her mind would drift back to that place full of bougainvillea flowering everywhere, the sun shining on the waves, the layers of colour in the sky, the volcano smoking in the distance, and Tony beside her. She would go home after work to her little flat, cook herself an egg on toast and look over at the railway station and Tesco in the distance, a mug of tea in her hand.

A few weeks after she got back Tony rang. She couldn't believe it.

"Have you forgotten me already, Sarah?"

"No, of course not."

"So, when are you coming back?" he asked.

"I don't know. Maybe next summer," she said, trying to play it cool.

"How can I wait that long? Come here and sing with me. It will work, I told you before." He paused. "You cannot forget how good it was. You and me. Come for the start of the season, after *Pasqua*."

"After what?"

"Easter."

"I can't."

"Later, then, but not too late."

"I shall try," Sarah said, trying not to feel too excited at this insane prospect.

"Please, promise me you will come back soon. I am waiting."

Could he mean it, she wondered, did he really want her to come back? Was she not just one of many pretty girls sitting at the bar catching his eye? How many girls got up and sang with him? There would be other girls and other hotels, she was sure.

He called her every week and sent her postcards of the places they had visited, churches and beaches, the volcano at sunset and views of the town, to remind her of that week. Not that she could forget, she thought of nothing else. So vivid was that week in her life it was as if she had lived no other. She kept the jasmine he had picked for her pressed between the pages of her diary, the fragrance didn't fade; for Sarah it was the smell of

Sicily. Sicily was in her blood now. Or was it Tony? Her frozen heart had defrosted, melted perhaps too quickly.

The long grey days of winter finally turned to spring and Sarah announced to her boss that she would be giving a month's notice.

"Well, this is all very sudden, Sarah, I must say. Can you not take some leave if you want to get away for a while?" Meredith sat behind her desk looking at Sarah over the top of her glasses that were attached to a chain round her neck, her fine grey hair pulled back into a tight bun.

"I haven't got enough leave, I intend to go away for the whole summer," Sarah replied, hearing her voice quaver.

"The whole summer? Well, I suppose we could stretch to giving you a month's leave or some extra weeks, unpaid of course."

"Thank you, Meredith, but I have made my decision." Sarah clutched the file of papers she was holding, feeling hot and red-faced.

Meredith coughed. "Well, I suppose you know what you are doing, but really you might have given me further notice."

"My contract does say a month."

"Yes, but, well, we are beyond a contract, Sarah, or so I thought."

Sarah bit her tongue so that the word sorry would not slip out. Four years of making tea for Meredith, collecting her dry cleaning and buying her cheeses from Covent Garden, in between cataloguing the department's collection had been quite enough. She was convinced she was doing the right thing.

Sarah's mother Margaret was bewildered when she announced she would be returning to Taormina for the summer. She had been secretly scheming rather than sharing her plan with her family.

"How many months in Tallomena?" her mother asked, incredulous. "Why on earth do you want to go back to that hole for that long?"

"It's Taormina, Mum, and it's not a hole, it's a beautiful place."

"I cannot think why you have given up your job to go there. That was a good job, Sarah."

"I'm going to Sicily to be a singer," Sarah stated as matter of factly as she could.

"You what?" her mother's tea cup clattered onto the saucer.

"I told you how good it was, singing in the bar, well I've been offered a job there for the summer."

"Singing? Where?"

"Oh Mum, I told you all about the jazz bar, remember?"

Her mother looked at Sarah as if she was speaking another language. "For goodness sake Sarah, that was a bit of fun, you're not serious, surely."

"Yes, I am. I was good in the choir at school, don't you remember?"

"But that was years ago. What singing have you ever done since then?"

"Not a lot, but my voice has been discovered."

"Discovered? By who?"

Her sister Lily came in from the kitchen carrying her cup of tea and a packet of shortbread biscuits. "What's all this?" she asked.

"I've never heard anything like it, Lily, our Sarah reckons she is going back to Sicily to be a singer. A singer!"

"With that man you mentioned?" Lily asked.

"What man?" Sarah's mother looked alarmed.

"Mum, I told you about Tony, I even showed you his picture, don't you remember?" Sarah sighed, wondering if her mother had gone batty. She noticed her mother had become very forgetful since her father had died, she had been so dependent on him, even relying on him to remember things for her.

"Oh Sarah, haven't you learnt your lesson, haven't you been hurt enough?" her mother asked.

"Yes, but this is different, Mum. I need to get over Michael once and for all and get on with my life."

"Giving up your job and running after some dreadful foreigner, you think that's going to do it, do you?"

"He isn't dreadful, actually." Sarah blushed, thinking of Tony. "He is handsome and talented. And he likes me. Actually he loves me."

"What? Loves you? And what on earth are you going to live on? Love?" her mother scoffed.

"I'm going to earn money. It's a proper job, you know. And anyway, I've got my savings, the money Daddy left me. I mean I am almost 25, it's about time I did something adventurous, and I've always wanted to travel."

"But that's not travelling. You've been there already."

"Yes, I know, but I like it."

"You've been strange ever since you got back from that wretched place. God knows what goes on there."

Her mother sniffed like she always did when she felt indignant.

"Mum, nothing goes on. Ruth is there too, so I have a friend. I can even get a job with her if it doesn't work out at the bar."

"What, doing what she does, a glorified Butlins hostess."

"Mum, she is no such thing. She works hard for that travel company and sometimes she feels quite lonely."

"More fool her then for staying. She's probably having a grand old time, always did like the men, and over there in the Mediterranean, well, as I say, it's a free for all in those bloody countries."

"Ruth is not immoral, she just falls in love easily."

"That's a good way of putting it. Looks like you do as well." Her mother finished her tea and collected the empty cups onto the tray. "Heaven knows what your brother will say about all this," she muttered, walking out to the kitchen.

Having remained silent, continuing to eat one shortbread finger after another, Lily put down her teacup and sat beside Sarah on the sofa. "Look, Sarah, Mum is only worried for you. I mean it sounds great on the surface, of course it does, like something from a movie. We are happy for you, course we are. But concerned, naturally. Especially Mum. You know how upset and ill she has been since Dad died, you know it hasn't been easy for her. She's more protective about you because you're her baby. Me and Andy, well, we're older, we've been married, made our own lives, we can look after ourselves and she can do without us."

"No she can't, she loves you and Andy just as much as me."

"Yes, but she doesn't worry about us in the same way. She will worry about you going away like this." Lily looked at Sarah. "We all will."

Sarah sighed. "Don't try to make me feel guilty, Lily. I have to grow up some time, I can't stay the baby forever," she said. Walking over to the fireplace she looked at the photo of her father on the shelf above it. She missed him and the talks they used to have, pottering about together at the end of the garden, tending to the patch of mint and vines of tomatoes and beans. "Dad told me to get on with my life while I was young. He said I mustn't waste it. He told me to follow my heart. And that is what I'm doing."

Chapter Two

Part of her knew she was being reckless, hardly stopping to think about what she was doing. She rented out her small apartment in Ilford to a professional couple for three months, teachers at the local primary school, pleased that this would more than cover her mortgage. A month later she packed her battered suitcase, full to bursting point: twenty pairs of knickers, various pairs of shorts, jeans, t-shirts, skirts, silky tops, satin nightdresses, bikinis and sarongs, seven pairs of sandals and enough toiletries to set up her own stall, including tubes of Immac and waxing strips that she had never used before in her life but felt sure she'd need.

Andy took her to the airport, leaving her with brotherly warnings as he kissed her goodbye. "Be careful, Sarah, and don't forget, you can call me for anything, whenever you want. Oh, and I expect a postcard."

Arriving at Catania airport in the late afternoon, she decided to take the train along the coast to the foot of the town. Emerging from the old elegant railway station, she stood on the kerb, the sun shining into her eyes as she gazed up at the buildings clinging to the steep slopes of Taormina. She couldn't quite believe she had returned. She didn't tip the lecherous taxi driver who took her up the mountain, dropping her at the top of the narrow street where Tony lived, the house where she had never quite managed to get to that week last summer. He had never invited her.

Lugging her heavy case down the few steps to his house, she stood at the front door, checking it was the right number. Suddenly feeling nervous, she tugged at her hair pulled up into a pony tail, wondering if she looked alright in her short skirt, strappy t-shirt and flip-flops. She could hear a piano. She felt uncertain, wondering what on earth she had done, not having warned Tony of her arrival, wanting to surprise him. She tapped on the door, hesitant, her fist a sweaty ball. The playing stopped. Silence. She tapped again, louder. The door opened slightly, his face appeared, dark hair falling into his blue eyes. "*Chi è*?"

"Hello, Tony," she said looking up at him, instantly devastated by his beauty.

"Sarah? *Mamma mia*! It cannot be true!"

"Yes, it is, here I am!" She threw her arms around him and he pulled her into the apartment, smothering her with kisses. Coming up for air, she stepped back. He looked even better than she remembered. "I wanted to surprise you, are you pleased?" she asked.

"*Certo*! Of course I am. Finally you have come back, my pretty English girl. I have been waiting for this moment." He took her in his arms again and held her tight. She closed her eyes as she clung to him, trembling. "Come on, let me get your case," he said. "You must be tired after your journey. I make you a coffee, are you hungry?" he asked.

"No, I ate on the plane. Plastic food, semi edible."

He laughed and walked across the untidy sitting room to the kitchen. She looked around her, trying to take it all in, noticing how dark and dusty and damp it was. In front of the silent flickering tv there was a low wooden table jumbled with photos, videos, keys, empty packets of gum and dirty glasses. On the other side of the room was a shabby sofa, piles of papers and books beside it, the electric keyboard in the corner. Following him, she sat on a chair full of clean washing thrown over the back, at least she thought it was clean. The kitchen table was cluttered: a plate with a broken brioche, an ash tray full of cigarette butts, empty coffee cups, stains and crumbs. He must have had people in. People. Friends. Women…

What a mess this place is, she thought. She hadn't imagined him living like this. His surroundings didn't match the glamorous image of him.

The tiny coffee pot heated on the hob, the coffee bubbling up through the spout, the smell surrounding them. He spooned brown sugar into the tiny cups and stirred and stirred. "Fresh espresso!" he said and smiled, handing her a cup. He drank his in one gulp standing by the sink. "*Buona*?" he asked, watching her.

"Yes. Very good." She sipped the bitter sweet coffee, looking at him, feeling it was all too unreal, as if the time separating them had faded. Their eyes locked together and she stood up to face him, the tingling desire running down to her toes. His kiss tasted of coffee.

"I want to play something for you," he said, pulling away from her. "It's something I have written myself." He sat at the piano. She followed him and watched as his fingers skimmed the keys, longing to reach out and touch them. She looked at his tall straight back, his hair shiny and black, sliced through with grey. "This is for you, Sarah, I have written this song for you. And later you can sing it." She sat on the sofa covered in dogs hairs and cried as he played something soft and romantic, looking at her, singing to her about love once found should never be lost. Afterwards he sat beside her on the sofa and kissed the tears from her face. "Sweet Sarah, I was not sure you would really come back."

"I didn't need much persuading." She smiled at him. "All those phone calls, all those postcards, you were very persistent."

"I don't give up so easily." He smiled then frowned. "Have you booked a room somewhere?" he asked.

"No," she shook her head, looking at him expectantly.

He took her hand. "Of course I want you to stay here tonight, but then we must find you a hotel. I have to think of my son."

"Your son?" she pulled her hand away. "You have a son?" She couldn't believe she had heard it right.

"Um, yes, I have a son, Roberto. He lives with me but he is away with his grandmother, my mother, visiting relatives in the country, they come back tomorrow."

"Oh." She stared at him as if he was a stranger. She realised he was.

"Look, here is a picture of him." He pulled out a crumpled photo from under one of the piles on the littered table. "It's an old one, but this is him, this is Roberto. He's seven now. That's his mother. We are not together now, of course. She lives in Paris."

"Oh. I see." But she couldn't look for long at the blurred image of Tony beside a tall blonde woman, a small fair-haired boy standing in between them.

She stood up and looked around her, realising there was no evidence of a child in the house, no toys or books scattered in the clutter. She walked to her suitcase, not knowing what to do, feeling hot and sticky and sick. "I have to use the bathroom," she said.

"Of course, are you okay, you look so pale?"

"I… I'm shocked, Tony. I mean, you never told me you had a son."

He shrugged. "No. But, it's no problem, you like children, yes?"

"Well…"

He put his arms around her. "Come on, Sarah, don't worry. You just arrived. *Stai tranquilla.*"

She didn't understand what he meant. "I'll just be a minute," she said, pulling away from him. She found the bathroom, locked the door and vomited. Splashing cold water on her face she looked up at herself in the spotted mirror. What have I done, coming here like this. Nothing is what I thought it was. He has a child. A son. And he lives in a hovel. She looked up at the blotchy black damp on the ceiling, a huge water boiler dripping into the bath. She shuddered, thinking of her tiled white bathroom at home, cool and clean. Clinical, Lily called it. But preferable to this. She shook her head and patted her face, smoothing the water on to her hair.

She returned to the kitchen. Tony looked at her. "Better?" he asked, without waiting for a reply. He took her into his arms. "Come here, Sarah, I know how to make you feel better." He kissed her and suddenly picking her up, carried her to his bedroom, like a bride.

"Tony!" she squealed, "what are you doing!"

From the open window the smell of jasmine filled the dark room. He laid her on to the bed and began to undress her, gently and carefully, as if he was unwrapping a precious gift.

Wasn't this what she had been waiting for, dreaming about for almost a year?

He was right, he did know how to make her feel better. After the ecstasy of their reunion they lay together quietly, listening to the birdsong outside the window and shouts on the street. "I shall cook something for us now, something special." He kissed her upturned nipple. "Why don't you have a shower and then you can watch me cook, okay."

The shower wasn't as awful as she had thought it would be. At least the water was hot. She changed into a cool cotton dress and watched him as he sliced the aubergines, fried them with garlic and olive oil, and boiled the linguine, *al dente*. He cleared the table and lit two candles. While the cooking simmered he opened a bottle of white wine from the fridge and poured it into crystal glasses taken from an ancient cupboard with doors that didn't close properly.

"Here's to our happy reunion," he said, holding out his glass to Sarah's. "Isn't it wonderful to be together again?" They sipped and kissed, the bubbly wine fizzing into her nose.

Struggling with the pasta, Tony showed her how to twirl the linguine on to her fork, feeding her a mouthful from his own. After dinner they sat on the shabby sunken sofa and he showed her dusty photograph albums of his childhood, his mother and father, his relatives, and the blonde woman and his son.

"I think it's sad to see time pass like this," she said, wondering why he was showing her his past, angry again that he had never bothered to mention he had a son and once had a wife.

"No, not sad, Sarah. We must live for the moment and be happy," he said, looking at her. She wondered if their moment had passed, that week of last summer faded already. He added fresh cold wine to the warmed remains in their glasses. "Let us drink to us, Sarah, to now. I am so happy you are here."

"Are you really?" she asked.

"*Certamente*."

And he spent the night showing her just how happy.

Spending the night with Tony was a dream but on waking, reality reminded her that she couldn't stay with him. The reality was he had a son. Had she really expected to arrive on his doorstep and move straight in? Maybe she had. But finding out he had a son changed everything. It was no longer just him and her as he had led her to believe last year.

"You should've told me, don't you think?" She looked at him as they drank coffee at the dirty kitchen table.

"Told you what?"

"That you have a child and he lives with you."

He sighed. "Yes, but I was afraid it would put you off."

"Well, it's a bit of a shock coming like this, so it would have been better if you had told me earlier, don't you think."

He sighed again. "But it doesn't change anything between us, Sarah."

"Oh no? It changes everything."

"It doesn't change how I feel about you. Wanting you to be here, to sing with me."

"Maybe that is the only reason you want me here." She felt so hurt she wanted to be spiteful, to hurt him back.

"Come on, please, don't start like this. I am so happy you have come back. You will soon get to know Roberto and you will see, everything will be fine. Let's take it slowly, hmm?" He kissed her softly and she felt her resentment subsiding.

After breakfast he made some calls and found her a reasonably priced apartment on the other side of town. Although everything was within walking distance in Taormina, the apartment was still a trek from the town, all uphill winding roads and steps. The narrow one-way streets were just as bewildering for the driver, not that Sarah had any intention of hiring a scooter as Tony suggested. The apartment was plainly furnished, old fashioned but clean, with a balcony and a view of the volcano dominating the horizon.

"Is it okay, Sarah, do you like it? I will pay the rent, of course." He kissed her as they stood on the balcony looking out at the view.

"Oh Tony, of course I do. Thank you." She flung her arms around him in a gesture of gratitude. She didn't question whether he could afford it, though judging by where he lived he couldn't be making that much money.

"You can start at the bar tonight, okay, we can go over some songs this afternoon."

"You don't waste any time, do you?" Sarah had to laugh despite wondering what she had let herself in for.

It wasn't going to be as easy as she thought. She didn't have a trained voice, nothing like it, but she was good enough, just about. It was still the beginning of the season so the bar wasn't full. She had to drink two glasses of wine before she could sing. But she pulled it off, somehow, still considering the whole thing to be some kind of fluke, for someone to stand up and tell her who did she think she was kidding. Instead, people clapped. Afterwards, standing at the bar beside Tony, his arm around her shoulder, being served more wine, she couldn't believe it was happening.

They drove back to her apartment on his Vespa, blasting on the road around the bay beside the dark beckoning waters in the coolness of the night, the stars shining above them, the moon lighting their way.

He stayed with her that night. His son hadn't returned as expected, they would come home the next day, but he explained it was better that she didn't sleep at his house again as the neighbours would only talk about her, and his son and mother would be told all kinds of stories.

"You did well tonight, let's celebrate," he said, opening a bottle of prosecco he had brought from the bar, kissing her lips softly as he handed her the glass. "Did you enjoy it, Sarah?"

"Yes," she laughed. "It was great, I could get used to this life." She sprawled on the wicker sofa, feeling dizzy.

"Do it then, do it for me, for us." He sat down beside her on the sofa.

"I feel drunk, Tony." She giggled again, feeling the room spin.

"Come on, let's go to bed," he said, taking the glass from her hand and putting it down on the table.

The next day, feeling sick at the prospect and hungover from the wine, she met Tony's mother and son. They were invited to lunch at his mother's apartment on the Corso. Signora Carlotta Agata Maria Pagano did not speak much English and Sarah didn't speak much Italian. Tony translated what he wanted when he wanted which resulted in Sarah sitting in silence for most of the lunch while Tony gabbled on to his mother in between mouthfuls of macaroni. Several times she imagined they were talking about her. Having been introduced as Tony's "friend from England", Roberto had looked at Sarah and then seemed to forget her, intent on his food as he was, while Carlotta maintained a grudging politeness, fixing her every so often with a stern gaze.

It was a cramped dark place with shuttered windows, threadbare furniture, old fashioned antimacassars on the fraying armchairs and dark wooden furniture that dominated the room. Sarah looked at the walls full of photos: Tony's father, long since dead of a heart attack, Tony as a child, the three of them at a picnic in the countryside, smiling. There were other photos of another family threesome, Tony with the blonde and the boy, various happy scenes that Sarah turned away from. She looked at Carlotta, dressed in black, her thick iron grey hair curling round her thin lined face. Her mouth remained turned down throughout the lunch, only turning up when Roberto directed his attention to her, demanding more pasta, the tomato sauce smeared around his mouth, or another glass of water which he slurped noisily. He was a chubby child with soft fair hair, big blue eyes and thick blond lashes, obviously taking after his mother, Sarah thought as she studied him, noticing the contrast with Tony who was dark and thin.

"How long you stay in Sicily?" Carlotta asked, offering her more of the red country wine with a frosty smile, which Sarah accepted since it seemed to make the time pass more tolerably. It seemed to be helping the hangover too.

"I'm not sure," she replied, looking at Tony.

"You see all the island, is better, no, not only stay here?" The dark beads of her eyes bored into Sarah's, almost threatening.

"Well, yes, I would like to do that," she replied politely, looking again at Tony who was laughing and joking with his son, oblivious to her discomfort.

"Yes, I think you should. Not stay here." She repeated the words slowly.

Sarah gulped more of her wine, unprepared for such hostility.

Finally they left Carlotta's house. Sarah couldn't wait to get away. "Looks like your mother has already heard some of those nasty stories if her reception of me was anything to go by," she said to Tony as they walked up the Corso.

Tony took her hand. "Please, Sarah, think nothing of it. She is just a little old lady, protective and jealous of her precious son and grandson. It will be better next time, you will see."

After many kisses and much fussing from his father, Roberto pulled away and ran off to meet his friends playing in the Piazza IX Aprile, the main big square. She watched him join the gang of kids shooting toy guns and kicking a ball. She thought most of the children were very spoilt, running wild at all hours, crying and screaming, every whim pandered to.

"Your son doesn't think much of me either," she said. "He didn't even say goodbye to me."

"He's just a kid, Sarah, kids are like that. He needs to get used to you, that's all. Don't worry. Now, come on, let's go back to your apartment," Tony said, taking her hand again.

She squeezed his warm strong hand, feeling proud to be seen walking beside him, tall and commanding as he was, practically every other person exchanging *Ciao* with him so that Sarah gave up asking who all these people were. Tony knew everyone and everyone knew him: people he went to school with, old friends, acquaintances, distant relatives, cousins of cousins. The whole town was related. "Interbreeds," Ruth called them. "That accounts for why they are all so strange and backward. Bloody interbreeds, that's what they are."

Tony made them coffee in her tiny kitchen and as they stood on the terrace facing the volcano, he told her the story of the lady who walked up Mount Etna in the nineteenth century, shedding her many layers of petticoats as she ascended. It was never certain if she ever came down to collect them. Sarah found it incredible that everyone lived beneath this presence, simultaneously moody and menacing as well as beautiful and bountiful. She watched the misty colours surrounding the mountain, pale pinks and blues, stretching sheaths of colour, as the sun behind the clock tower lit up the sky like sparkling gold. Below them a car passed, top down, playing KC and the Sunshine Band, '*Rock You Baby*', while the volcano smoked, spreading a white cloud across the sun.

He took her hand. "Let's take a rest, eh?" he suggested.

Sitting on the edge of the bed he took off his leather shoes and sighing, lay back on the bed. "Come here, beside me," he said, looking up at her. She slipped off her flip-flops and jumped on to the bed. His head on her lap, she stroked his hair, so black and shiny though grey streaks were clearly visible, and studied his face; his classical Roman nose, his mouth a cupid's bow, his eyes almond shaped, deep blue with a fringe of black lashes. Looking at him made her feel dizzy with desire.

He looked up at her, serious and silent. "You make me feel better," he said, finally. "You're so beautiful, and the best thing of all, you're mine." She smiled down at him, her silky hair falling into his face as she kissed his perfect mouth.

They started to practice every afternoon and perform every night except Monday when the bar closed. She walked to the bar each evening, wobbling over the cobbles and up the uneven steps. There she was plied with unlimited prosecco and romantic love songs. "This one is for Sarah," he would say and she would raise her glass to him, drinking happily until the moment she was asked to join him for a few numbers. Her heart would raise to her throat as she toppled down from her stool, but once she stood up and sang, the adrenalin kicked in and she was flying. *Love Letters. Body and Soul. All of Me*. Sometimes tourists would speak to her after, wanting to buy her drinks and talk about music and the beauty of Taormina. Tony would get jealous if men stood talking to her for too long. He would join her quickly, his arm around her shoulder, establishing immediately that she was his.

She hadn't actually been paid anything yet, but Tony said he was agreeing with the manager of the bar that she would get about thirty euros each evening. At least she didn't need to find money for the rent and hardly spent any money on food, not wanting to pile on the pounds with overdoses of pasta. Not that she was ever invited to the daily family lunches at Carlotta's. Tony would come to her apartment after, make them a small pot of coffee after which they would make love. She was aware that she wasn't being included in the family scene but kept apart, on the other side of town, almost like a mistress. She thought about this, telling herself she didn't mind, as she sat on the terrace eating crackers and cheese, olives and fruit. It was romantic and thrilling like this, she thought, looking out at the volcano, smouldering in the distance.

One afternoon Tony arrived earlier than usual. "I'm taking you shopping," he announced.

"What?" She put down her book.

"You cannot continue to wear jeans and t-shirts, you know. You have to look the part. You are sexy, Sarah, don't you see, but look how you dress. This is not England. Come on, let's go."

Sarah felt insulted, thinking her look of jeans, high-heeled sandals, halter-neck tops and silver hoop ear-rings was sexy enough in an understated way. Obviously not.

He took her to Marisi, one of the many expensive designer shops on the Corso, making her try on every dress available in her size, parading before him as he sat in the viewing chair provided. He chose which ones he liked on her, elegant red chiffon, fitted sexy black satin, deep azure blue silk, and white low cut jersey. She was amazed at how good she looked, the colours and fit showing off her figure. She looked dramatically different. She felt different.

"Tony, I can't believe it, you've spent hundreds of euros on me," she said as they left the shop laden with bags.

"And you are worth it. You are beautiful, Sarah, you need to be decorated. And you have to look good if you are going to sing with me. I am thinking of adding more numbers for you, okay."

Sarah gulped and nodded, not sure that it was.

“And that’s not all, we are not finished yet. Next, we need what goes on underneath.” He winked at her.

From Intimissimi, the glamorous lingerie shop, he chose black lace thongs and push up bras, white silk camisoles and red satin slips. Everything fitted like a dream and she marvelled as she twirled herself in front of the mirror in the small cubicle, never having worn such racy underwear. Tony came to peek around the curtain to give his approval, unable to resist demonstrating it by grabbing her around the waist and kissing her slowly, his hands sliding down to her peachy soft bottom. She pushed him out before the sales assistant discovered them.

Sitting on her bed alone painting her toenails and waiting for Tony, hidden here in a paid apartment on the other side of town, being bought fancy clothes and sexy underwear, once again she felt like a mistress. But Tony no longer had a wife: the blonde had left him over a year ago.

“She loved me for about five minutes,” Tony told her as they ate *granita* one afternoon, sitting outside a café in the big square at Letojanni. It was like sorbet but more slushy, Sarah thought as she licked her spoon, the lemon cold and bitter sweet, a perfect combination on a hot afternoon.

“But you were together for longer than that, surely,” she said.

“Of course,” he replied seriously without acknowledging her attempt at humour, dipping a chunk of the brioche into his coffee *granita* mixed with cream. “But she was always unfaithful. The whole town knew, everyone knew except me. I didn’t believe it. One night I followed her. It was true.”

"That's terrible."

"I worked away a lot then, touring with a small band, so she had all that time to see other men. And she took every opportunity."

She could hear the bitterness in his voice. "But her son, your son, how could she leave him?"

Tony shrugged. "Her freedom. She needed her freedom."

Sarah shook her head. "My boyfriend left me too."

"It happens. It hurts. But we move on, no?" He looked at her and smiled, feeding her a morsel of his brioche.

Sarah nodded and chewed thoughtfully. She hadn't really believed she would ever be able to move on after Michael, devastated as she had been by his sudden departure, but meeting Tony had changed all that. He might be older and have more 'luggage' as her mother called it, but somehow that only added to his attraction. Here he was, this handsome worldy-wise man, this singer-musician, in one of the most beautiful places on earth and she was with him, not only his lover but his singing partner. He made her feel sophisticated and special, he had made her a singer.

Spending some afternoons alone, when Tony was too busy to come and see her, she liked to stroll around town or sit outside the many cafés lining the Corso Umberto. There were so many men flitting around the town, bombarding her with their looks and smiles and corny chat up lines that sometimes she had to change direction just to avoid the more persistent ones who would follow her along the street, trying to entice her. It was futile of course, but she didn't like to tell them to piss off. Slimy and unappealing most of them but they didn't really mean much harm. Sipping her *caffè freddo* she would watch the playboys pass by, mingling with the tourists, elegant women in stylish dresses tripping from one shop to the next and lanky men in shorts revealing their hairy white legs, cameras around their necks, hats that didn't suit them, their wives drawling that they wanted to stop at that ceramic shop down the way as they licked their dripping *gelato*. She bought cherries and olives from the market, read her book in the shade of the public gardens and cleaned her little apartment. She sat on the terrace and watched the volcano smouldering in the distance, fantastic and foreboding.

Sometimes she would take the steep descent down the hill to the beach, in the cable car if she was feeling lazy or by walking down the many steps. Steps with stops over the picturesque views of the bay, jagged rocks, hidden grottos and Isola Bella, the small island below with the empty broken house on top. Looking out at the layers of sea and sky melding into one on the horizon she would hold her breath at the beauty. Once below she would lay her towel on the rocks, the pebbles digging into her back since she couldn't afford a sunbed at ten euro. Remembering to put suncream on her elbows, Tony's warning that girls with black elbows look nasty, ringing in her ears, she would stretch out and sweat in her black Calvin Klein bikini, sitting up at intervals to look at the sea, letting the sound of the waves wash over her. She might take a squashed peach from her bag and think of the first time she ever came to this enchanted island.

Landing at Catania, the hot blast of air hitting her as she stepped down from the plane, she had felt a wave of emotion totally unexpected, her eyes filling with tears, and contained within that emotion was a promise of something. She hadn't known then what it could be.

It was all thanks to Ruth, of course, that she had ever met Tony. Ruth turned up one night at the bar. They hadn't really spent much time together since she arrived as Ruth was busy working and seeing Saro when she wasn't. She raised her glass to Sarah who was singing something seductive and came to sit with her after. "God, love, look at you, who would have thought it. You look fabulous in that dress. And you can sing, I can't bloody well believe it!" Ruth poured her a glass of wine from the bottle she had cooling on the table.

Sarah laughed. "It's becoming quite addictive."

"Bet he is too," Ruth nodded her head towards Tony, playing and singing alone now.

"He certainly is."

"So you really came back to live the dream, didn't you? You jammy cow."

"You know I got a shock when I first arrived." Sarah took a gulp of her wine.

"What do you mean?"

"Tony has a kid, a son."

"What? No. Don't tell me he's married?"

"No, he isn't. Not now. But he has a kid who lives with him."

"But he didn't tell you that before, did he?"

"No, of course not. I didn't have a clue."

"Good grief. But what's he like, the kid, I mean how old is he?"

"He's okay, cute, I suppose, he's only seven."

"Bloody hell, seven? And where's his mother?"

"She left them. She lives in France."

"Bloody hell," Ruth said again. "Sounds a bit complicated, love."

She sighed. "It's not quite the dream I expected. It's not all jasmine and romance, after all."

"It rarely ever is. This place, the men…seductive on the surface, but underneath there are so many hidden layers."

"He's also got a mother hanging round his neck," Sarah continued, pouring them another glass of wine from the bottle.

"Oh love, they always have, a mother or a wife, usually both. Course Italian men are notorious for their mothers, you know that. And Sicilian men are worse, let me tell you."

"Well, I can't say I have warmed to Tony's *mamma*, that's for sure."

"The mothers are to blame for everything. Do you know it's the mothers giving their sons enemas from the time they are born that turns them into homosexuals."

"What?" Sarah laughed. "What on earth are you talking about, Ruth?"

"They do, and that is why they run from the mum to the bum."

Sarah screamed with laughter.

"This is no laughing matter, I am telling you, Sarah, most men here like it up the arse and that is because they have had tubes up there from birth. They go with men on the sly, usually behind the rocks on the beach, going back home to the mother or wife afterwards. Disgusting."

"Oh Ruth, wherever did you get all this nonsense from?"

"It's the truth. Closet homos all of them."

"Tony certainly isn't, I do know that much."

Ruth hesitated. "No, well and neither is Saro. You know I'm still seeing him. Course, I knew he was married. Married with three kids, I might add."

Sarah could see the man with the bad teeth, a lifeguard at one of the beach clubs.

"It's just a bit of fun, love, that's all. I advise you to treat it the same. Your Tony's handsome, love, but don't take him too seriously. It's best not to take any of them seriously."

But Sarah knew she was serious about Tony. Just as serious as he was about her. Peeling off her layers, reaching the very core of her every time he made love to her.

The summer was slowly stretching on. The town became very crowded in August and unbearably hot. They were becoming quite a double act at the Stella Luna.

"You know I want you to stay, Sarah," Tony said one night as they lay in bed together, the air conditioning droning above. "I mean, we're doing well, aren't we, at the bar. You are becoming quite popular, you know that, don't you?"

She couldn't help wondering if she detected a note of jealousy in his voice, but dismissed the thought. "I'm loving it. It's like a dream," she said.

"We could tour as well, you know, in the winter months. That's what I used to do, before."

"Touring where?" she asked.

"Sicily. Italy." He sat up stroking her tummy. "Anywhere."

She smiled up at him, directing his hand to where she wanted it to go.

"So," he stopped. "Will you stay?"

She shrugged. "If you like." She was teasing him, playing it cool.

"I'm serious, Sarah, I don't want you to go back to England. I want you to come and live with me, at my house."

She sat up too, suddenly in shock, her heart beating fast. "What? You never even invite me to lunch at your house and now you want me to move in?"

"Yes, I've thought about it and made a decision. Please come and live with me, Sarah."

She didn't waste any time, the next day she packed up and pulled her heavy suitcase down the hill from the apartment and up the old cobbled Corso, the sun burning her shoulders. She negotiated her suitcase along the dusty narrow streets, fumes from the cars choking her as they almost ran her down, scooters roaring dangerously close.

Approaching the small square near Tony's house, she passed the elderly ladies sitting in their fold-up chairs outside their houses in the narrow back streets, wearing cotton print dresses and talking animatedly as they made paper flowers to hang across the street in honour of yet another saint, the flaps of skin hanging from their arms. The end of their summer, Sarah thought sadly, but still they sit outside, smiling and talking. Gossip, she discovered, is what actually kept them alive. They would discuss and dissect everyone's business, no one was left undiscovered. They eyed her as she passed them, some staring with stone faces, perhaps only one smiled at her, the stranger on the street. She thought of the old ladies with their curled white hair back at home in England, congregating and chatting at the bus stop with their shopping bags, laughing and lumbering with sticks, unsteady on their feet, off to collect their pensions at the post office. Her own mother looking so young yet not feeling so well. And the men? Here they were outside cafés and bars, playing cards. In England, inside betting shops, in their slippers in front of the telly. Dead.

She unpacked her case in Tony's dark, cramped bedroom, and looking at the bed she realised she had slept there only once, the first night she arrived back in Taormina. Tony had made a thing about her staying at the house yet now she was here moving in. She couldn't believe it. Wasn't this what she had wanted all along?

"I want you to feel at home," he said, standing at the door. "I have explained to Roberto that you will stay here."

"Does he understand?"

"Don't worry, he will. He stays with my mother more than here anyway, because of my working late. It's always been like this, since she left."

She, of course, was Vivienne, the blonde. Sarah wondered why she had left Tony and her son. What had happened to make her do this? She didn't want to ask him. He didn't seem to like being questioned about anything.

Although she tried to be friendly to Roberto, she could see it wasn't going to be easy. He was shy and seemed to cling to his father when she was around. But most of the time he wasn't there, spending his days at the beach or rampaging the streets with his friends, eating and sleeping with Carlotta. The family lunches seemed to have stopped, she noticed.

Sarah met Carlotta in the street one hot morning. She was wearing a thin black dress, a shopping bag over her arm, buying artichokes at one of the vegetable carts.

"You still here?" Carlotta said, unable to disguise the disappointment in her voice. "You like Taormina, I think?"

"Yes, it's very beautiful."

"You like my son also?"

"Yes, of course I do."

"And my grandson?"

"Yes, he's a lovely boy," she replied, not meaning it. Sarah watched the old dragon as she paid for her artichokes, counting out the coins from an old leather purse.

"You cook?" Carlotta asked.

"Not much," Sarah admitted.

"English very bad cooks."

"I wouldn't say that."

"You thin, very thin." Carlotta looked her up and down, making her feel self-conscious.

Sarah shrugged. "It's fashionable."

Carlotta shook her head and walked away without even saying goodbye.

Rotten old bag, Sarah thought as she watched her walking up the steep road. The man stood beside his cart looking at her. She pointed to the crate of grapes. "*Mezzo kilo, per favore*," she said.

"Your son and your mother clearly don't like me, Tony," Sarah announced, thumping the bag of grapes on the table.

"Don't say that, Sarah, it's not true, they have to get used to you, that's all. It was hard for them when

Vivienne left, hard for me too. But now I have met you and everything has changed. I'm so happy you have come into my life." He kissed her.

"I don't think they are," she said, pulling away from him.

"Of course it is different for Roberto, his mother left him and it is difficult for him to accept you."

"I am not trying to replace her, I can't."

"No, of course not."

"And your mother doesn't accept me either."

"But she will. I promise. Once they realise how happy I am with you they will be happy for me, you see?"

"I am not so sure."

"You are my sweet, simple Sarah," he said, stroking her cheek.

She looked up at him and laughed. "Hey, I'm not sure I like the sound of that, I'm not so simple, you know, and sometimes I am not so sweet."

He smiled. "You misunderstand me, I mean you are not complicated. My life is complicated enough." He sighed.

She wondered what he meant about his life being complicated. Since moving in she noticed there was something elusive about him, something she couldn't reach in him. He disappeared a lot, not telling her where; he always had something to do or someone to see, always rushing somewhere immediately after breakfast, business of some kind or another. He would leave the house looking immaculate in his designer suits and shirts, smelling of soap and expensive cologne. It didn't add up. His appearance and the awful dump he lived in.

She was finding it difficult to adjust to living in a dark damp house with the mess of two males, three if you counted the dog: Sammy, she discovered, only ever having seen evidence of his hairs on the sofa, was a fat brown and white beagle, very affectionate but his hairs were everywhere. The house was always a wreck, mess upon mess, no matter how hard she tried to clean up.

Of course their intimate times always made up for any misgivings she had, making her forget everything else. Tony often came home with more sexy underwear, scraps of black lace that she had to model immediately. He was passionate and loving, tender and caring. She had never known such continuous desire and excitement, it was a whole new world for her and she was always left wanting more as if it were a new intoxicating drug.

She renewed the contract on her apartment in England, extending the rental to the same couple for another six months then called her mother, telling her she would be staying in Sicily.

"Oh, Sarah, are you sure you want to stay there, do be careful, won't you? We miss you terribly," her mother said. "It's been over three months. You said you would only be away for the summer."

"Yes, but we are doing really well, Mum, I mean my singing career has taken off. We are going to start touring soon, you know, doing gigs in other towns."

"I see, well, if that's what you want, what can I say?"

"Tony is lovely. We are happy together. Be happy for me, please, Mum."

"I am, but…" She could hear her mother trying not to cry. "I miss you, Sarah, that's all."

"I miss you too, Mum, I won't leave it too long, I'll come home and visit soon."

"I hope so."

"I shall come for Christmas, I promise."

She called Lily. "Mum hasn't been too well, that's probably why she got upset," her sister explained.

"What do you mean not too well?" Sarah asked.

"We're not sure exactly, a combination of things, stomach mostly. She's going to have some tests soon. She wasn't well before you left, was she?"

"No, but it wasn't anything serious, are you saying now it is? Don't keep anything from me, Lily, please."

"Course I won't, Sarah, don't be daft. I shall keep you posted, don't worry. Now give me your number so I can call you sometimes."

"Is Andy alright?" Sarah was always slightly afraid of her older brother, he had been very protective since her father died. When Michael left her he wanted to find him so he could kick his brains in. He meant well but he made her feel as if she couldn't look after herself.

"Same old Andy, you know," Lily replied.

"I don't want to call him."

"But you should."

She did so, wanting to get all these tiresome calls out of the way, not wanting to hear any dissent or lectures from her family.

"Bloody hell, Sarah, what's all this about you staying over there in that poxy place?"

"I see Mum hasn't wasted any time telling you my good news," she replied.

"Good news. Are you sure? What are you doing over there?"

"Singing. Living with a man I love."

"What, you, singing? You've got to be having a laugh."

"You wouldn't say that, Andy, if you heard me."

"Oh wouldn't I? And this bloke you've shacked up with?"

"Tony."

"Yeah."

"What about him?"

"How's he treating you, that's what."

"Wonderfully. We are fine. Happy. You know? But then you don't, you're never happy are you, Andy?" She knew she was being a bitch.

"Oi, don't get cheeky on me, Sarah."

"I'm sorry, but you might be glad for me, and not so distrustful of everything and everyone."

"Yeah, well, that comes from experience."

"Anyway, I have to go now, I'll call you again soon."

"Make sure you do."

As the busy season finally quietened down, there was less work for them at the Stella Luna. Tony arranged for them to do a gig in a bar in Catania with his friends, Joey playing sax and Giuseppe double bass. She had met them before but it was the first time she had ever sung with other musicians. At the rehearsal they had made her feel at ease. But still she was nervous, the Coco Club was a bigger venue with its small stage, technical lighting and sound; the set up was much more sophisticated. She wore a new deep violet low cut silky dress Tony had just bought for her from a new shop in town and high silver sandals. At Tony's suggestion she had her hair cut and styled at a trendy salon in the afternoon. She dramatised her make-up, heavy-lidded smoky eyes and a violet mouth to match the dress.

She twirled for Tony. "You look amazing," he exclaimed. "*Bellissima.* In fact, too beautiful." He frowned. "I cannot let all these men look at you."

She laughed. "What men?"

"Here in the bar. Drinking, watching you sing."

She noticed Joey and Giuseppe were having enough trouble keeping their eyes off her, but they knew better than to let Tony see them ogling. She could tell they were a bit in awe of him. Maybe that was due to his age and experience. And his own devastating looks. He didn't look like the average Sicilian man who was short, balding and pot-bellied. Thank God for that. He was tall, distinguished, handsome, every corny description from a romance novel, that was Tony. And he was hers.

The gig went so well the manager of the Coco Club booked them to come back in a few weeks time. They celebrated with champagne, which went straight to her head.

"Maybe we are hitting the big time, Tony!" Sarah clapped her hands, excited.

"Calm down, Sarah," he said. "I've done all this before. It is hard work, you know, if you start gigging or touring around, don't think it is so easy."

She felt squashed. "No, but it's fun, isn't it?"

"For now, but don't get above yourself."

But the second time was even better. Sarah wasn't so nervous and enjoyed looking so glamorous, gaining confidence, singing stronger than ever before. The audience really responded and she felt like a starlet. But the following week, Tony told her the Club didn't want her to sing, they just wanted the band.

"You're joking, what do you mean?" Sarah was horrified.

"That's what they said."

"But that's not fair, Tony. You didn't accept did you?"

"What could I do?"

"But didn't you fight for me? Tell them it was all of us or nothing?"

"Of course I did, but it was no use. Better that we have some money coming in. I could not refuse."

But Sarah didn't understand. She was furious. "I am going to call him up," she said, remembering the smarmy manager looking her up and down, his greasy face leering, a cigarette permanently hanging from his mouth.

"No you will not, you leave this to me. Understand." Tony went out, leaving her simmering.

By end of October the Coco Club didn't want them back at all and the Stella Luna had closed until December. While Tony seemed to spend more time away from the house, out with friends, doing business, going off for evenings without her, she was stuck with the housework she hated in a house she was beginning to loath.

"Two peach hibiscus today. Look, flowers for you," Tony called to her through the window one morning.

All she could see from the bed was the brick wall. She sat up and sipped her coffee. Lukewarm again. He stood outside the window looking in at her, smiling. "Two flowers. Come and look," he said.

She sighed. Her feet touched the cold dusty stone floor as she searched for her slippers. Pulling her black baby doll decent she walked to the window. Sunlight shone outside, a patch of blue sky just visible if she stretched out far enough. And there before her were the two hibiscus, flowering overnight, now facing each other as if poised for a kiss. Behind them the brick wall was topped with ivy, below which were stacked large fragments of a Roman temple that Tony had somehow procured. He was balancing on these stones, tending to the jasmine trailing above the window, one leg out, glasses on the end of his nose. "Beautiful," she said, smiling up at him.

He looked down at her over the top of his glasses. "Come outside and see the others," he said, jumping down from the wobbling stones. "Come."

She sighed again. Walking through the apartment, she stepped out from the gloomy kitchen into the yard. She looked at the pot of red hibiscus standing on the rusty iron table and noticed the fallen heads left to shrivel on the side. "Lovely," she said. This romance was all very well, but she was getting fed up with the grim reality.

"Sarah," he said, taking her hand, "I have an idea. I want to make a garden full of flowers, plants and pots, a terrace where the sun shines, somewhere Roberto can play and space for Sammy to run."

"Rather than a yard always in the shade smelling of dog's piss you mean?"

"Don't say that, I washed here this morning." The hosepipe lay unravelled on the paved ground.

"Well, it still smells," she said, wriggling her nose.

Smiling and squeezing her hand he pulled her towards him. "But we can make a garden, jasmine smelling sweetly in the night, sunshine, colour and beauty all around us every day." He held her close to him, breathing in the just-risen scent of her.

She pulled away from him. "A paradise waits for us, Tony. But the reality? The reality is the piss and shit of Sammy. The dust from the building works all around us. The brick walls blocking out the light. The proximity of every bloody neighbour, coughing, spitting, crying, crashing their cutlery and shouting the odds. This place is a nightmare, Tony, don't you see it?"

Turning back to the dark kitchen she began clearing the worktops, trashed as usual the day before: ice cream wrappers and sticks, ashtrays full of cigarette butts and chewing gum, oily plates shoved in the sink, empty milk bottles, others half full left out of the fridge, salt and sugar scattered over every surface, chipped cups and spilt coffee on the stove. She didn't know how it all happened. She opened the dishwasher, the stale smell hitting her as she realised she'd forgotten to put it on last night.

"Bugger it," she said to herself, slamming the dishwasher door shut.

He stood in the doorway watching her. "What's wrong, Sarah? Let's be happy, look, the sun is shining."

"I would if I could find the sun. Can you see it from this dungeon, because I can't?"

"You talk like this house is a prison, but this is your home now. I thought you would be happy here with me. Instead all I hear are your complaints. I'm going out," he said.

"Yes, you do that, you're always going out, God knows where, since you never bother to tell me. And I will, of course, clean up the kitchen, left a wreck once again by you and your delightful son." She threw the tea towel at him, walked back to the bedroom and slammed the door. Kicking off her slippers she flung herself onto the bed and burst into tears.

It was their first real argument, but she didn't know why she was so upset or what had really happened. Something wasn't right. Ever since she had moved into the house. Ever since they didn't want her at that bar in Catania. She didn't know any more. She had thought it would be so easy living with Tony, keeping house, loving him, singing with him. But it wasn't. She was trying hard to do it right but the more she tried the more it went wrong.

Leaving the mess in the house, she got dressed and took Sammy out for a walk in the public gardens, looking out at the sunshine glittering on the waves down below at the bay of Giardini. She bumped into Joey whom she hadn't seen since their last show together.

"Hey, Sarah," he stopped and kissed her cheeks. He was an American Italian so she didn't have to stumble over sentences and speak baby broken English with him. "How's it going?" he asked.

"Okay," she said.

He bent down to stroke Sammy then stood up looking at her. "Are you sure? It was too bad you gave up the singing with us, you know, at the Coco Club, it wasn't the same without you those last few gigs."

"What?"

"Well, when Tony said you wanted a break it was a shame for us, we were all so good together, didn't you think so?" His warm brown eyes studied her.

"But I didn't. Want a break." She stopped. "I mean, Tony told me it was the Club who decided they didn't want me all the time. I was so upset about it."

"Oh, was it that way, I must have misunderstood," Joey said quickly. He looked away from her, suddenly nervous. "Anyway, I gotta run, Sarah, I'll see you around." Before she could reply he was gone.

She went home, stunned. She sat on the shabby sofa waiting for Tony to come home.

"How dare you do that to me," she said as soon as he walked in through the front door.

"What?" he said, throwing the keys down on the table. "What are you talking about now? Are you still angry from this morning? I thought you would be calm by now. I don't want to hear all this moaning all the time."

"Moaning? I'm talking about the Coco Club."

"What about it?"

"You know exactly what. You stopped me playing with you. Why? Why did you do it when we were all doing so well together, why Tony?" She sprang up from the sofa, wanting to lash out at him, tears spilling out with her anger.

"I had to do something. It was getting out of hand."

"What was?"

"All those men looking at you. You wriggling around on that stage. I couldn't watch it any more."

"What?"

"You were becoming too much."

She laughed through her tears, unable to comprehend. “Too much for what?”

“For your own good. Don’t forget, Sarah, I created you.”

She realised how serious he was. “Created me?”

“I made you a singer. I changed how you look. It was me who did all this.”

“But you don’t control me, Tony, so don’t try to.”

“You are mine now, you belong to me.”

“What, like a trophy on a shelf that you can take down and dust whenever you feel like it?”

“You don’t understand how to live in this country at all, do you? As a woman you hardly have a voice. As a foreign woman, well, you can forget it. You owe everything to me. Just remember that. You are nothing without me.”

“You have to be joking, Tony.”

“I didn’t want everyone looking at you, you are mine, not for the public to look at and speculate, wondering if they can fuck you after the show. You can become a slut like this.”

“What? This is not the Victorian era, you know.”

“Men are like that here, they see you looking so sexy all the time, they think you are available for them. But you are not, so I had to do something, don’t you see?”

“Bloody hell, Tony, no, I don’t see. You are mad. And jealous. Not just about me but of me. Because I was doing so well. I was too good. You want all the attention, isn’t that it?”

“No, that’s not it. You understand nothing. If you carry on like this you never will.” He snatched up his keys suddenly and left before she could say another word.

Sarah called Ruth and met up with her that evening. Tony still hadn't come home. They sat in a small wine bar, down one of the side streets off the Corso. It was quiet in town now, not so many people around. Sarah lit up a cigarette and sipped her red wine.

"Hey, love, since when have you started smoking?" Ruth said.

"Oh, ages ago. Goes with the singing, moody mellow jazz and all that stuff," she laughed through the smoke haze.

"But does nothing for your voice, you ought to watch out."

"I only have one now and then, on the quiet, Tony doesn't like it, of course. But then what does he like."

Ruth looked at her. "Is everything alright, you don't seem yourself, love."

Sarah sighed. "To be honest it's all going a bit pear-shaped, Ruth. I suppose it had to didn't it?"

"Why, what do you mean? What's happened?"

"It's Tony." She paused, putting out the half finished cigarette. "Tony stopped me singing. We did a few gigs at this place in Catania, the Coco Club, remember I told you about it?"

"I wanted to come, you know I did."

"Yeah, well it was short lived anyway, he said they didn't want me to sing with them which I thought was odd. Turns out he didn't want me to sing with them."

"Why? I don't get it."

"He wants me locked in the house, his dolly daydream, not out running wild in the big wide world."

Ruth shook her head. "What did I tell you, love, these men are like Arabs, worse sometimes. It's the same mentality. There is no equality with them."

"Doesn't look like it."

“What are you going to do?”

“I don’t know. He says we will start up again at the Stella Luna when it opens, the beginning of December. But everything seems so different now.”

“Everything is different here. I did warn you about what lies beneath the surface. Course, in the winter it gets even worse, it can be depressing. There are loads of suicides here, you know.”

“Stop it, Ruth, you’re supposed to be cheering me up.”

“I’ll get us another drink then, that should do it.”

Chapter Three

Any place that advertises its dead must be peculiar.

Sarah shivered as she stood in front of yet another poster naming the most recent death to occur in the town. Here you died one day and were buried the next. She looked at the poster. Everyone in town would know who this person was. Except her. She didn't know who anyone was and she wasn't sure she wanted to. Taormina, of course, was the jewel of Sicily: a tourist town full of beauty, charm and warmth. But, as she discovered the longer she stayed, the climate was growing colder, along with the local hospitality, and the beauty was being eroded by the constant corruption which led to deterioration and neglect, rubbish accruing, the historical left to ruin, amenities poorer, prices higher and conservation forgotten. Small town mentality made of concrete. She sighed as she walked down the street like a building site, full of works on houses that were never finished because the money was always running out. Paradise it might look from the public gardens: the spread of mountains, the countryside and the sea, the sun setting behind Mount Etna; but there was something oppressive and foreboding about the place, a more sinister side of the street if you cared to walk down it.

Pushing her cold hands further into the pockets of her long beige quilted coat, she wondered if this early Christmas present was part of Tony's campaign to make her look less attractive and therefore attract less attention. The coat was hardly flattering, all that padding made her look about twenty stone, but it did keep out the cold, the dampness of winter that was seeping in. The long summer had eventually given way to winter; the happy holiday feeling had turned to a darker reality and it wasn't turning out quite as she had expected. They hadn't gone touring in November. She wasn't surprised. Not after the Coco Club fiasco. But she was disappointed. His ridiculous jealousy had ruined everything. And now something else was going on. Just minutes ago she'd overheard Tony talking on the phone in the bedroom. Hushed tones that she couldn't make out but didn't like the sound of. There was something intimate in his voice, something too intimate. She had stood at the closed door, holding her breath, her heart thudding loudly. He was talking to a woman. She was sure of it. Turning away in shock, unable to confront him, she had left the house. It was then that she remembered the letter he had stuffed into his pocket the other morning as if to hide it from her. The implications were too awful to consider.

The December darkness had descended like a heavy curtain. She weaved through the empty narrow streets, crammed with higgedly piggedly apartments, not even a doorstep separating the private from the public, the dust outside and the dramas within, the smells of jasmine and rubbish. Reaching the small dark square she arrived back at the house, hesitating a moment at the front door before she continued walking on, up the uneven steps taking her further into the town. She couldn't bear to go home yet.

Walking along the almost deserted Corso Umberto, she didn't stop until she reached the big square lined with oleander trees now bare of blossom, cafés on one side and the magnificent view on the other. It all looked so different in the winter. She crossed the chequered square and stood facing the Ionian Sea, the outline of the volcano barely visible, the lights of the nameless towns flickering in the distance below. Looking at the full moon shining low in the darkness over the bay, the waves shimmering in silence, she was overwhelmed by the heartbreaking beauty and turning her back on the moon, she continued along the empty Corso until she found herself walking into Roland. He was the tall American always propping up the bar at the Stella Luna, watching her sing. He would sit with a notebook beside his wine glass, working on his latest novel, often stopping to talk to Sarah when she wasn't singing. She liked him, he was amusing. But if she thought Tony was old, then Roland was even older. He was a bit of an ageing hippie, always in jeans and baggy shirts, loose fair curls framing his strong rugged face half hidden behind a beard. He was one for the ladies, she'd heard, but that must have been in his past.

"Hey, Sarah, how are you? I haven't seen you in ages." He held out his arms to her.

"I could say the same to you, Roland, where have you been hiding?"

"In my cave, I don't go out so much in the winter. I hate the cold." He hugged her as if they were long lost friends and she buried her face into his chest. He was like a big winter bear, warm and comfortable, in his baggy cord jacket, a red woolly scarf looped around his neck. She could feel his warmth through the layers of cashmere and cord and she suddenly thought of her father. Gently he pushed her back from him. "Hey, what's all this, what's up, Sarah?" he asked as the tears ran down her cheeks.

Sarah shook her head, feeling embarrassed. "I'm sorry, Roland. Just ignore me. I'm fine."

"You sure don't look fine to me. Let's go and have a drink, you look like you could do with some company."

She looked up at him. "Do you have time? Are you on your way somewhere?"

"Of course I have time, I always have time for you, Sarah. I'm not going any place special. In fact, you know me, I would have wound up having a drink anyway, if I can find somewhere open that is." He put his arm around her shoulder. She found a crumpled tissue in her pocket and dabbed at her nose and under her eyes, imagining the mascara streaking down her face. How embarrassing, she thought to herself as he steered her down some steps off the Corso. "Course, the Casanova Bar is always open," he said as they walked in. "But let's hope there are none of those in here tonight." She looked around, it was quiet and cosy, soft sofas and low lights. It was empty. "Now, shall we have wine or do you want a brandy or whisky perhaps, I don't know?"

"I think a brandy, actually." She pulled off her blanket coat, glad to be rid of the stifling layer.

"Right. I'll have some wine, for now." He ordered for them and from his jacket pocket presented her with a pale blue folded handkerchief. "Here now, dry those big sad eyes of yours." He hesitated as she took the handkerchief from him. "Is there any chance those tears have something to do with that fine fella of yours?"

"Roland, what a suggestion!" she replied quickly, standing up. "I'll go and wash my face, repair the damage," she said.

"Well, okay, you do that, though I can't see much damage from here." He winked at her, his soft brown eyes crinkling at the corners as he smiled.

In the cool clean bathroom she studied her reflection in the square mirror above the sink. Surprised at the tears in front of Roland, her sad puffy eyes blinked back at her as she blotted the black smudges beneath them. Odd of him to say that about Tony. She often had the feeling that Roland didn't like him. Maybe they were old rivals, fighting over the women in town. Sarah studied her face. Could he really be cheating on her? Wanting her tucked away at home while he went out to play? Yet despite the discord between them he still wanted to make love to her: in the bedroom he was always able to convince her everything was the same. But was it? Or was she just fooling herself?

"Better?" Roland asked when she returned.

"Yes, I think so. Shall I keep this or do you want it back?" She held the still folded handkerchief in her hand.

"Keep it. A memento, huh? Now come on, get some of that brandy down your neck. I ordered you a large shot, though in here that means almost a full glass."

"I can see that. Thanks." She took a sip. "Just what I need. Though I'm afraid I seem to need this stuff too much lately," she said.

"Nah. Don't worry about it, I never do. Drink every day. Never does me any harm."

"But how can you be so sure?"

"Well, I'm still here. I've made it this far and I don't look to be giving up yet."

"I suppose I should say Cheers to that."

"Certainly." He raised his glass and looked at her expectantly. "Are you really okay now?"

"I'm fine."

"So you keep saying but I am not convinced. Why don't you tell me what's happened?"

She bit her lip to stop herself from crying again, her hand trembling as she put the glass back down on the table.

As the wine flowed, so Sarah confessed her fears to Roland and they sat drinking and talking all evening until the bar closed. She found herself clinging onto him as they tumbled down the road. "I'm not going to make it, I can't see," she said. The only lights visible were those in the far distance, twinkling beyond the bay.

"Your feet will find the way. Now come on, we're nearly there." He almost carried her, his arm around her waist, she could feel her feet leaving the ground. She struggled beside him, thinking she really should have gone home. He put her down as he fumbled with the key. They entered the dark passage and he found the light. She found the sofa, soft brown leather, and slumped onto it kicking off her boots, the high heels hurting her feet.

"That's right now, you make yourself at home and I'll do the coffee."

"Cook the coffee, that's what Tony calls it," she said, hearing herself slurring the words.

"Does he? Well, I don't cook anything much and certainly not coffee." He stumbled out to the kitchen.

"I can't cook either, unless you count toast and Tony doesn't have a toaster. He's a fabulous cook, of course." Sarah suddenly realised she wanted to be home. Home with Tony. But of course he was hardly ever at home. She checked her mobile phone. No calls. No messages. Just his face, her screensaver, her wallpaper, her everything. She got up. "I want to go home now, Roland, but I think I need some water first."

"Go right ahead, help yourself. Glasses are up there. Tap's okay I hope, no bottled at the moment. Must get some."

"Tap is fine." She gulped down half a glass. "Ugh."

"That bad?"

"No, but I feel a bit sick."

"Oh dear. Brandy and wine *and* sambuca is some combination."

"Yes, not advisable."

"I'm just a wine man myself. Cuts out the crap." From the coffee machine he poured them two mugs and added some milk. "This okay for you?"

"Yes," she said, without looking. She took the cup and they walked unsteadily to the sitting room.

"Now, you can stay here, Sarah, on this sofa. I've slept here before, it's very comfortable, and I can walk you back home tomorrow morning."

"Thank you, Roland. You're very kind."

He sat next to her and took her hand. "Sarah, I know that it's difficult for you right now, but you will come through this." She nodded and looked down at her hand in his, small and pitiful, and dry. Why did she never remember the hand cream, she wondered vaguely. "Now let's drink this coffee," he said.

The light woke her. She was wrapped in a blanket, still fully clothed, her boots where she had left them overturned. Her mouth was sticky, her head throbbing. What on earth am I doing here, she thought, why did I stay, why did I drink so much? And why, oh why, did I spill my heart out to Roland? She didn't wake him but left a note of thanks, balanced on top of the cup of cold coffee.

She let herself in. Tony was clattering in the kitchen, cursing, steam rising from the pots on the hob. She crept across the room, not wanting to look at him, she wasn't ready for a confrontation.

"Sarah, I didn't hear you come in!"

She turned at the kitchen door and faced him. She didn't know what to say.

"Where have you been? I was so worried."

"But you didn't call," she said.

He blew on the wooden spoon full of sauce. "I did, but I couldn't reach you. There was no line."

"Well, it doesn't look like you've been searching the streets for me," she said, thinking he had more interest in the pots and pans.

"But what happened? You look terrible."

"Nothing happened."

"But where were you? How could you stay out all night?"

"I don't want to talk about this now, Tony," she said, walking through to the bedroom, her heels clicking on the cold stone floor. Passing Roberto's bedroom, she could hear the noise of the TV, cartoon shouts and shootings. She went into their room, dark, damp and cold, and sat on the bed in her thick coat feeling frozen, hungover and unwashed. Tony followed her and stood in the doorway looking at her.

"A hot shower, eh?" he said, as if reading her mind. Instead of being angry as she imagined he would be, he appeared almost indifferent. "I am cooking some bolognese for tonight, but now we'll have some meat and salad, okay, in half an hour we'll eat." He returned to the kitchen. So worried about her but he still had time to think about his stomach, she thought.

It was always lunch time. Father and son time. Tony pinched Roberto's chubby cheek, messed his hair and mashed up his salad with balsamic vinegar and olive oil, force-feeding him mouthfuls of grated carrot when the boy wanted only to eat his meat. Sarah sat at the table and chewed on the fresh country bread, sullen-faced and silent. Looking up at the once white walls of the kitchen, she wondering how many years of dirt were splattered there. If he could afford all these expensive clothes she wondered why they couldn't afford a few pots of paint to brighten the place up. She noticed the cobwebs hanging from the high ceiling, the patches of damp spreading from the corners; the cracked stone floors and old boxes stacked everywhere, empty of shoes, computer games and last year's mobile phone, now stuffed full with papers and receipts, disintegrating scraps of nothing. And that huge ominous painting. Dark reds and blacks, a disturbing image of a man sitting awkwardly, somewhere desolate and surreal, the bones of his legs protruding under the cloth wrapped around him. She looked up and shivered, it was darkly disconcerting, she thought, as the figure looked out from the shadows to an invisible horizon while she sat at the table below him, trying to eat her *involtini* and salad. The lumps of lamb stuck in her throat, along with the words left unsaid. Her head ached. She cleared the dishes.

Having left the table as soon as he could, Roberto dashed back through the kitchen with a huge plastic water rifle, blasting water everywhere before he ran out into the street to terrorise the neighbours. Sarah screamed after him to be careful. Tony turned to Sarah, smiling, remaining infuriatingly magnanimous. Shaking her head she retreated to the bedroom. She called her mother.

"You don't sound yourself, Sarah, are you sure you're well?"

"Yes, of course I am, Mum, I was phoning to see how you are. Are you feeling better?"

"I'm fine."

"Really? But what did the doctor say this time?"

"Oh, the usual nonsense. You mustn't worry about me. I shall be getting better soon. As long as you're alright, that's the main thing."

"Everything is fine, Mum."

"And we shall see you soon, you will come home for Christmas, won't you?"

"Yes, of course I will." But she hadn't yet mentioned her plans to Tony.

Sarah went back to the kitchen. Tony was at the table reading the newspaper. She sat down and watched him, glancing at the words she couldn't read. She started picking at the skin on her thumb. She knew she wanted to pick a fight with him, wondering how he could sit there so calmly.

Tony looked up from his newspaper. "Well?" he said.

"Well what?"

"Are you going to tell me what's going on, Sarah?"

"Nothing."

"What do you mean, nothing?"

"Nothing's going on."

"And last night? Where were you all night?"

"I was out."

"Out? Out where? Who with?"

She was silent.

"You cannot live here with me and go out where you like and do what you want."

"Why not?" she said, knowing she was being unreasonable. "You do."

"I do what?"

"Go where you like, do what you want. You're always leaving me on my own, I never know where you are."

"I have to work, Sarah."

"We were supposed to be working together, remember?"

"You know I have been looking around for us. It isn't easy. You know I am taking whatever work I can."

She didn't believe him, not any more. "But when can we go back to the Stella Luna, it's December already?"

"They will let me know, I told you that. Now, are you going to tell me where you were last night?"

"Why should I? I need my freedom too."

"Freedom? Freedom to stay out all night? I don't think so."

"I need friends."

"Friends? But you have friends. You have me."

"Do I?" She looked at him.

"Of course."

She remained silent.

"So, don't you think I have a right to know?" he asked.

"What?"

"Where you were? Who you were with? Did you and Ruth meet some men in town and go back to her house with them?"

"Don't be daft," She laughed.

"This isn't funny, Sarah."

She looked at him, realising he was angry but that he was making a great effort to suppress it. "I wasn't out on the pull, if that's what you think. I was with Roland," she said.

"Who? Roland?"

"Yes."

"That creep who hangs around the bar?"

"He's not a creep."

"You spent the night with him?" Tony suddenly stood up. The newspaper fell onto the crumbs left unwiped on the table. For a moment she thought he was going to hit her.

"Nothing happened," she said quickly.

"Am I supposed to believe that?"

"Yes, because it's true."

"You spend the night with another man and tell me nothing happened?"

"He's not another man, he's just Roland." And getting drunk with him hadn't made her feel any better she realised.

"And nothing happened?"

"Nothing," she replied. "I told you."

"I don't believe you."

"Look, I drank too much. I slept on his sofa. That's all."

"That's all?"

"Yes. I didn't plan on staying, I just passed out." She looked down at her bitten nails and picked again at her thumb.

"But why did you go home with him? Tell me the truth, Sarah." He sat down again grabbing hold of her hand, twisting it, hurting her.

"Stop it, Tony."

"What's going on? Are you having an affair?"

"No," she pulled her hand away, feeling the tears sitting in her eyes, waiting to spill. "Are you?" She looked at him, the look was a challenge.

"What?" He stood up again. "You are the one who stays out all night and now you accuse me?"

Her tears fell, dropping silently onto her jeans. "So who were you talking to on the phone yesterday?" she asked.

"What?"

"I heard you. Who is she?"

"What are you talking about?"

"That call."

"What call?"

"You tell me."

"I don't know what you are talking about. You mean my mother? The only woman I call is my mother."

"Yeah, right." She sniffed.

"Enough of this, now, Sarah, you're being ridiculous." He walked away from her. "Do you want a coffee?" he asked.

"No, I do not," she replied.

"Tea, then? I shall make you a tea." He opened the cupboard above the sink: tightly bound packs of Lavazza coffee, sachets of hot chocolate, a yellow box of Nesquik, a small box of Relax herbal teabags and right at the back, the familiar small blue package of Tetleys. "Ah yes, here it is, ninety nine teabags of English tea."

"Fifty, actually," she said, wiping the tears across her cheeks. "All the way from England." She sighed, remembering how she had packed them in her suitcase many months ago. But there were no kettles here and her travel kettle was too full of limescale to use so she had chucked it away. She thought about her chrome kettle at home on her always clean granite worktop from Ikea. Her pretty mugs collected over the years in her cupboard, neatly stacked in rows. The semi-skimmed goats milk from Tesco. Tea never tasted the same here, even if the teabags were Tetleys. Perhaps it was the water. At home she might have a jammy dodger or a toasted tea cake. And sit down. Here you stood up at the bar in a café for a quick espresso, black and bitter, a small crisp sachet of sugar in the saucer, shake it and stir, two sips and it was gone, pay and bye-bye. Tony would talk to the owner behind the bar, hardly aware of Sarah standing beside him as he gabbled away. She would feel shaky later, certain the caffeine was unsettling her nerves even more.

He made them tea in the saucepan, boiling the teabag, milk and sugar together. "I learned this in India," he said, watching the bubbles begin to surface. "This is real *chai*." He switched off the gas and poured the hot milky tea into the cups, slopping it over the worktop. Getting up from her chair, Sarah stood beside him. She didn't know he had been to India. "Here," he said, handing the cup to her. "You like it?" he asked, watching her take a careful sip. He slurped from his cup. "Be careful not to burn your mouth," he laughed. "I just did in fact."

But she didn't want to talk about the sodding tea. She felt like throwing the cup in his face. She looked at him, wanting to find the truth there in his eyes, but something else caught inside her and she looked away. Holding the cup in both hands to warm them, she shivered. "It's freezing in here, as usual," she said.

He walked over to the thermometer hanging on the wall. "It's 19. Perfect. Not cold at all."

"Well, I am."

"You need more calories," he said.

"No, I don't. I need central heating."

She lay in bed the next morning, feeling the burden of everything that was left unsaid between them. She sat up and sipped her coffee from the chipped mug, watching Tony as he stood dressing, feeling the distance between them. He pulled on his sweatshirt and jeans and stamped into his shoes. It was cold in the room.

"Tony, I've been thinking about booking a ticket," she said, wanting to shock him, to get some reaction. Maybe he wanted her to go, to get her out of the way.

"A ticket, what ticket?"

"For home."

"Home? England, you mean?"

"Yes."

"But it's Christmas soon, how can you go to England?"

"I haven't been back home for months. You know my mother isn't well. She wants me home for Christmas. She needs me."

"But I need you too, Sarah. I need you here with me," he said.

"Do you?" She looked at him, tall and handsome and as cold as the room itself.

"Of course I do. We shall be busy at the bar."

"You mean they do want us back there?"

"Of course. But not just that, Sarah, I need you. You are practically my wife now. I had hoped one day you would be."

“What?” She looked at him, stunned, clutching the covers up to her chest, feeling the goose bumps rising on her bare arms.

He looked back at her. “I thought that is what you wanted too, but it is clear from your behaviour that you do not.” He turned and left the room, leaving her speechless. She heard the front door slam.

She sat up in bed, in shock. Maybe she’d got it all wrong, suspecting Tony of deceiving her, when really he wanted to marry her. She couldn’t believe he had said it, so matter of factly. Was that a proposal? Had she ruined everything, getting drunk and staying out with Roland like that?

A banging on the front door startled her and she jumped out of bed hoping it was Tony coming back. The banging persisted. She pulled Tony’s old blue dressing gown from the back of the door, draped it over her flimsy flowery nightdress and ran on tiptoes over the cold stone floor. She opened the door, still standing on her tiptoes. In front of her there stood a tall thin blonde woman wearing a black suit and big black sunglasses, a small trolley suitcase behind her. She smiled, thin lip-glossed lips. “Hello, I’m Vivienne, Antonio’s wife. Is he around?”

The dressing gown fell from Sarah’s shoulders.

Chapter Four

"He's not here." Sarah picked up the dressing gown, quickly slipping it back on, tying the cord tightly around her waist, aware of how ridiculous she must look.

"And you are?" She looked Sarah up and down, swinging her sunglasses in one hand. Her eyes were green with glints of gold.

"Sarah."

"Are you Antonio's new housekeeper?" she asked, one side of her mouth turned up in a smile.

"No, I'm not. I'm his girlfriend."

"Really? He's kept you well hidden." Vivienne stepped into the apartment, pulling the suitcase behind her.

"I could say the same about you," Sarah said, as she moved aside to let her in, noticing her pointed black shoes, smart black handbag, bare brown legs, looking more American than French, more slick than chic. And she'd got a bloody cheek turning up like this.

"Didn't Antonio mention I was coming for Christmas?" Vivienne asked.

"No, he didn't." The phone call, the whispers in the bedroom, the letter. It all fell into place. This was the other woman.

Vivienne smiled, looking around the shabby front room, cluttered and littered, piles of papers, stacks of plates, discarded toys. "I can see some things have changed around here, it was always so neat when I lived here. So, do you live here now?"

"For the moment," Sarah replied.

"A temporary arrangement, you might say?"

"Not exactly."

"And my son? Where is he?" She turned around as if he might pop out from behind the sofa or from under the table.

"At his grandmother's," Sarah replied.

"Ah yes. He would be." She looked at Sarah. "And how do you find him?"

"He's fine, I like him."

Vivienne shook her head and smiled. "He's a bad boy, just like his father."

"I wouldn't say that."

"Wouldn't you? I shall go to see him. The case I leave here. If it does not disturb you?"

"Of course not."

"We meet later then," Vivienne held out her hand to Sarah, cold and thin.

Sarah showered in shock, her mind scrambling, unable to believe what had turned up on the doorstep. She had said she was his wife. His wife. They were still married. She wasn't an ex at all.

Dressing quickly, leaving her duvet coat hanging in the damp wardrobe, she pulled on her thick cable jumper and wrapped a long woollen scarf around her neck. As she approached the front door she saw the suitcase standing in the middle of the sitting room. It did disturb her. She wanted to kick it out onto the street. Sammy yapped at her heels. She left the house, banging the door behind her.

Outside in the narrow street she looked up at the apartments opposite: ugly irregular stacks built to each owner's specification without any thought of aesthetics. Rock music blared from the one where the young couple lived. Below them she could hear the Russians talking, two girls who worked in restaurants and cleaned bars, working wherever they could; it was always word of mouth, the work in this town, serving, cleaning or cooking. After the bar work had ceased up Sarah had hoped to work with Ruth at SunStops, the travel agency, but nothing ever came of it. She knew she wouldn't have been much good at dealing with complaining tourists, not that there were many of those around now.

It was a cold but bright December day, the blue sky just visible above the buildings. She stood for a moment, trying to breathe, to suppress the waves of panic and shock rising through her chest. She didn't know what to do, where to go, but walking up the small side street from the house, the stray cats scattering on the steps, she turned onto the road, passing the fishmongers, the knick knack shop where the old woman sat outside on a chair knitting, and the ceramic shop which was always closed whatever time of day. She stopped at the Pasticceria Condorelli, her favourite café on the corner, with its glass tables, chrome chairs and marble topped bar where she usually stood to drool at the pastries while the noise of the coffee machine spitting out her cappuccino deafened her. She would smell the freshly baked *pasti di mandorla* before she reached the door; the sugar-crusted almond cakes, crumbly and soft inside. But this morning she couldn't eat, she felt sick.

Standing outside the café, she took out her mobile and called Ruth, explaining what had happened.

"Just go in and have a coffee, wait for me, I won't be long."

She did as she was told, sitting by the window, looking out at the street, empty but for a few locals passing by. By the time Ruth joined her she was in a terrible state.

"Come on now, love, don't cry. I'll get you another coffee. And let's have some cake, I'm starving." Ruth was flushed and pink from hurrying, her hand in her bag searching for her purse.

"How can she still be his wife, she's supposed to be his ex," Sarah cried, her tears almost spilling into her cappuccino.

"That's what they all say. At least Saro didn't pretend."

"But only this morning Tony said one day I would be his wife."

"Did he? A lot of men say things like that," said Ruth.

"Yes, but how can he say what he doesn't mean?"

"What did I tell you about men saying one thing and meaning another. Anyway, maybe he does mean it, only just not yet."

Sarah sniffed into her soggy tissue. "No, not when he's still married to someone else."

"But how do you know he really is? Maybe she just said that to be spiteful."

"Why would she lie? No, Tony is the liar."

"They're all liars, love."

"I thought Tony had another woman but this is worse, he still has a wife. And now she's back. What on earth shall I do?"

"God, love, search me." Ruth bit into her pastry, a *cannolo*, the ricotta cream dotted with candied fruits oozing out of the end. "I've got enough problems of my own with that prick. Do you know what Saro did last night?" She blotted her perfect painted lips with a napkin.

"What?"

"Let me down again, didn't he. Supposed to be taking me out to dinner. A rare event in itself. There I was, all done up, nails, face, hair, clothes, the lot, all ready to go, final coating of lipstick and wham. He calls. He can't come. Something happened at home. His wife's brother arrived unexpectedly and they had to eat together. He couldn't get out of it. For fuck's sake."

"Oh no." Sarah did wonder what she saw in that man but never said so.

"That's what they're like here, you see. Raise your hopes and then shatter them. Bastards, all of them. I warned you, didn't I?" Ruth flicked her fair curling hair behind her, the gesture defiant and defensive. "Maybe we should both go home. To England. I'm not sure there's anything here for me any more. Maybe you feel the same now?"

"I don't know how I feel, I'm in shock." She blew her nose. "But what about your job?"

"That is over now anyway to be honest, for this year at least. I can do better at home in the winter. And the summer too, come to that. I earn a fraction here in this bloody toy town. Sometimes I wonder what on earth I'm doing here." Ruth sipped her caffè latte and sighed. "Think I need a brandy with this coffee, what about you, love, too early?"

"No, I'll have one with you. Though I seem to be drinking far too much these days."

"Why not, I say. All the bloody grief they give us, no wonder we turn to drink."

She couldn't reach Tony. He wasn't answering his phone. But she couldn't bear to go home so she walked through the public gardens, the high heels of her boots wobbling over the cobbles. She stood looking out at the sea far below down at Giardini, the volcano in the distance above. Snow on it now but she remembered the summer when it was hazy with sunshine, the colours of the sea and sky shifting around the magical monster it was. She wandered up to the avenue where stood her favourite tree; there she would sit under its generous shade during the heat of the day in her denim shorts and sunhat, watching the butterflies dancing on the lavender, dancing all around her. In paradise. A paradise now tinged with poison.

By the early evening she was sitting outside one of the expensive cafés in the Piazza Aprile, a glass of wine on the table in front of her, the bowls of peanuts, olives and other savoury *salatini* untouched. The panic had subsided but she still felt sick. There was no response from Tony, no matter how many times she called. She could imagine them all at his mother's, the happy family reunited, and of course she just didn't fit in. She'd always felt like a mistress, maybe she really was.

She could see a mist rolling in from the sea, illuminated by the lamps and the white hanging decorations lit and looped across the street like lumps of fluffy cotton wool. "Imagine if it rains, they will be dropping with water over everybody," Tony had laughed as they strolled through the Corso last week. But there was no rain tonight. Only fog. She took a sip from her glass, watching lone predatory men stroll past, some staring boldly at her, a woman daring to drink alone. Here, in this holiday paradise, it could only mean one thing. In the summer the whole town was on the pick-up: the would-be greasy gigolos on the prowl at night in their same old shirts, thinking they looked sexy, hoping to strike lucky with the impressionable lone female tourist sipping a glass of wine at one of the many bars and cafés. He'd buy her one drink and she'd spend the night with him - and the rest of the holiday buying him drinks. She would go back home to England or Finland or wherever home was, and that same evening the playboy would be back on the prowl and some other woman would fall into his trap. In the winter fodder was more scarce. She despised all of them.

She felt imprisoned by paradise now, surrounded by the sea, hemmed in by the looming moody beauty of the volcano, and now this fog.

"So romantic, huh, this fog, just like London."

She was startled, lost in her thoughts. "Roland, I didn't see you there, how are you?" She stood up to kiss him, smelling his cologne, a smell she almost didn't like.

"Well, I'm fine. How about you, did you recover from the other night?" he asked, hugging her to him.

"Yes, but I think I need to begin again."

He laughed. "Don't mind if I join you then?" He took off his woolly hat and shook out his shaggy hair. Pulling out a chair he sat down beside her. "Vino for me too. Don't you find the wine very good here? And surprisingly cheap, though I guess we get a good price because we're locals."

"Yes, I suppose so." She hadn't really thought about it, realising she was sick of always having a drink in her hand. But not so sick that she stopped.

"And will you just look at this fog. So damned romantic, don't you think? Look at it. Rolling in on us. Just like that. Just like London, huh?"

"Well, no, actually it isn't. London isn't like this. We don't have fog, not like this. It's a myth. It was smog years ago. It was different. People here have a false concept." She could hear herself jabbering on, almost hysterical.

"Well, it's a small town," he said.

"Small town, small minds," she snapped.

"In some cases, yes, but not all." Roland held up his glass. "Now let's drink to this fog."

Sarah clinked her glass with his and smiled into his eyes, soft and kind.

"Now, that's good stuff, isn't it?" he said.

"Yes, but…" Sarah stopped, took a quick gulp of her wine, her hand shaking as she placed it back on the table. Roland put his hand on hers, she could feel the warmth from it.

"Are you better now, or not?" he asked.

"Not. Worse, in fact."

"Oh, I see."

"No, I'm not sure you do. But I don't want to talk about it."

She did want to but thought better of it. Instead, she made him talk about his life, the wife and kids he had left behind in California ten years ago, how he was washed up and burned out in those days, while here he felt there was a quality of life he savoured, along with the wine.

The smell of jasmine perfumed the night air as she walked the streets home, not so drunk that she would go back to Roland's again. It was becoming a habit, getting drunk with him. But these were exceptional circumstances, she told herself. She let herself in, stumbling through the dim sitting room to the kitchen, dark but for the small lamp on the table. Looking down at Sammy curled up in his basket she could feel herself swaying. Tiptoeing carefully into the bedroom she peeled off her clothes where she stood and left them to crumple to the floor, slipping into bed in her bra and panties. She could smell the smoke on her skin.

"Tony, are you awake?" she whispered in the dark. "I need to talk to you."

"I don't want to talk to you about anything now, I am tired, we can talk in the morning. Goodnight." He turned over, away from her, leaving a cold empty space between them.

Sarah lay on her back looking into the darkness, biting her thumb and thinking of the unmentioned, unwelcome visitor. She had noticed the suitcase was gone.

Tony brought her coffee the next morning as usual, placing it on her bedside cabinet. He stood looking at her saying nothing. Sarah sat up, blinking. Her mouth felt dry, she couldn't speak or swallow. She picked up the cup and sipped the coffee, too strong today but she needed it. She looked at him standing in his jeans and brown shirt, all clean and shiny, always effortlessly handsome, while here she was still in bed, stale from the night before. Noticing her skirt and jumper rumpled on the floor as she had stepped out of them, she remembered what she had been drinking to forget.

"So, are you going to explain what is going on, Sarah?" he asked, still looking at her, his arms folded.

"I was just about to ask you the same thing."

"What? You were the one out drinking all night while I was working and don't think I don't know who with."

"I was out drinking because I was upset yesterday, very upset."

"Upset? Why?"

"I could ask you why. Why is she here?"

"Who?"

"You know very well who. Your wife." Sarah spat out the words. "You certainly haven't been in a hurry to mention her since she arrived."

"Oh, that."

"That? Her. Your wife. Who just happened to turn up on the doorstep. You lied to me, Tony."

"How lied?"

"You told me you were divorced."

"We are."

"But not legally. She said she is your wife."

"Yes, but that is a formality only."

"A formality? You are still married!"

"Only on paper."

"Only by law. You even said you wanted to marry me, how could you?"

"I do, Sarah, I do. This does not affect us."

"Oh no?"

"No, of course not."

"But you didn't even tell me she was arriving."

"I didn't know."

"You are lying to me, Tony. You knew she was coming. That's who you've been calling."

"Look, don't get angry."

"Angry?" She laughed. "No, I'm ecstatic. As if it wasn't enough that I've had to look at photos of her ever since I've known you, now she's here in my face. It's great."

"She is here to see her son for Christmas. Our son. She is staying with my mother and Roberto is there with her. At first I didn't want her to come. I didn't want to see her again, or have Roberto see her, but I couldn't stop her. I had to agree. She is his mother after all. So, you see, that's it, that is all."

"That's all? And the rest."

"What is wrong with you, why are you making this a problem?"

"Oh, it's no problem for me to find out you are still married. I am so happy for you."

"Look, we are separated, it's no big deal, it changes nothing between us. There is nothing for you to worry about."

"But I am worried. How can I not be?"

"Sarah, you need to calm down."

"Calm down?"

"In fact I am the one who should be angry with you. Just what do you think you are up to? I know you were with Roland again."

"How do you know?"

"I have my spies."

"But it's not how you think it is. Nothing is going on."

"Of course not, you need freedom and friends. You are totally innocent."

"Tony, I am, believe me. He is just a friend. I don't like him, not like that. How could I?"

"Forget it, Sarah, I don't want to hear it now." He turned away from her and left the room.

"Tony, come back," she shouted after him. Seething with anger and frustration, she threw the coffee cup at the door, watching it break into pieces all over the stone floor, the remains of her coffee splattering the white wall.

Chapter Five

Her first Christmas in Taormina. The big fir tree erected in the main piazza. Garlands hanging across the streets. The shops full of lights. Poinsettias in pots outside the doorways. Everything green and glittering. The trees were laden with the famous Taormina mandarins, many scattered and squashed where they fell, unheeded. She walked along the Corso, seeing it differently, though it was always the same, with the same staff hanging out of the designer shop doorways of Miss Sixty, Max Mara, Stefanel, Deborah of Fifth Avenue, Benetton. Beautiful girls tossing their long curling hair, cigarettes in hand, talking, laughing, revealing flat brown stomachs whatever the weather, women with names like Olympia with thick eyebrows and hard faces, chewing gum; the stylist with the pink strands of hair, pancake make-up and lipstick outlined outside her lips having a quick puff outside the hairdressers; the big-bellied men congregating outside their jewellery and ceramic shops, guttural voices growling; the waiters of the café in the square wearing red cummerbunds and joking with tourists still wanting ice cream in December.

Sarah glanced at her reflection in the successive shop windows, glimpsing her thin girlish body and serious pale face, all the colour of summer washed out of her. The summer of sunshine and song. She found Tony in the Stella Luna, he was at the piano practising, she knew he had been working there without her. She stood beside him while he continued to play, obviously trying to ignore her.

"Tony, I came to say I'm sorry," she said, putting her hand on his shoulder. He stopped playing. "I know how it looks, but really I was using Roland."

"What? Using him to do what?"

"Get at you. I thought you were the one having an affair, so in my despair I turned to Roland, but only as a friend."

"But why did you think I was having an affair?"

"The call I overheard, that letter you hid from me. You've been acting secretive. Now I know why."

He sighed and took her hand. "I kept it all from you, Sarah because I didn't want you to worry. But there is nothing between me and Vivienne now."

"But you could've told me, I would have understood. Instead we've both misunderstood each other."

"But why did you go out with Roland? I still don't understand."

"I was upset. It wasn't deliberate. It wasn't because I wanted to be with him, I don't. How could I when I love you?"

"You are not acting as if you love me."

"And neither are you. I thought there was someone else. There is in a way. She is still your wife."

"But just in name, not in feeling, I promise you." He stood up and put his arms around her.

"I'm sorry, Tony, I really am. I over-reacted. I've been building it up." She kissed his neck, breathing in the fresh smell of him.

"So, don't tell me you are still thinking of going to England?" he asked, pulling away from her.

"No, I'm not. As much as I want to see my family, I think I need to be here."

"Of course you do. Here with me," he said.

"And Vivienne too, by the looks of it."

"Yes, but don't worry. It will be fine, I promise. Come on," he said. "Let's go for a walk while it's still light. I'm so glad you don't want to go away." He kissed her cheek and she smiled up at him. She wasn't looking forward to telling her mother. It was their second Christmas without her father and she knew it would be a difficult time for the family who wouldn't understand why she wasn't coming home.

"While we are clearing the air there's another thing. You've got to let me sing, Tony. If I am staying you have to let me back in. I don't understand why you are shutting me out. We were so good together."

Tony sighed. "It was wrong of me, I know that now. Let's start to go over some numbers for the Christmas holidays, okay?"

On Christmas Eve Sarah sat in Ruth's tiny flat, all white walls and stone floors. All the apartments were designed as if the island existed in a perpetual Mediterranean summer when in fact the winters were damp and cold. Ruth had managed to make it warmer and more homely with rugs and throws, as well as a blow heater she had brought from England.

Sarah looked at the silver parcel placed on the coffee table. "But why was this delivered here?" she asked.

Ruth set down the tray of tea and cinnamon biscuits. "God knows, just left outside my door, found it this morning. Come on, you might as well open it."

Sarah tore open the tissue paper and pulled out a black nylon transparent thong with feathers and tassels at the back.

"Blimey, don't they wear those at Playboy?" Ruth said, choking on her biscuit.

"Gosh." Sarah could feel herself going red. She looked at the label. "Cheek. It's a size 14. I'm not a size 14, my bum isn't that big."

"Obviously a bad guess!" Ruth laughed.

"But who on earth can it be from?"

"Isn't there a card or a note?"

"No, nothing." Sarah checked inside the box.

"Well, whoever it is they know you know me and they know where I live. Not sure I like the sound of that."

"Everyone knows everyone here, no one is allowed to be anonymous."

"Yes, but not everyone knows my address. Hey, it had better not be Saro, I'll kill him."

"Don't be silly, Ruth, course it isn't. Maybe Tony is having a joke on us both."

"I wouldn't show him that feather thing if I were you, he'll only be jealous."

"He's jealous enough as it is. That reminds me, I can't stay too long, Tony's cooking an early supper just for the two of us."

"How romantic."

"I'm so excited to be singing again at the bar tonight. You are coming, aren't you?"

"Course."

"So you're glad too that you've stayed on, even after everything you said about going back home?"

"Yeah. Saro begged me not to go." Ruth smiled, biting into another cinnamon biscuit. "He is very hard to resist."

The candlelit supper made her feel special, like the old times with Tony. He cooked spaghetti with tuna, olives and capers. They drank Nero D'Avola red wine which made her feel warmed and flushed.

After, as she was touching up her make-up, she realised she felt nervous: it was the first time they were performing together since the Coco Club. Watching Tony as he stood looking at himself in the mirror, combing his hair, she noticed he was wearing yet another new suit, beautifully tailored as usual from his man in Milan, and once again wondered how he could afford these expensive clothes. She never asked him. His carefully co-ordinated silk ties and perfectly pressed shirts were nothing to do with her either. His mother took care of all that and she had never offered to take over. He turned to her and smiled. The vision of him always left her feeling weak in her stomach, as if she was seeing him for the first time.

She suddenly remembered the mystery gift. "Tony, I have something to show you," she said, putting down her eye-liner and rummaging in her bag. She pulled out the feathery thong and dangled it in front of him.

"My goodness, what is this?" He snatched it from her. "Who gave you this?" He frowned and threw it back to her.

Sarah looked at him. "Isn't it from you? I thought you were playing a joke."

"A joke? No. My gift is much more serious. Which reminds me, here it is." He took a box from his bedside drawer and placed it on her pillow. "Merry Christmas," he said, kissing her softly.

She looked up at him, surprised.

"Open it!" he commanded.

Inside the red velvet box sat a thin platinum band with a small sparkling diamond. "Tony!" she gasped.

"You like it?"

"Yes, but..."

"Here, try it on," he said, taking it out of the box for her.

"Which hand?" she asked, looking at him. He slipped it onto her left hand. "But Tony, I don't understand. This is impossible." She looked at him, waiting for an explanation.

"Just believe me. This is a promise of my love." He kissed her again and she was silenced.

She studied the ring twinkling delicately on her finger. It all seemed so complicated. How could he give her an engagement ring when he wasn't even divorced? He wanted to marry her but he was still married to someone else. His baggage seemed to be accumulating the longer she knew him. First a son and now a wife. Was there anything else he was hiding from her?

At the Stella Luna, Ruth and Sarah sipped prosecco and shared from the same plate a very sweet, sloppy cream cake concoction. Sarah had sung a few old numbers with Tony, delighted to be back there again, feeling the thrill. But that was all she was allowed to do. A few numbers. She started to protest but Tony told her she couldn't stand up and sing all night, she wasn't used to it. He promised she could come on later and do a few more at the end of the evening. Disappointed, she was grateful that Ruth was there and glugged down one glass of prosecco after another.

"Tony's mother made the cake for Christmas, don't you like it?" Sarah asked Ruth, watching her mash the mixture with her spoon.

"What I'd prefer right now is a nice bit of real Christmas cake, full of fruit, with proper icing and thick marzipan, not all this gooey, soft mush," said Ruth, draining the last of her prosecco. "And a proper drink, not this soppy soda pop. I need a whisky."

"I quite like both."

"Ah, well, you're being loyal, love. Got to be, I suppose." She nodded at Tony. "Just look at him. Loves it doesn't he, never gets tired of the sound of his own voice, does he?"

"No, but he obviously gets tired of mine. Am I that bad?" she asked Ruth, feeling deflated.

"Oh love, you were good, you really were, a bit croaky but that is sexy jazz for you, I suppose. Look, don't worry, just see it as a bit of fun and enjoy it."

"Maybe I am taking everything too seriously, I don't know any more."

"Well, I suppose he must be serious too, he has just given you this ring. Let's have a proper look at it then."

"It doesn't fit."

"What?"

"It's a bit loose." Sarah held out her hand to Ruth, the glittering stone, the shiny band, it slipped down her finger, only the knuckle barring the fall.

"He'll have to get it changed. Stupid sod. Didn't he check your size?"

"Said it was the smallest they did."

"Bollocks! The crap these men come out with. A ring like that and it's too big!"

"I know. It's so beautiful." A sob caught in her throat.

"Oh no, you've not gone all silly now, have you? I mean what is this ring, an engagement ring or what?"

"I don't know. I suppose so."

"What d'you mean you don't know? It looks like one. But then he's hardly in a position to propose is he?"

"At the moment, no, but it's a promise. That's what he said."

"Promise of what, that he'll divorce her and marry you?"

"I hope so."

"Are you sure you want to marry him?"

"I think so. Oh, look, here she is. That's his ex, just arriving."

Ruth turned to look. "So that's her. Quite a stunner isn't she." She jumped down from her stool, tottering on high heels, her low-cut dress revealing her still tanned cleavage which Sarah put down to the sunbed. "I'm off, love."

"No, Ruth, you can't go, not now," she pleaded.

"I have to, I'm meeting Saro, he's escaping for a few hours and as it's Christmas he'll be folded into his family the rest of the time so it's my only chance and I have to take it. Merry Christmas, love, and I hope you're wearing that thong." Ruth winked at Sarah as she kissed her goodbye.

The crowd applauded Tony just as Vivienne walked in, flowing blonde hair, glowing skin, golden silk dress, gold stiletto shoes. Would he look at her and desire her again, Sarah wondered, wanting to escape, not stay and be sociable.

"Hello, Sarah, here you are and so we meet again." Vivienne stood beside her at the bar.

"Yes, hello," she said, noticing Vivienne looked tired beneath the glow.

"We are all here for a Happy Christmas, I think."

"Let's hope so." Sarah smiled back, draining the last of the prosecco from her glass.

"That looks good," Vivienne said, stepping up onto a stool. "Maybe I shall have one of those."

"No, we are having this now," Tony said, arriving with a bottle of wine. "This is *passito di Pantelleria*, a sweet wine of superior quality," he assured them, pouring them each a flute. Tony wedged himself between Sarah and Vivienne and raised his glass. "*Buon Natale* to us all," he said.

"It's very sweet," Sarah said.

"Yes, of course it is," Tony replied. "It is supposed to be."

Vivienne inspected the pale golden liquid. "Are you sure this is good, to me it looks like off wine," she said, grimacing before she took a sip, after which she drank it back in one go. Roberto, having followed his mother into the bar, was whining, pulling on his mother's dress to go home. "He blames me because he is not in bed," she said to Sarah, her slender legs wrapped around the bar stool.

"Oh dear," Sarah looked at her watch, it was approaching midnight.

"Spoilt," Vivienne pronounced, swaying as Roberto pulled her. "But, you know, it is Christmas, so we can make exceptions."

"And you are his greatest Christmas gift, I bet." Sarah said, smiling, trying to be nice though she didn't feel like it. She couldn't help feeling the irony of the situation, here they were altogether, Tony, his wife and the other woman. Wondering which role she was playing, she slid the ring from her finger and slipped it into her jeans pocket, not wanting it to be seen by the wrong eyes.

At midnight they stood in the piazza where a huge fire was lit, giant logs of wood burning fiercely; there were fires outside all the churches, a symbol of giving warmth to the poor. On this one night at least, the rest of the year they can freeze, Sarah thought as she stood looking at the flames. She didn't like the heavy dark atmosphere. The air felt oppressive, there seemed to be no rejoicing, no fun or laughter, no carols of comfort and joy, no mulled wine or mince pies. Panettone and prosecco however was not a poor substitute: she loved the slices of sweet bread with raisins and dried fruits and the sparkling dry wine. She had drunk enough of it tonight and was glad of the cold air to sober her up. Tony had made her wear the thick blanket coat and she put a padded arm through his as they stood watching the fire. "Merry Christmas," she said as she kissed his cold cheek.

The Christmas Day lunch was skilfully arranged by Carlotta. Tony sat with Vivienne, their son between them, while Sarah was placed at the other end of the table with the elderly aunts and uncles visiting from out of town. Carlotta sat beside Tony and looked across at Sarah. "*Tutto bene*, everything okay, yes?" she asked, smirking.

"Yes, of course," Sarah replied, even though it wasn't. She smiled back, sipping her Martini aperitif. The only concession to Christmas evident in Carlotta's small apartment was the *stella di natale*, the poinsettia in the middle of the table. Sarah thought of the real

Christmas tree her mother always had, the tinsel and lights, the baubles and small wooden angel fitted at the top of the tree.

"We did not expect you stay so long in Taormina," Carlotta said.

Sarah caught the flicker of hostility evident in her eyes. "No, I'm sure you didn't."

"Is a long time you are here. You not miss family? Your home. So far away."

"I'm surviving," Sarah could feel the false smile fixed on her face.

"But soon you go, I think, no? You cannot stay here forever."

"Who knows, maybe I will," said Sarah, feeling those black beads boring into hers. Carlotta looked like a thin black crow in her widow's weeds, her beaked nose, lined face and hair of steel. Sarah raised her glass and finished her bitter Martini in one gulp.

There was pasta for Christmas lunch: penne with tomatoes and baked cheese on top. No turkey here then, Sarah thought, suddenly yearning for the brussels, stuffing and cranberry sauce, for the smiling faces of her sister Lily and her brother Andy, her nephew Benjamin and her poor dear mother. She imagined them all gathered round the table wearing paper party hats from crackers with jokes that Ben always knew the answers to, crackers spilling key rings, puzzles and tiny packs of playing cards. No Christmas pudding, no brandy butter and cream, no mince pies. Sarah sighed. She drank more of the red wine to make herself feel better, only to make herself feel worse. Tony busied himself with taking pictures, forever getting up to get the angle right, so many shots of Roberto eating and drinking and making faces. Vivienne chain-smoked and talked in French on the phone. Everyone gabbled away in languages Sarah couldn't understand. She escaped in between courses to stand on the balcony overlooking the quiet street and cried to her mother on her mobile.

"Come home, Sarah, if it's that bad. We're all here missing you. You should've come home. We are your family. Your father is missing but you shouldn't be." Her mother sounded tearful.

"I'll be alright, Mum, it's just the wine making me blubber," Sarah replied, feeling guilty she had upset her mother.

"Well, whoever eats pasta for Christmas dinner, I ask you, what a strange lot you've got involved with. Come back, dear. Brussels are waiting," her mother laughed, trying to sound more cheerful. "We've got plenty of those left."

Sarah could see them altogether in her mother's house, full now after the pudding and pies and cake but with the promise of turkey sandwiches later, sitting at the table playing cards with pennies, Newmarket and Sevens. How she wished she could be at that table now.

"Why did you sit next to her, your place is beside me, yet I am left an outsider while you play happy families." Sarah couldn't help feeling annoyed as they walked home, the festivities over.

"That's just my mother, it was no big deal," Tony said.

"No big deal? Your mother's a spiteful old cow." She knew the red wine was making her more volatile and she shouldn't be so bitchy.

"Don't get upset, Sarah, she doesn't mean anything."

"I can see what she's playing at even if you can't."

"She knows there is nothing between me and Viv so she is wasting her time. In fact Viv insulted me, she told me I look old and tired," he said.

"Did she? That's not true at all." Tony was looking as handsome as ever.

"And I think she looks old and fat, but I didn't tell her."

"But that isn't true either."

"It doesn't matter. Come on."

The late afternoon sky was a deepening dusky blue. She took his hand and they made their way home through the Corso, buzzing with after luncheon displays. How these people love to show off, she thought. Stout ladies walking in their finery, fur coats and stiff glossy shoes, their arms linked through their husbands; young nubile beauties strutting the length of the street, flinging their hair about, wanting to be worshipped on their way to an assignation; effeminate, coiffeured, perfumed pretentious men stalking the streets for Christmas girls or boys; couples strolling leisurely; tourists here for Christmas lunch in the hotels or just for the day from the cruise ship; children running and riding bikes, parents following or sitting at a café nearby. All the shops, cafés and bars were open. Piped music blared out from speakers set up the length of the entire Corso, tired old tunes that no one really wanted to hear, while Christmas lights flashed like falling snow. "Kitsch, eh?" Tony laughed as he looked up at the plastic Santas hanging from the balconies, an arm around her shoulder. She could see women looking at him as they passed, their impossibly black hair long and crinkling. She could see he looked at them too, but he was with her, she reassured herself.

"You see my love, there is nothing to worry about," Tony said, taking Sarah in his arms once they were home. "Your fears are unfounded."

"Well, I'm not exactly happy in her presence, but…"

"You need only be happy in my presence, Sarah, that's all I ask." He twirled her round until she was dizzy. "Just be happy, for me."

The next day wasn't known as Boxing Day but Santo Stephano. Every day was named after a saint, not just holidays. Sarah remembered family Christmases when her father was alive; he would always have a bet on Boxing Day and would want to eat cold turkey with pickled onions. He pickled the onions himself, jars all over the kitchen marinating and stinking, Sarah hated them. Here there were no pickled onions. They were back at the bar for an early evening set, playing the same familiar tunes, jazz ballads old and new. Having sung two songs Sarah was sitting at the bar having yet another enforced, extended break when Vivienne walked in and sat beside her, pulling herself up onto a high stool. She ordered a Campari and started smoking immediately, talking and laughing with the staff like they were old friends. Sarah had never made friends with the handsome barman or the pretty blonde barmaids standing all in a row, flittering around the tables in their black fitted aprons. She realised she hadn't really made friends with anyone. Except Roland, of course.

Finding her courage as she drank her gin and tonic she turned to Vivienne. "So how long are you staying?" she asked, trying to sound casual.

"I am not sure, I have not decided. It has been a long time since I have seen my son, of course. I miss him, that is for sure. But I make a choice, no. But now I can stay a while."

"But do you work in France?"

"In Paris, of course. I have some problems there at the moment. With my boss. He is difficult. And I have a boyfriend but he is becoming possessive and I do not like that. And then I have a neighbour who declared his love for me just before I come here, when all I ask of him was to water my plants while I am away! And, well, you know, I am a business woman, I meet a lot of men, so many men, but I get so tired of them all."

Sarah looked at her, unable to find an adequate response.

"But Antonio, he is, I suppose, a good father. He tries to be a good man."

"But you left?"

"Sure, I left, I had no choice. It was terrible for me. Under chains here, lock and key, night and day. A woman like me cannot stay here forever. Maybe you are different?" Vivienne looked Sarah up and down, blowing smoke into her face. "But be careful, I say," Vivienne continued, raising her voice over the music. "Tony isn't everything he appears to be. Nothing is here."

Sarah didn't understand, she wondered if Vivienne was drunk. She looked at the other people, couples and groups, locals and tourists. Some were talking quietly while others were listening to Tony sing. She noticed one woman sitting at a table alone staring at him, her chin on her hand, a glass of red wine in front of her. The bar was strung with tiny lights and there were candles on each small table shedding shimmering intimate shadows everywhere. Tony was a romantic figure in his dark grey suit and white shirt, tie-less and casual, his black hair falling into his blue eyes looking out into the distance as he crooned about love and longing. Sarah felt momentarily mesmerised as she had done so many times when she watched him.

"And you, why are you here?" Vivienne startled Sarah from the spell. "Please don't tell me you are in love."

"Well, yes, I am."

"Then I pity you," Vivienne laughed. "You are lost.".

"What do you mean?"

Before Vivienne could answer she was distracted by Roland approaching, waving and shouting across the bar to her. "My darling Vivvie, you are back, I cannot believe you are here." He swept her off the stool into his arms.

"Back to see you, Rollie, of course!" she laughed.

"You bet. And don't you look exquisite. My word, just look at you. Glamorous, by God!"

Vivienne stood tall and shining, sequins scattered through her sheer black dress setting off the golden sparkles of her hair. "You don't look so bad yourself," she giggled. "You've lost weight I see."

He patted his tummy. "Yeah, this is just padding, you know. But when this sweater peels off, well you know what's underneath, eh, Vivvie?"

She poked him in the ribs. "Rollie, you are as naughty as ever."

"And let's hope that never changes, huh."

He managed to drag his drooling eyes away from Vivienne to look at Sarah. "And here you are too, Sarah. Fancy that!"

Sarah smiled, feeling far too casual in her trendy torn jeans and halter-neck top, wishing she had worn a dress. "Let's have another drink!" she said, holding up her empty glass, trying to feel brave but knowing it was just the gin talking.

The next day her brother rang from England. "So you couldn't even come home for Christmas, could you?"

"Merry Christmas to you too, Andy."

"And who rang up crying? Upsetting Mum."

"That was just too much red wine at lunch."

"Since when have you been a wino? You an alcoholic now then or what?"

"No, Andy, it's Christmas, everyone drinks at Christmas."

"You could've come home, you know, Mum ill as she is, missing Dad."

"Don't try to make me feel worse than I do already."

"And so you should. We haven't seen you for months. Family has to stick together, you know, at times like this."

"Mum's okay without me."

"And how would you know?"

"She said so."

"Yeah, well she's not going to tell you, is she?"

"She knows I have commitments here. I'm working."

"Yeah, right." She could hear the sneer in his voice.

"I am. And Tony has his family here too. It's been a bit complicated."

"How?"

Sarah hesitated. "Well, Tony's ex turned up. And, you see, it turns out that they aren't divorced like I thought."

"You what?"

"They will be, it's just a matter of time. It's no big deal really. But, anyway, I…"

He cut her off. "And you're still there, what the fuck for?"

"I knew I shouldn't have told you. But that's why I wanted to stay. I'm with Tony now, I can't just ditch him, he needs me."

"Needs you when he still has a missus, that's rich."

"I got upset at first, but they are separated. She's here to see her son."

"Bloody hell, Sarah, what have you got yourself into, racing out there after some old married guy."

"I'm not running after him. And he's not that old."

"What? He's nearly twice your age."

"Don't exaggerate, he isn't. And anyway, I didn't know he was married, did I."

"No. But you do now."

"Yes, but it's not how you think it is. It's not like he's married and I'm the bit on the side."

"No, I'm sure it isn't."

"Andy, I'm not that daft, give me a bit of credit, will you."

He sighed. "Look, do what you want, Sarah, it's your life. I've gotta go now."

"Merry Christmas to you too, big brother."

She hung up the phone and went back to cleaning the house, a never-ending battle with the dust and mess, trailing the vacuum cleaner over the uneven stone floors. Andy's call had disturbed her. Was she mad to stay here like this and was that why she was drinking so much, turning to alcohol like so many of the locals. Like Roland. Sammy ran around her, then out into the yard, away from the noise of the vacuum. She half-heartedly dusted the surfaces, stacks of music books and papers and toys scattered around the room, there wasn't a clear surface anywhere. Giving up, she sneaked out into the yard, having taken a secret cigarette from the packet she kept in one of the kitchen cupboards. Slim Merit. Just one, now and again. Despite Tony's disapproval. It was alright for him to smoke, of course. Sammy licked her toes, cold in her flip-flops as she stood on the fallen leaves. It was dark already, she looked up at the evening sky, at the faint glimpses of stars. She thought about her mother, lonely without her father. Of course she felt guilty, but she didn't need Andy rubbing it in. Stepping onto the cigarette butt she picked it up and threw it into the kitchen bin.

The next morning Tony was dressing, the drawer of the old wooden chest wide open.

"Where are all my socks?" he asked.

"They should be there. Haven't you noticed my systematic pairing so you don't have to spend hours looking for a matching sock?"

"But I can't find any, not one."

She got out of bed and rummaged under the pants and vests he'd tossed aside. "Look, here they are. Men can never see what is front of them," she said.

He sat on the edge of the bed pulling on the socks.

Sarah stood and looked at him. "Tony, how long is Vivienne staying here?"

"I don't know. She will go soon, don't worry."

"But I do worry."

He sighed. "Look, Sarah, we have gone over this so many times. Try to understand." He pulled on his shoes and laced them. "Don't think she has come back for me." He stood up and kissed her forehead. "It's not true. Whatever she has told you."

"How do you know what she has told me?" Sarah asked, alarmed at his suggestion.

"I know women. They are witches."

"Oh, really?"

"Most of them, yes. But you, no. Only sometimes."

"Thanks."

"Look, I say again, don't worry. She will go soon, probably after the *capodanno* celebration."

"The what?"

"New Year."

"Are you sure?"

"Yes. Now come on, get ready, we have to eat at my mother's today."

"Oh no, not again. I don't want to go."

"But you must go. I want you to go."

She looked at him and realised she couldn't refuse.

Once again Sarah endured Carlotta's matriarchal exhibitions, her exaggerated fussing over Tony and Roberto, and the evident affection and closeness between her and Vivienne who helped to serve and clear the table, a part of the family, while Sarah watched, feeling like the excluded onlooker.

"You not like the pasta?" Carlotta asked Sarah, looking at her with barely disguised disgust.

"Yes, of course I do, sorry to leave it but I am so full," she said, patting her flat tummy. She'd hardly managed to eat any of the linguine with *zucchini*, even though courgette was her favourite vegetable.

Carlotta didn't understand. "You not like. You not cook pasta?"

"Yes I do like it. But no, I don't cook." She remembered the time she had tried to prepare a simple pasta dish for Tony at her little apartment before she moved in with him, wanting to impress him. The spaghetti was all soft and sticky, and the fresh tomatoes burned in the frying pan. Tony had to start all over again.

"Sarah, that is terrible, a woman must cook, no?" said Vivienne.

"Well, my mother can, or at least she used to when my father was alive."

"But you? I suppose you live on baked beans? That is normal for English, no?"

"Something like that. Though I prefer toast."

Vivienne laughed.

"*Mamma mia*!" Carlotta was shaking her head and waving her hands, gabbling something which Sarah couldn't understand, though she caught the look of contempt on her face as she took away her plate.

"It's considered an insult," Vivienne said.

"What is?"

"Not to eat the food."

"I can't help that. By the looks of her she wants to stuff it down my throat." Sarah helped herself to another glass of *vino rosso* and tried not to let the old crow bother her.

As they left the house after lunch, climbing down the many steps to street level, Vivienne linked her arm through Sarah's. "Come, little Sarah, let's go and have a coffee shall we, just you and I?"

"Oh, okay, if you like." Sarah was surprised by this suggestion.

"Or do you have something to do at home?"

"No. Not really." But she felt uneasy.

Vivienne steered her up the street. "Tony wants us to be friends, you know."

"Does he?"

"Of course."

"But where is Tony?" Sarah asked, turning around, scanning the street behind them.

"He's taken our son to the cinema. Didn't you understand that?"

"No, not really."

"You English with your language, you never have the ear for another, do you?"

"No, as the saying goes we just speak louder."

"Ah yes, that seems to be true, all those rowdy Englishmen. I met many."

"Have you been there?"

"In England? Oh yes, many years ago. Lots of lovers in London. But they are very narrow-minded, your Englishmen, don't you find?"

"Not all of them. Where are we going?"

"I like this little bar at the end of the street. It's been there for years, never changes. So much here stays the same. You can be sure of that. Let's have espresso, yes?"

"Think I need some sobering up, that red wine at lunch is lethal."

"Ah, the grandmother's good strong country wine."

The only thing about her that is good, Sarah thought.

"Do you know it here?" Vivienne asked as they entered the bar.

Sarah looked around at the red painted walls, the floors of dark stone, wooden beams above them. "No, I've never been here before," she said.

"Marvellous cocktails. The owner and I were once such good friends." Her green eyes twinkled at Sarah.

"Really?"

"But these men, you know, they have limitations."

"Like Tony?"

"Ha! You think I mean him?"

"Well, maybe."

"He does too, but in different ways. You'll see."

"Do you still love him?" Sarah asked.

Vivienne laughed, spitting her coffee across her silk shirt. "Excuse me, but that's quite funny." She wiped at the spot of coffee with a napkin. "Still love Antonio? No. I don't know if I ever did." Vivienne shrugged. "But you are young. You are free to love him. I am done with him."

"Thanks very much."

"If you really want to know, and you do of course, I am here to take Roberto home with me. To Paris."

"What?"

"Yes. It's where he belongs. With me. My son cannot stay here. I left him because… well, the truth is Antonio would not let me take him. It was impossible. He made sure of that. But now he cannot stop me. Antonio cannot take care of him. I see that. He runs around town, so wayward. Not that I want the boy to be tied to his father's shoelaces, you understand. But there is no control here. The schools produce illiterates. I do not want this. Not for my son. No. He must go to a good school. I have plans for him. He cannot stay here and work in some shop or restaurant. He must have some ambition. Some sense of self that these islanders do not possess. The man is the lion here, ripping his way through life, chaos is left behind him. Nothing is achieved."

Sarah was shocked, she didn't know what to say.

"And you. You think you are mothering him?"

"Your son? No, of course not. I wouldn't presume to do that. His grandmother cares for him mostly. And Tony, of course."

"Yes, when he feels like it."

"He tries."

"Tries and fails."

"But you said he was a good father."

"I don't always say what I mean. And Antonio does not always do what he says."

"Does Tony know?"

"That I take Roberto home? Not yet. I have told Carlotta. She is devoted to him and it will break her heart when he goes. She wants me to be here of course. Never wanted me to leave. But Antonio makes life impossible." Vivienne lit a cigarette. Camel. She inhaled deeply, looking at Sarah. "Do you know him at all?" she asked.

"I hope I do, after all this time." Sarah looked at the smoke hanging heavy in the air, wondering if she really did know him, feeling there was always something elusive about him. She sipped at the shot of coffee not sure if she was feeling more sober or more drunk.

"I wouldn't be so sure." She looked at Sarah and shook her head.

"But does Roberto know he is going with you?"

"Of course. He is happy to come back with me."

"I see."

"You think I am a bad mother. I go away. I leave him here. But I never wanted to leave him, you understand? Except you don't, you cannot. You have no idea what I went through." She put out the cigarette. "So, now I come back. I take him away. And to hell with Antonio." She downed the last drop of coffee. "Come on. Let's go. This is between us, you understand, do not talk to Antonio, *va bene*?"

Sarah nodded.

She didn't know what to make of it all. Tony had stopped his wife taking their son away from him? He hadn't exactly put it that way. He said Vivienne had left the kid, left them both. But why had Vivienne been so desperate to leave?

It was the day before New Year's Eve. Tony was ranting and raving, storming around the house. "She cannot do this to me. I told her. It's impossible. She must stay here with us or she goes alone."

"What do you mean she must stay here with us?"

"With me and my son, of course."

"How?"

"I don't know. But we are still married. She cannot take him away. We have an arrangement. I let her go. But not my son. She cannot come back and do this. I cannot allow it."

"Oh, so you are married after all, when it suits you, it's not just a formality now is it."

"What?"

"So now you want her back? Your wife, you want to be with her?"

"Not exactly. No. That is not what I want. But my son. He is at stake."

"And me?"

"Please, Sarah, you are nothing to do with this."

"I'm not?"

"No. It's better you stay out of it."

"Fine. I bloody well will."

She ran out of the house in tears, taking her ghastly gigantic coat with her. What was she, just a dolly sitting on the bed to wind up and play with when he felt like it? And how could he want Vivienne to stay? It would be far better if she left and took the boy with her. She sat seething and sobbing on a cold iron bench in the public gardens, looking at the snow on the volcano, the cold pale sea below. Sometimes she hated the sight of it, always there, dominating the horizon, its enormity was overwhelming, too threatening. Thunder rumbled like an empty stomach, darkness in the distance. Her phone rang. It must be Tony, he must be sorry. She took it out of her pocket. Crestfallen. Private number. "Hello?"

"Sarah? How do I get out of this fucking airport?"

"Andy? What do you mean, where are you?"

"I'm at the airport, here in Catatonia or whatever it's called."

"What, you're at Catania? You are joking, right? Where are you really, Andy? Stop messing about."

"I'm here, for real, trying to get a taxi."

"But you can't be. What are you doing here?"

"Come to save my long lost sister. Now, quick, just tell me how to get to you, this call is costing me a fortune."

"Well, you could get the big blue bus. There is a sign just outside the airport, turn right, you can't miss it, wait there. It will have Taormina on the front, it's the last stop, so it will take about an hour or so, but it's cheap."

"Alright, I'll call you when I'm on the bus then."

"I'll meet you at the terminal, when you get off the bus I'll be there. I just can't believe you are here."

"Well, you'd better." He hung up.

She stood in the dark bus terminal and burst into tears when Andy finally stepped down from the coach, carrying a small rucksack.

"We're late cos something in the engine blew up on that bloody bus, took ages to get it going again."

They hugged and she started to laugh through her tears. "Things like that are always happening here. You get used to it. Gosh, Andy, what a surprise. As I waited I was still wondering if you were having me on."

"Here I am, large as life, though I wasn't sure we were going to make it."

Andy was booked into a small *pensione*, nothing fancy but decent enough. Sarah took him back to the house for dinner, not having returned since the argument. Tony was in the kitchen cooking spaghetti carbonara. Roberto was on the sofa playing on his gameboy.

"Tony, I have a surprise, look who's here, this is my brother Andy. He's come all the way from England to see us. Andy meet Tony."

"You didn't tell me he was coming." Tony said, shaking hands with Andy after wiping his hands on a tea towel.

"I didn't know, that's why."

"Intended as a big surprise," Andy said, returning the handshake. He was wider and bigger than Tony, and Sarah couldn't help feeling he looked a bit threatening.

"Of course you are welcome," Tony said to Andy.

Vivienne opened the kitchen door, emerging from the hallway.

"It looks like there is a surprise for me too," Sarah said. "I didn't realise you would be here. This is all very cosy, I must say."

"Well, Tony and I have a matter to discuss, as you know," Vivienne replied, looking at her meaningfully.

She noticed Vivienne had cleared the clutter and found an ancient flowered tablecloth on which to set the plates and glasses, knives and forks. Vivienne opened a bottle of red wine and tried to flirt with Andy but he pretended not to notice. Tony dished up the pasta and they sat down to eat. Sarah twirled her spaghetti, half of it falling from her fork every time she tried to take a mouthful. She had never got the knack of it and hated the humiliation of trying to eat the stuff. She glanced at her brother. He looked like a rugby player, big and burly, his face always scrubbed and serious, his eyes a bit too small for his full face, his hair cropped to cut out the curls. She wasn't so sure she wanted him here.

"So, tell me, what do you do in England, Andy?" Vivienne asked, helping herself to more wine without offering the bottle round.

"Drive a cab. A London taxi, you know, the big black taxis?"

"Of course I do. I have been in one. I do know London. It's not so far from Paris. Have you ever been there?" she asked.

"Paris? No," he replied.

Sarah looked at him, she knew he couldn't stand the French but to say it would be asking for trouble.

"And you have never been here before?" Vivienne continued

"No."

"So, I can tell you it is a good time to see Taormina."

"It's colder than I imagined." Andy replied.

"Bet you're glad you wore that thick sweater, Andy." Sarah could see it was one of their mother's knitted numbers.

"Yeah, Mum made me bring it. But I didn't think it would be this cold."

"Oh, you English, always talking about the cold and the weather," Vivienne laughed.

"Well, we prefer the sunshine, but I don't suppose it gets hot here this time of year," he said.

"Oh, you'll be surprised how hot it can get." Vivienne looked at him and giggled, drinking off the wine in her glass.

Sarah was looking at Tony who didn't seem to be paying attention. He hardly spoke, eating his spaghetti in a determined way, stabbing at the elusive strands and gathering them quickly around his fork so that nothing escaped. "What's going on, Tony?" she asked quietly.

"What?" he looked up from his plate.

"I want to know what's going on here," she lowered her voice.

"I don't understand, Sarah, what do you mean?"

"No. That's typical. And so very convenient." She sighed, pushing the small cubes of fatty bacon to one side with the rest of the spaghetti already congealing in the dish.

"Antonio is angry with me," Vivienne said to Sarah.

"I don't want to talk about this now, Vivienne," Tony said.

"I am taking his son away, that's why he is angry."

"No, you are not, you will not take him," Tony shouted.

"It's for the best, Antonio, you had him for a year, now it is my turn."

"I will not let you take him, he's my son."

"And mine too. I gave birth to him."

"You have to let him go, Tony, the boy needs his mother," Sarah said.

"And whose side are you on?" Tony glared at her, throwing his fork down on the plate.

"Look, I think it's better if I go." Andy got up from the table.

Sarah got up too. "I'll come with you Andy, walk you back to the hotel."

"Right. Thanks for the meal. Nice to meet you all."

"I shall see you later, Tony. I hope you'll have calmed down by then," Sarah said.

"Yes, you leave us to the discussion. We will sort things out," Vivienne said, lighting a cigarette.

"There is nothing to sort out, Vivienne, just go will you, leave me in peace." Tony sat at the table with folded arms.

Roberto had already left the table and was back with his gameboy on the sofa, Sammy lying on the floor beside his feet.

Sarah and Andy walked in silence. "Look at Etna," she said. "Isn't it amazing?" They stood to look at the view over the bay. Etna at night, covered in snow, a paler shade of the dark blue of the sky, the line of red lava just visible, the stars and moon above. She breathed in deeply, the cool night air filling her lungs. "Sorry about that, Andy. I think we could both do with a nightcap, don't you?"

"Hadn't you better get back?"

"No, I'd rather sit with you for a bit," she said. They were the only two in the bar below the *pensione* as they sat with their coffee and brandy. She sighed. "It's lovely to see you, Andy, but why have you come?"

"To find out what is going on here."

"Well, you haven't come at a very good time."

"I can see that."

"It isn't usually like this."

"What, happy cosy families you mean?"

"It's hardly that. Vivienne wants to take their son back to France with her and Tony wants him to stay."

"Yeah, I got the gist. If that scene we walked into was anything to go by, maybe they're both staying."

"Andy, don't say that."

"You'd better open your eyes then. You're living in a fucking fantasy."

"Andy!"

"Well, who the hell is this tosser who tinkles the piano? You don't really know him do you?"

"Of course I do, I live with him. And how dare you call him that, you've only just met him."

"Yeah, and I didn't get a very favourable impression either." Andy shook his head. "I just don't trust the bloke, there's something about him."

"How can you say that?"

"Come on, what have you got yourself into, Sarah? It's a good job I came out here."

"But I didn't ask you to come, Andy. You're supposed to be looking after Mum at home, not running out here to interfere in my life."

"I am looking after Mum, it's all I do. Not something you'd know about since you upped and left her. Didn't care then, did you, cos there was some poxy Italian stallion on the scene."

"It wasn't like that."

"Oh no, what was it like then, go on, do tell me. How long do you think you can go on like this. I mean, what about money? That money Dad left you won't last forever."

"Tony is looking after me."

"But you're a big girl now."

"And I don't want you to tell me how to live my life."

"But look at you, Sarah, you look terrible. You on drugs or what?"

"Course I'm not, what are you talking about?"

"I've never seen you so thin. What do you weigh, three stone and a paper bag?"

"Very funny. I'm just off my food at the moment."

"Yeah, but on the booze, I can see. You watch out. You'll be getting yourself knocked up next. Stuck on this poxy island. Call this a civilised country. It's more like the third world if the airport is anything to go by."

"Andy, stop it, what do want?"

"Just this, if you want to start the new year with any dignity, you'll come home with me."

Sarah lay in the dark going over her talk with Andy. He always made her feel stupid, as if he knew better. Turning up here, checking up on her, as if she was incapable, how dare he. Ever since Dad died he was always interfering. He took over when Michael did the dirty on her. She was grateful then but sometimes it was too much. This time she ought to tell him to sod off. She couldn't sleep. She turned over to face Tony, she could tell he was awake, his breathing shallow as he lay beside her. "You have to let her go, Tony," she whispered.

"And take my son away from me?"

"So she stays here then, great, one big happy family."

He sighed. "I don't want to talk about this now, Sarah, I am trying to sleep," he said.

He felt as cold as stone beside her. "But how can you sleep at a time like this?"

"Because I am tired."

"Well, I can't sleep. You must talk to me. We have to sort this out."

"What do you want me to say? I cannot solve this problem tonight. Go to sleep now. We can think of this tomorrow."

"Everything is always tomorrow, *domani*, always *domani*." She got up and went to the kitchen to make herself some hot chocolate, noticing how clean and tidy Vivienne had left it. How dare she clean up the kitchen, how dare she make herself so at home, setting tables, opening bottles of wine, acting as if she had come home. The sooner she left the better.

Chapter Six

Whenever Vivienne appeared it was like opening a bottle of champagne. On New Year's Eve she fizzed and sparkled, overflowing with glamour and charm. Slender and elegant in her slinky red dress and silver high shoes, her hair piled up on top of her head. Sarah was pulling out all the stops to compete. Having tried on all her beautiful dresses, hardly worn since last summer, she discovered many of them were too big, forcing her to revert back to her uniform of jeans and tops. Come on, Sarah, get a grip girl, she said to herself, knowing she had to look more glamorous tonight. She was singing with Tony and his musician friends once again, Joey and Giuseppe. She hadn't sung with them since the Coco Club fiasco but she knew Tony often joined them for late-night drinking and gambling sessions. Looking at herself in the mirror, she sighed. Andy was right. She was definitely too thin. She looked pale and tired with dark circles under her eyes. Finally, she settled on a simple short black silk sheath, high red heels, dramatic red lips and dark charcoal eyes. She couldn't help feeling the look was more anorexic model chic than the voluptuous steamy singer she wanted to be.

She felt nervous singing in front of her brother and Vivienne, and that was after a drink. She was allowed to sing a few of her favourite numbers *Love Me or Leave Me* and *I'm Through with Love*. But for the first time she was relieved when it was over, her legs like jelly as she rejoined Andy at the bar. The place was packed with locals from the neighbouring towns of Catania and Messina. Thin girls in heavy make-up and short skirts. Young boys with gelled hair and jeans, overdosed with aftershave. Smarmy men in suits, draped in as much jewellery as their Barbie doll girlfriends. Everyone was looking at everyone else, talking and squealing at the same time. Sarah pushed her way through to Andy and squeezed onto the bar stool beside him.

"Not bad, sis, got to say it, you're quite impressive." He raised his bottle of Moretti to her as she sipped on her waiting glass of white wine which she drained almost in one gulp.

She didn't know whether to laugh or cry with relief. "Really, Andy? Was I?"

"To be honest, I didn't know you had it in you, where's all this come from then?"

"I don't know. It was thanks to Tony."

"But are you serious about all this then?"

"I'd like to be, but…" she sighed. She didn't want to tell him Tony had put the dampeners on her brilliant career. "Well, it's all luck and not much stardom really."

She noticed Andy was watching Vivienne who was bopping around the bar, a glass of wine in her hand, talking to everyone as if it was her party. Waving at Sarah, she teetered over to her. "I could not imagine you would have a voice," she exclaimed.

"Thanks for the compliment," Sarah replied, noticing Vivienne was drunk.

"No, really, I mean it, you are good, *vraiment*." Vivienne was jostled by a handsome tanned man who obviously thought every woman would fall at his feet. "Hey," she said, about to push back when she realised it was someone she knew. "Maurizio, *ciao*!" they hugged and he pulled her out into the crowd.

"She's quite something, isn't she," Andy said, taking another swig from his bottle of beer.

"Succumbed to her charms too, have you?"

"No, I'm just the observer here."

"What do you make of Tony's mother? She doesn't like me. She was only nicer to you because you're a man." They had all eaten together at Carlotta's before they came to the bar. For Sarah it had been rather traumatic, she felt tense and on edge and could hardly eat a morsel.

"Well, course I expect she is a bit of an old bag, but she does cook well."

"Mamma's cooking. Always is the way to get round a man. So you liked the pasta then?"

"Well, I couldn't eat it every day, but I've got to admit, this is the real stuff."

"Being a good cook doesn't make up for being an old witch."

"No. I can see she must give you some stick, the old girl." Andy finished his beer.

"Course she does. I'm sure she'd be delighted if Vivienne got back with Tony."

"Who knows, maybe she has."

"Come on, it isn't like that, Andy."

"Oh no? You still insisting on living in this cuckoo land of yours, I see."

Sarah looked over at Tony sitting at the piano. He appeared oblivious but then he looked up at her and smiled. She smiled back, feeling formal. As she expected, Tony had left the house early that morning to avoid any discussion. She sighed. "Sometimes I do feel as if he'll never be mine, Andy," she said, continuing to look at Tony. "Not really mine. He belongs to his music, his mother, his son."

"And maybe his wife," Andy added.

"Will you lay off, Andy, and mind your own business. I'm not so sure I want you around here interfering."

"You should be glad I'm here to look out for you."

"I don't need you to look out for me, thanks very much."

Andy snorted.

"Oh look, there's Roland." She stood up and waved. In another baggy pullover he looked as scruffy as ever, but he didn't care and she admired that about him.

"Who's he, another father figure?"

"He's an American, lived here a while. He was a journalist but now he writes novels."

"Is he any good?"

"I haven't read anything."

"Sounds dodgy then."

"Happy New Year, Sarah, though it is a tad early, I know." Roland kissed her on both cheeks.

"Roland, I want you to meet my brother Andy, he's here on a surprise visit from England."

"Just to see your little sis for New Years, huh? Hey, I am supposing right, that she is your little sis or have I just offended you?" He held out his hand to Andy.

"No, you're right, I am her older and wiser brother," Andy said, giving Sarah a looking as they shook hands.

"Oh really, well our little Sarah here isn't so dumb, are you now? And have you heard her sing?" He winked.

"Yes, he has, but you missed me, I've sung already." Sarah said.

"Damn, surely you'll do a few more numbers, hmm?"

"Only requests," she teased.

"Well, now, it may be too early to celebrate the arrival of the new year but it's never too early for the vino, don't you agree?"

"You go ahead, but I'll stick with the beer thanks," said Andy.

"Sarah?" Roland smiled at her, his head on one side.

She held up her empty glass. "Yes please, it is New Year's Eve after all." She looked at Andy who shook his head.

"That's my girl. You know Andy, you should try some of the vino while you are here, we have some great wines in this region, the best coming from the soil of Etna, the volcano, would you believe. Can you imagine? It's supposed to have magical properties, acts like a love potion, and the way I see it that's what we all need, huh?" Roland laughed.

"Nah, I'll stick to the beer, thanks all the same, though you sound very convincing, are you a wine rep?"

Roland laughed again. "No, but I drink enough of the stuff so I should know. We'll have prosecco later, of course, to toast in the New Year. Do you not go for that either, Andy?"

"What the hell is it?" he asked.

"It's sparkling wine, but not the cheap stuff," Sarah explained. "It's a celebratory drink for birthdays and new years."

"And actually just about any other time. I drink bottles of the stuff," Roland said. "I've even been known to have prosecco for breakfast."

"Roland, for breakfast, how could you?" Sarah grimaced.

“Well, I was staying in a palace in Venice for Christmas one year and we were served prosecco with our porridge, except we didn’t have it with porridge, of course, but you get my drift.” Roland chuckled.

“How grand, drinking prosecco in a palace in Venice.” Sarah sighed.

“It was very romantic,” he grinned.

“I suppose I will try some of that then, since I’ve never had it before. But I warn you I may well be forced to go back to the beer,” Andy said.

“Well, you Brits are obsessed with your beer, I guess. So, this your first time here, Andy, what do you think of it?” Roland asked.

“Not much, to be honest.”

“Really? But maybe it does take some getting used to. It’s Disneyland, that’s what I call it.”

“Unreal and unbelievable, you mean. All lit up and nowhere to go.” Andy said.

“It’s Disneyland for adults. Sure, it’s a man’s world, but I guess that’s why I like it so much. Been here a long time. My home. Haven’t been back to the States for years.”

“You don’t miss it?”

“Nah. Just a bad memory for me.”

“I’m hoping Sarah is going to say the same about this place.”

“Andy, stop it. Ignore him, Roland” she said. “How was your Christmas?”

“Just the same as any other day really. Drank too much. Didn’t eat too much though.”

“But did you have pasta for your Christmas lunch like I did?” she asked.

“Nope. Can’t say that I did. Actually had a frozen microwavable hot pot, how’s that?”

She laughed. "I missed the brussels."

"Yuck, I can't stand those things. Had them once and that was enough." Roland put down his glass of wine. "Hey look, there's Vivvie, will you excuse me a moment, I must say hello, but I'll be right back," he said, disappearing into the crowd. Sarah watched him as he grabbed hold of Vivienne.

At the end of the set the musicians stood drinking and talking with Vivienne. She was laughing loudly, leaning against Tony. She put an arm around his shoulder since she was almost as tall as him. They make a glamorous couple, Sarah thought, but wasn't she supposed to be the one by Tony's side, laughing with him, holding his hand, his singing partner and his lover. She was about to jump down from her stool and march over to him, to break up the party going on without her, when the clocks struck twelve.

Hundreds of bottles of prosecco exploded simultaneously in every bar and home. Bubbles spilled everywhere. Outside, the fireworks exploded in the piazza. "Come on, *andiamo*," Vivienne shouted, and grabbing Tony's hand they ran out onto the Corso. Andy and Roland followed Sarah as she pushed her way into the crowd on the street. The sky was alight with shooting flames of colour, sparkles of falling light. Not to be outdone, Mount Etna was still erupting, putting on its own display to herald in the New Year: a livid red stream of lava was threading down the volcano in the darkness, visible from the square in the night sky amidst the twinkling lights of the towns beyond. Sarah felt like exploding too. Where the hell was Tony?

She found Andy down a side street, holding his bottle of beer, shouting at Tony.

"You don't go screwing around with my sister like she's some old slag."

"What is a slag?" Tony asked.

"Andy, what's going on, what are you shouting about?" She was alarmed at her brother's sudden belligerence.

"Think you were kissing the wrong bird, mate."

"What are you talking about?" She looked at him and back at Tony. "Tony, what's going on? Are you going to explain?"

"Yeah, he bloody well wants to."

"It's nothing, just a mistake. Vivienne, tell them."

Vivienne shrugged, a bottle of prosecco in her hand as she staggered away from them. "He's my husband, I can kiss him if I want to."

"What?" Sarah was stunned. "Kiss who?"

"Antonio, I can kiss him, or whoever else I want to kiss." Vivienne stumbled up the street towards Roland, laughing.

"Oh no you can't. Come back here, how dare you walk away," Sarah shouted after her.

Vivienne was caught off guard as Sarah ran at her and losing her balance went flying across the street, the bottle smashing along the wall of the ceramic shop. Vivienne fell, laughing hysterically, far drunker than Sarah realised. Roland was beside her instantly.

"Tony, how could you!" Sarah screamed.

"It was nothing, Sarah, you must believe me." He grabbed hold of her hands but she pulled away from him, noticing now the smear of red lipstick across his cheek, knowing full well it wasn't hers. They hadn't even exchanged a happy new year greeting.

"You tried to sleep in my bed." Vivienne sat sprawled on the street in a puddle of prosecco, broken glass all around her. Roland was on his knees, trying to pick up the pieces.

"What are you talking about?" Sarah stood over her.

"The bed that was mine, not yours. It was not for you to take my place."

"How dare you. You were the one who left."

"But now I have come back."

"To take your son."

"Antonio does not want me to leave."

"So I can see."

"For a man like Antonio you were just a diversion until I came back."

"Really? Was I?"

"He is not a man you can trust."

"Looks like I am finding that out."

"Sarah, do not listen to her, she's crazy. Vivienne, you are drunk," Tony said, adding something in French which Sarah couldn't make out.

"I'm sick of your lies, Tony, in fact, I'm sick of you. You can have her and I hope you both rot in hell."

"I don't understand," Tony held out his hands to Sarah.

"No, I bet you don't," shouted Andy. "Not when it suits you. I've stood by long enough."

He punched Tony, overflowing with temper and beer. Tony fell back, surprised by the hard knock to his jaw.

"Andy, what are you doing?" Sarah grabbed hold of his arm.

"He had it coming, Sarah, believe me. And I'm not finished yet."

“Oh yes you are,” she clung to him as he tried to fling her off, his strength nearly knocking her sideways.

“Don’t try to protect him, Sarah, he’s just a worthless shit, can’t you see that now?”

“Leave him, just stop it, Andy. I want this all to end now!” Sarah screamed so loud the silence after was deafening.

“I’ve got so much stuff, Andy,” she said.

Andy sat on a chair by the window watching Sarah pack her case. “It doesn’t matter,” he said. “Take the essentials, leave the rest here.”

She was crying. “I don’t know what I’m doing.”

“No, but I do, someone has to around here.”

“I’m not sure I can go.”

“You are coming with me, Sarah. I’ve got you a ticket. We leave tonight.”

She couldn’t stop crying, her tears falling into the suitcase as she folded her jeans and sweaters into neat squares.

“Sarah, he was kissing his wife. I was the one who saw it. How many times do you want to go over it?”

She remembered the fireworks, the colour, the noise, the people; the nightmare that followed. “I still can’t believe it,” she said.

“You’d better believe it because it happened.”

She looked at him. “But Tony explained. Vivienne was drunk and she just got too heavy with him.”

“From what I saw he wasn’t exactly pushing her off.”

“Now I’ve calmed down I want to believe him.”

“Don’t get sentimental on me, Sarah. Just come back to sanity for a while, you need some perspective, you’ve been in this madhouse far too long.”

"But he gave me a ring."

"A ring?"

Sarah took out the ring from its box and slipped it on. She hadn't been wearing it.

"For crying out loud, what does he want, to marry you too and be a bloody bigamist?"

"I know it's impossible." She sniffed, putting the ring back into the velvet box.

"Yes, it bloody well is." Andy sighed. "Look, you told me Frenchie was going back home with the boy, right, when was it?"

"Yesterday."

"And have they gone?"

"Okay Andy, we all know they didn't go."

"Need I say more then? Now come on, hurry up and get packed, will you."

She took a last walk in the gardens. A winter blue sky spread over the sea: it was like looking at a magical fairy tale land. The sight of the volcano was like no other: magnetic and moody, it drew her every day, just to have a glimpse, to check it was still really there. It held the people of the town in its thrall, subjected to its power as they always had been over the centuries. The energy affected them all. She wondered if that was why she constantly felt unsettled. Living under the shadow of this splendid, slumbering monster surely led some to madness. Etna madness. Spitting and simmering calmly enough now, at any moment it could erupt ferociously and devastate the towns below it, throwing down its fistfuls of burning red lava, like it did years before onto Catania, destroying the city. Tony took her there once and they walked through the streets now paved with grey black lava stone. She looked up at the cloud formations around the volcano, sometimes strange shapes and rings would appear, drifting away from the smoking summit. She wanted to clear the clouds of confusion in her head. Maybe going home for a while would do that.

But when it came to it she found it harder than she thought. "How can I say goodbye to you, Tony?" she asked.

He shrugged. "This doesn't have to be goodbye. But your brother is in charge of you it seems. You do not listen to me any more."

"But you kissed her."

"No, she kissed me."

"Oh, and that makes all the difference."

"It meant nothing. I have told you so many times. We were all drunk."

"That's no excuse."

"But you know how sorry I am."

"And why is she still here, she should've gone home yesterday."

"I'll sort it out."

"What is there to sort out? She needs to go. You need to get a divorce. Unless you still love her, of course."

"I do not love her. But I love my son. It is more complicated when you have children. You do not understand this, Sarah. You are still the child."

She looked up at him. They had driven down to Letojanni, a small town by the sea, holiday apartments empty for the winter, streets deserted except for the hardened locals: wizened old women sitting on the pavement benches, men congregating in cafés drinking coffee and playing cards. No one smiled. The sea was rough, the daylight bright and harsh. Her eyes watered in the wind as she watched the high waves, white frothy cappuccino foam sweeping the beach, leaving a shoreline of cigarette butts. He took her hand. "Let go, Tony, there's no point."

"Stay, Sarah, please, I don't want you to go."

She shook her head. "After all that's happened how can I stay?"

"But nothing has happened. You are making too much of this."

"Oh am I? Well, I don't think so. Her exhibition proved she wants something more from you and it isn't just your son."

"She didn't mean it, she was drunk, she is jealous of you."

"Of me?"

"Of course. Look, all I ask is that you trust me, Sarah. Let me take care of things. It will be done. And quickly."

"Yeah, it looks like it."

"I promise. Just give me some time. Please, Sarah." He took her hand again and kissed it. "It is you I love. Love doesn't happen so easily."

"No, but words do."

"Trust me."

She pulled her hand free. "I think it's too late for that."

Chapter Seven

Sarah looked down from the window as they flew over the miniature patchwork of green, a new world emerging through the clouds. She sat with a planeful of pale middle-class couples drinking G&T, red or white wine with their pre-packed chicken and salad roll, coffee to follow, bitter instant nasty stuff that Sarah refused to sip. She couldn't eat or drink anything. Andy ate hers, seeming oblivious to her discomfort. As she looked out of the window over this other world, she wished she hadn't been persuaded to leave Tony.

Back home, straggly tired Christmas decorations lit up the greyness of Gatwick. Her sister Lily was waiting for them at the arrival gates. "My poor Sarah, just look at you." Lily hugged her. "You look terrible."

"Thanks!"

"She hasn't stopped crying, this one," Andy said.

"You know what you need?" Lily said. "A nice hot cup of tea. Bet you don't get good tea in Taormina, do you?"

"No." Sarah laughed and hugged her sister.

"Let's get you home then. Always was Andy to the rescue, wasn't it?" Lily put an arm around Sarah's shoulder. "Still, whatever happened out there, I'm just pleased to see you."

"Even if it has all ended in tears," Andy said as he pushed the trolley to the car park.

The grey green fields, the endless grey of the motorway, all sped by in a blur of tears. Sarah remembered the drive along the highway from Catania last summer, the yellow genestra and mimosa blossoming, the orange and lemon groves, the olive trees and villas dotted in the distance, Etna watching over it all. Now it was January and she was back to urbanity, driving through the run-down centres of Croydon, Streatham and Brixton. She hadn't been away for so very long, just over six months, but it felt like forever. Everything was familiar yet everything was strange. She noticed the diversity on the streets not found in the small town of Taormina. There everyone looked the same. Here there were so many people you got lost in the crowd. There everyone knew your face, your past and your present. Here no one knew you and no one cared. Here were high streets full of every kind of shop, kebab shops, betting shops, grocery stores, ethnic shops: Turkish, Indian, Caribbean, Polish; every nationality catered for. There you got Sicilian and got on with it.

Finally, they were back in the familiar streets of home. Grey uniform streets, regular residential roads. She stayed in Lily's house not far from her own flat. All her things were kept at Lily's since she had been renting out her flat and as the renting agreement had another three months to run she couldn't go back there. But there was plenty of room at Lily's three-bedroom house, her son Benjamin having moved out to share a house with some university friends. Lily was reassuring and welcoming, making sure everything was clean and tidy and comfortable in the spare room, Sarah's new bedroom: a big cold bed with crisp clean sheets, colourful curtains and bedspread, and thick soft carpet; no more dusty stone floors beneath her bare feet. It was a cheery room which only depressed Sarah further.

She sat at the small dressing table brushing her hair, feeling lost and lonely. Lily brought her some tea and madeira cake she had made. She took the brush from her and continued brushing her long hair. “So lovely and glossy, your hair. You are lucky, Sarah. Look at my messy mop, I can never do anything with it. I used to brush your hair when you were a little girl, do you remember?”

“I remember the tangles. I used to scream. Remember that stuff you sprayed in it after washing, 'no tangles, no tears', something like that.”

“Yes, but it never worked.” They laughed. Sarah looked at Lily’s reflection in the mirror as she stood behind her brushing her hair; she looked tired but contented. She was a manager in a florist’s, her passion for flowers and plants was evident in her own garden which was small but particular; she was very creative and loving. “Thanks Lily, you are making me feel better,” she said.

“I want you to feel better. I want you to feel at home here. I’m glad to see you Sarah, you’re my little sister, but I hate to see you suffering.” She put the brush down and kissed the top of her head. “Now drink your tea or it will get cold.”

Tony called her a week later. “So, have you forgiven me? Are you coming back?” he asked.

“That depends on you.” She tried to sound cold, unconcerned.

“Of course I want you to come back. I never wanted you to leave. You know that.”

“I’m not so sure, Tony. Is your wife still there, is she staying?”

“No, Vivienne is leaving. She will go back to France.”

“Oh, really?”

“She does not want to be with me any more than I want to be with her.”

“It didn’t look that way to me.”

“It was all a mistake, you know there is nothing between us, let’s not go over it again. Please come back. We can work things out.”

“And your son?”

He sighed. “I have agreed she can take Roberto. I thought to do the right thing by him but I cannot.”

“The right thing?”

“Please understand, Sarah, I didn’t want to lose my son. But I don’t want to lose you too.”

Sarah was silent as she took in his words, her heart pounding.

“We will get the divorce. We will have things legal between us for Roberto’s sake. It cannot happen overnight but slowly, slowly things will be resolved. I promise.”

“I hope so.”

“Sarah, please, it will not be easy for me. I need you. I need you to be with me, to support me. Can we not try again? Just the two of us. If you still love me you will return to me.”

“I’ll think about it.”

But she didn’t need to think, everything he said was what she wanted to hear. He wanted her, not his wife. He even prized her over his son, willing to give him up. For her.

A week later, she arrived in Taormina to hailstones, the nuggets of rain clattering on the pavements as she pulled the case down the steps of the street, her shoes splashing in puddles, muddy and gritty. She wanted to surprise Tony, arriving on his doorstep, just like she had last summer. She was horrified when Vivienne opened the door.

"What on earth are you doing here?" Sarah could not disguise her astonishment.

"I can say the same to you. But do come in. Poor little Sarah, you look frozen. These Mediterranean winters are not so warm, more like England, no?"

"Where's Tony?" Sarah asked, stepping inside, feeling the roles were reversed, here she was turning up with her suitcase just as Vivienne had done a month ago.

"He's here, outside in the garden, protecting his plants, you know how he loves those plants, growing in pots all over the place. Antonio, here is a surprise for you," Vivienne called out into the yard.

Sarah looked around and saw everything clean and bright, as if the whole room had been sprayed with bleach. Here she was, the lady of the house back at home, Sarah thought, thinking not of herself, but of Vivienne. The knowledge of her terrible mistake rose up to her throat nearly choking her.

The shock on Tony's face was evident when he saw Sarah standing by the open front door. Vivienne was silent, her arms folded, watching and smiling. His hands were covered in soil which he wiped on an old tea towel, his hair wet from the rain. "Sarah, you could have telephoned, what are you doing here?"

"That's a nice greeting. Nothing like being pleased to see me. I am here, Tony because you asked me to come back. Or had you forgotten?" She wanted to spit at him, tear him apart. She felt blind and stupid, dumb and deaf, as if she had been sleeping and only now had woken up to reality.

"But Sarah, you do not know what is happening here and you just arrive without a word."

"Oh, I can see what's happening here quite well enough." She turned around, out of the door, back to her suitcase standing in the rain.

Tony followed her into the narrow street. "Please, Sarah, stop, we can talk about things. Do not be in such a hurry to jump to the wrong conclusions."

"I think I have taken far too long to come to the right ones so now I'd better stick to them. You lied to me, Tony. Again."

"No, she's leaving, I promise. I didn't expect you so soon."

"I can see that. I didn't expect to find her living here with you. But I've caught you out. Goodbye Tony."

"Sarah, come back, don't go like this." he shouted after her down the street, the dirty tea towel still in his hands.

Rivers of rain flowed down the streets. Wading through the water her feet were soaked through to her socks. She wheeled her case behind her, tears of anger mingling with the raindrops lashing her face. How could she have believed him and come back like this? She had wanted to surprise him, make him happy. Instead he had made a fool of her. She walked in the rain all the way to Roland's house. Banging on his door, she was trembling with the cold.

"Sarah, my word, what are you doing here? I thought you'd gone back to England with your brother."

"I did, but I've just returned." She stood shivering, looking at him.

Roland looked confused. "Well, eh, I guess that's great."

"No, it isn't. Tony asked me to come back but I cannot even stay with him."

"I don't follow you."

"Look, Roland, here is my suitcase. I cannot stay with Tony. She is there instead of me. I'm sorry but I don't know where else to go."

"Who is?"

"Vivienne, who else?"

"Oh no, I get it. Come in quickly, Sarah, I'll grab the case."

"Sorry, Roland, I just didn't know who else to turn to." She stood dripping in the dark passageway.

"I am always here for you, Sarah. You know that. I didn't realise what was going on."

"She's moved in Roland, that's what's going on."

"No, are you sure?"

"Well, she's there now."

"I knew it was serious when your brother socked him one that night but, hell, we were all so drunk."

"Andy's very protective."

"Needs to be, I'd say."

"I'm sorry to land on you like this. Will you take me back to the airport?"

"Hey, hold on a minute, Sarah. Just calm down. Let's check the flights first. You can stay here, at least for tonight. Now, let's get you warm and dry." He put his hand on her shoulder. “I’m so sorry, Sarah, you didn’t deserve this.”

“I’ve been a fool.”

“Maybe. But fools for love we have all been at some time in our lives.”

Since she couldn’t get a flight till the next day, Roland insisted on taking her out to eat at Caprice, a small restaurant, its walls painted with floral murals. It was set on a noisy, narrow road, so narrow and unpaved it was almost impossible not to brush with the passing cars as they walked up the steep street, but the food was so good it was worth the risk.

“You’ve been so kind, Roland,” Sarah said, eating slivers of the grilled swordfish. “I do appreciate it.”

“It’s the least I can do. I’m just trying to cheer you up, I can imagine you’re feeling pretty rotten now. You can count on me, Sarah, I hope you know that. Hey, don’t get me wrong, I like Vivvie, she is a wow. Vivvie the vamp we used to call her. I admit I was dizzy about her. We had a thing once. Very brief, as I think most of her encounters are. But I can wise up, unlike most men.” Roland cut into his steak, blood streaking across the plate.

“Unlike Tony, you mean.”

He looked up at her and put down his knife and fork, swallowing his mouthful of bloody meat. “Well, she was the one who broke his heart and maybe he’ll never get over that. Maybe he can’t let her go.”

Sarah sipped her wine. “It looks that way.”

“Maybe you have to face up to the facts, Sarah, that’s all I’m saying.”

“I have now, don’t worry, I’ve learnt my lesson this time. I’m out of here and out of his life, for good.”

"I guess that means you're out of mine too, sadly for me. But you don't have to rush away, Sarah. You can stay with me for as long as you like. Sort out your feelings. Take your time." He reached across the table and took her hand.

Sarah woke up early, remembering the last time she had slept there on the sofa, a drunken sleep. This time she hardly slept, going over the scene she had returned to, feeling more than ever that Tony had made a fool of her. How would she ever live it down at home. Andy had been right all along, how could he see it all so clearly while she remained the blind, pathetic fool?

Roland's place was a mess, newspapers, manuscripts and books were scattered around his sitting room, the bathroom needed a good scrub and the tiny kitchen was a tip. She slipped out to get some fresh air and buy rolls from the bakery. On the street corners were the familiar carts selling vegetables, small old ladies in their coats and handbags were gathering to gossip. No one queues, everyone talks at the same time, it's a wonder anything ever gets sold, she thought. Tony used to buy broccoli, aubergines and leeks from the carts, to cook with pasta. What would he be cooking today for his wife and son, she wondered bitterly, clutching the bag of just-baked sesame seed rolls.

Back at Roland's she stood in the kitchen at the cluttered worktop buttering a roll. Roland was still asleep, she could hear the snores coming from his bedroom, she would wake him soon. There was a knock at the front door. She wasn't going to open it but the knocking continued so she put on the safety chain and opened the door as far as it would go.

"Tony, what on earth are you doing here? How did you know I was here?" She took off the chain and opened the door wider.

"It wasn't difficult to guess you would be staying with Roland," Tony said. "Who is it you go out with in the night. Even before Vivienne arrived you were out on dates with him."

"Hardly dates, Tony. We just shared a few drinks, nothing major."

"No? Staying out all night is nothing major? Staying in his apartment is nothing major? Sleeping in his bed is nothing major? It is to me."

"I have never slept in Roland's bed or anywhere else with Roland."

"But if I had behaved in the same way, what then?"

"In case you hadn't noticed you are behaving far worse, that's why I'm leaving."

"It is not what you think. You understand nothing."

"Well, you can always try to enlighten me, but you haven't got long, I'm leaving for the airport in an hour."

"But we must talk, Sarah."

"No, I don't want to hear any more lies from you, Tony. I came back because you begged me to and what do I find, it's worse than when I left, she's living with you now."

"No, she isn't. Please, Sarah, listen, let me explain. At least let me take you to the airport."

"No, Tony, there's no need for that. This is it, it's over. Goodbye." She shut the door, slamming it in his face and went back to the kitchen. She looked at the hot buttered roll and suddenly lost her appetite.

But Tony hadn't left, he was banging on the door, shouting at her to open up. "I am not leaving, Sarah, let me in."

"Go away, Tony, I don't want to see you."

Roland came running out of his room in a t-shirt and baggy boxer shorts, his hair dishevelled, looking like a wild man. "What the hell is going on here, what is all the racket?"

"It's Tony." She couldn't help noticing Roland's bandy, hairy legs.

Roland opened the front door. "Hey man, you got a problem or what?

"Yes, I have, what is Sarah doing here with you?"

"Well, since she couldn't stay at your place as you have another little lady in tow she came here."

"Always running to you, isn't she?"

"What a cheek you've got, Tony," Sarah said. "This is about you and Vivienne, not me and Roland but here you are turning it around again."

Tony looked at her suitcase in the hallway. "But you cannot go like this, you cannot leave me again, Sarah, please, I beg you."

"What do you want me to do, move in with you and your wife, how cosy."

"No. It's not like that."

"Look, just leave, Tony, now. I don't want to see you any more. It's over."

Roland stood at the door. "I think you had better do as she asked."

"It's not over, Sarah, you will see." Tony rammed his fist into the wall and cursing he turned and left.

The drive to the airport in the rain, mist hiding the volcano, the view rolling by. This is the last I shall see of the island, she thought, I'm never coming back, never, it's all over. It should have been paradise, it could have been paradise, but now there was no chance, perhaps there never had been, perhaps I was naïve to have thought it might ever work.

"Are you all set, you sure you want to leave now?"

She had checked in her case and joined the queue to go through to departures. "Yes, Roland, I'm ready."

He kissed her and held her to him. "Promise you'll keep in touch, Sarah. Call me, anytime."

"Yes, I will. And thanks for everything." She pulled away, eager to be alone.

She sat in the departure lounge biting her lip, refusing to give in to the tears.

Chapter Eight

Back in England, Sarah watched the black crows from her bedroom window, always there on the rooftops of the flats opposite. Silent and black. She took them to be a bad sign. She stood in the silence wondering how she could have gone back to Taormina. She felt ashamed and humiliated.

Back in the ugly urban surroundings: as she walked down the road, she noticed the deterioration, rubbish everywhere, the shops along the dirty high street forever closing and reopening as something else. The accountants was now a travel agents, the computer shop once sold lingerie, the halal kebab shop was once a dry cleaners and the carpet shop was now an oriental nail salon. There was still the hairdressers and tanning shop, the massage parlour over the estate agents and the herbal specialists claiming to cure acne and impotence.

She had arranged to meet Andy in one of his regular haunts, the Crown in Romford. It was familiar, shabby and comforting; a contrast to the glamorous and pretentious bars of Taormina. She sipped her glass of house wine. Not the quality she was used to.

Andy looked at her. “I told you not to go back, Sarah. I knew it could only end in tears. Hadn’t it already ended in enough?”

“Yes, Andy, but I believed him.”

“Why?”

She sighed. “Because I wanted to and because it seemed possible. If Vivienne was going back to France and taking the boy then it would just be me and Tony. What more could I want?”

“If it had been true.”

"Yes, of course, and it wasn't. So now I'm back for good. That's it. It's over. No more running back to Taormina. No more running back to Tony."

"I can't say I'm sorry to see him out of your life, Sarah, but I know you're upset and you're putting on this brave hard front."

"Hurt and heartbroken, course I am," she said flippantly, sipping her wine. "But I'll be okay, I have to be. It's happened before."

"Don't remind me about Michael. You really do choose the good ones don't you, Sarah."

"Maybe there aren't any good ones."

"You'll get over it, you will, but give yourself a chance, you've only just got back. I know it's not great around here. I mean we are surrounded by flat-heads, rag-heads, and wide-screens, but…"

"What? Can you translate that, surrounded by what?"

"Eastern Europeans. Our old colonial friends. And those stupid cows covered in black but for the slits for their eyes."

"Andy, you really are getting worse, have you joined the BNP?"

"No, I don't mean it like that. What I'm saying is I still prefer it here, multi bleeding cultural and all, than what I saw over there in your poncy paradise."

"That's good of you."

"I saw it out there, Sarah, I saw it for what it is. A fucking fantasy fuelled on cocaine, alcohol and designer shops."

"Alcohol, yes, but cocaine? I never really saw any of that going on."

"Come on, didn't you see those blokes going to the toilets all the time, especially in that bar where Tony plays?"

"Well, yes, I did, I suppose, now you come to mention it. But you know how vain and posy these Italian men are."

"Yeah, but they weren't going to the loos to look at themselves, believe me. Didn't you notice how long they were gone for, and that wasn't to touch up the eye-liner."

Sarah shrugged.

"If you ask me it's all drugs, booze and fancy shops, and not a lot of anything else going on in town."

"There are concerts and exhibitions, you know."

"And as for your jazz man, well, he loves himself but he's not that brilliant, wouldn't see him lasting long in London. He's a bit of a chancer."

She sighed.

"Look, there will be someone else, Sarah."

"Maybe there will or maybe there won't. But I don't want to be alone forever. Surely you don't either. I mean you can't live with Mum for much longer."

"Don't worry about me. Besides, Mum needs me, I don't mind being there. And as far as women go, well, I think I've given up."

"You've never got over Donna leaving you, have you?"

"Not really. But maybe I deserved it." He shrugged, finishing the remains of his pint. "But you're only young, Sarah, you'll meet someone else."

"So you keep saying. But I did love Tony, perhaps I still do."

"Love? How can you love him? He's old. He's got a kid. His still got a fucking wife, for Christ's sake. Are you telling me he's the right man for you?"

"Well, if you put it like that..."

"That's how it is."

"Andy, as bad as this wine is, just get me some more, will you?"

"So what do you think has happened back there in Taormina now you've left?" Lily asked the next evening while cooking spaghetti bolognese. Sarah didn't have the heart to tell her it was the last thing she wanted to eat.

"I saw what was happening. He's with her and the kid, back together, a happy family. His mother will be pleased." She sat at the table, watching Lily as she opened the can of plum tomatoes.

"It's awful to think you went back to find that mess when you expected a happy reunion." She stirred the tomatoes with the fried onion, adding tomato puree, which Tony would never do. Tony was a wonderful cook. "But we all wondered if you were right, you know, to go back so quickly like that."

"It seemed right, but of course it was terribly wrong. What a fool I was."

"But is it really over?"

"It has to be." She sighed, putting the plates on the table, taking out the knives and forks from the drawer in Lily's tidy, homely kitchen. She noticed Lily was boiling the pasta for too long.

"You have to pick up your life, my love. You've done it before. We've all done it. Look at Andy and Lily, both unlucky in love and they were married." Sarah sat beside her mother, holding her thin, lined hand. Her mother shook her head. "We all knew you were asking for trouble, Sarah, going out there like that. Pinning your hopes on this man. Running from one bad deal to another."

"I know, Mum, but I didn't think it would work out like this."

"No, course you didn't. But there usually is a wife somewhere on the scene, especially with these foreigners. Hidden all over the show they are."

Sarah sighed.

"But men his age do have pasts and often the past is not resolved as we would like to think it is."

"Oh, Mum." Sarah hugged her mother, noticing she was thinner than ever and dark under the eyes. "How are you feeling, really, because I can see you don't look well."

"Thank you very much."

"No, I mean it's worrying, what's happening Mum, tell me? Are you eating anything because you don't look as if you are." She remembered when her father was alive her mother would cook every day: wonderful roast dinners, casseroles with dumplings, steak and kidney pies and puddings, steak and chips, egg and chips, scrambled eggs, toad in the hole, jam tarts and apple pies, bread pudding and chocolate gateaux. Her mother had gone to pieces when her dad died, her world had fallen apart and she'd never recovered. She had stopped cooking and stopped eating. Now Sarah drank economy tea with her mother, nibbling on a Rich Tea biscuit.

"Please stop going on, Sarah. Your brother does enough of that. I'm just pleased to have you home, and this time I hope it is for good."

Walking back to the bus stop Sarah felt sad thinking about her mother; having continued oblivious in her own selfish little world, she hadn't realised just how ill her mother must be. Now she could see it for herself.

Sarah found a part-time job imputing data for a national archive in a big open-plan office with rows of workers. As she made her way to work on her first day, commuting to the city, she looked at the tired faces on the train, some dozing, others reading the free newspapers given out at the stations; for them it was just another Monday morning, not the start of a new life. Getting out at Aldgate she walked through the desolate shopping mall, the shops all shut except for the coffee kiosk. She bought a paper cup of coffee and burnt her mouth as she took a sip too soon.

The work was going to be relatively mundane but she was glad of this as she slipped into her assigned computer terminal with a batch of papers for her training session. At lunch time she joined the black and blue rivers of city-suited people flowing through the city streets, everyone walking fast, talking loudly on their mobile phones, stuffing sandwiches in their mouths. Laughing, talking, walking and eating all at once. Sandwich shops and pubs lined the streets. She looked at the skyline. London was beautiful, the glassy magnificence of the Gherkin was a man made match for Mount Etna. She sat outside the coffee shop, her cappuccino all froth and no substance, not like the Sicilian style. But at least London seemed more friendly than she remembered and they all spoke a language that was hers. She took her book and read, feeling less guilty as she lit a cigarette since her fellow café dwellers did the same. Tony would never know.

He didn't know anything about her now. But although she tried not to, she missed him.

Ruth had returned to England for good too, having finished with Saro who was back with his wife after a temporary estrangement. "See, you cannot trust the bastards over there, what did I tell you, Sarah? You and I can start again, they can't. They are stuck in their sorry little worlds while we can do whatever we want, meet whoever we want."

Sarah sipped her expensive Cosmopolitan cocktail in ZeeZee, a noisy new bar in central London full of very young people. "I know, but I'm not sure I want to. Not like this. Meat markets, that's all these places are." She looked across at the group of girls giggling and squealing, a pitcher of some kind of yellow cocktail on the table in front of them.

"Oh, love, don't take that attitude. Just have a bit of fun."

"But isn't it better to meet someone when you are sober and in control of your faculties? It was your fault I met Tony in that bar, drunk as we were."

"Please don't remind me, I feel guilty enough about that as it is. Then again, I've met just as many sods when I'm sober."

"But what about meeting men at work, you work for an international bank now, surely there must be lots of eligible men?"

"If there are they are hiding under their desks, I can tell you. Come on, drink up and I'll get us another."

"Do we have to stay, I don't like it here, Ruth. Can't we just go back to your place and have a coffee?"

"No we cannot, I've made such an effort to get ready I'm not leaving now. We have to start on the circuit again, love. Get going, get out there, get seen." Ruth stood up, shouting over the music. "We can do it!"

Sarah smiled, hoping to convince herself that they could.

Chapter Nine

"I'm coming to London."

"What?" Sarah couldn't disguise her astonishment, shocked that Tony had called at all. It was almost two months since she had left Taormina. A Sunday morning, she was sitting at the kitchen table eating toast and marmalade, flicking through the Sunday papers. She thought he had given up since she always refused to speak to him every time he called.

"I am coming to England," he said.

"But why?"

"To see you, of course."

"Don't bother, Tony, I don't want to see you."

"But I have the ticket already."

"More fool you."

"I am coming the first week of April. I haven't forgotten it's your birthday."

"Well, don't bother as I've forgotten you."

"Have you?"

"Well, what did you think I was going to do?"

"So, you do not want me to come?"

"You can do what you like but don't expect to see me."

"I'll call you again next week to let you know what time I arrive."

"Don't bother, Tony." She put down the phone, stunned.

What a nerve he's got, she thought, returning to her hard toast and cold tea, to think he can just walk back into my life. The conceit of it. She was about to make some more tea when Lily returned from a car-boot sale, having left very early in the morning.

"Did you get anything?" Sarah asked.

"Mostly a load of old rubbish, but I did get this." Lily pulled out from newspaper wrappings a blue and lilac ceramic soap dish. "It was only a fiver."

"Oh, Lily, that's awful," Sarah said. "But look, it doesn't matter, I've got something to tell you."

"What?" She looked up at Sarah. "What's happened?"

"Guess who just phoned."

"No. Who?"

"Who do you think?"

"You don't mean Tony, do you?"

"Yes."

"And?"

"He said he's coming to England."

"What? Surely not?"

"Yes."

"When?"

"Beginning of the month."

"I don't believe it. What did you say?"

"I told him not to bother."

"Good for you. But do you mean it?"

"Yes, course I do. He's got a bloody cheek." Sarah went out to the kitchen and put on the kettle, Lily followed her.

"So you don't want to see him then?"

"No, I bloody well don't. I can't believe he's rung up like this out of the blue. I'm not going to be taken for a fool again." When she thought about her last visit to Taormina she could still feel the humiliation burning. Since then she had been trying to forget all about Tony. This call could undo all the hard work of the past few months but she wasn't going to let it.

One evening a few weeks later she opened the door thinking it was Lily home early from work only to find Tony standing on the doorstep like a vision from another world: tall and thin, in a smart grey overcoat, a huge bouquet of red and white roses in his arms, a suitcase by his side.

"Here I am, Sarah," he smiled.

"What on earth are you doing here?"

"You could at least say hello."

"I can also say goodbye." She was about to close the door.

"Sarah, please."

"Where is your wife, then?" Sarah asked, peering round the door, half expecting to see her.

"What are you talking about?"

"Surely Vivienne is here with you on this visitation?"

"Why would she be with me?"

"Where is she then?"

"Not here, and not in Sicily. She has gone."

"Gone? Gone where?"

"To Paris, of course, and she has taken Roberto with her."

"Oh, really, and am I supposed to believe that?"

"Yes, because it is true. Look, Sarah, we can talk about this. If you let me come in."

"I don't see the point of letting you in or the point of talking."

"Sarah, please, I have come all this way to see you. Don't you remember you surprised me this way too?"

"Once, long ago."

"So, here I am." He opened his arms to her.

"How did you find me, how did you get here?"

"I have a car, I hired a car from the airport."

"And where are you staying? Don't think you can stay here."

"No, I do not presume that. I am staying in Brighton."

"What? That's miles away."

"Yes, I realise that now. Please, let me in, Sarah, just for a moment."

"I don't think so." She looked at him, trying not weaken.

"Sarah, don't be like this, don't turn me away." He looked at her, his magnetic blue eyes pleading with her.

"Five minutes then." She opened the door wider. "You don't need to bring that in here, you can leave it in the car," she said, indicating the suitcase.

"No, I have some things inside the case I must give to you."

He looked thinner, she noticed, and was there more grey in his hair or was it just the light. Her tummy tightened as she studied him. Handsome as ever, she thought.

"Ah, this is a nice house," he said, looking around, still holding the bouquet.

"It's my sister's house, not mine."

"Ah, yes. Of course. Oh, look, please, these are for you." He held out the heavy cellophane-wrapped flowers.

"Thank you. My sister will love these. She's a florist."

"A what?"

"Someone who works with flowers."

"Where is she?"

"Still at work. She'll be back later." She took the flowers out to the kitchen and left them on the table.

She stood for a minute trying to compose herself, her heart beating fast.

"We must talk Sarah, I need to explain."

"I don't think I want to hear it, Tony, not any more."

"But you must. When you came back to Taormina it was not how you think. Vivienne was not living there with me, she did not move back to the house like you assumed."

"It looked that way to me."

"Yes, you could see it that way, she was there in the house, but she didn't live there. She came every day to see Roberto who stayed with me. I knew he would not be with me for much longer so she agreed he could spend the last weeks in his home with me."

"I see."

"Do you?"

Sarah shrugged. "It doesn't matter now."

"Yes, it does. I want you to understand she wasn't there living with me, not as you think, we were not as husband and wife."

"Maybe she wanted it to be like that."

"No. Anyway, I didn't want that. She knew. She was jealous, that's all."

"Jealous? Well, she can have you."

"Sarah, don't say that, don't be childish. I don't want to be with her. She doesn't really want to be with me, she was just being…"

"A bitch."

"What?"

"It doesn't matter."

"Sarah, stop saying that, it does matter. Listen to me, I am serious. There is nothing between me and Vivienne. We are getting a divorce."

"Oh."

"Yes, the process has begun."

"I see."

"Stop being so formal, Sarah, please." He tried to take her hand but she pulled away.

He knelt down to his suitcase and unzipped it. "Look. These are for you." He took out various parcels exquisitely wrapped and tied with bows, exotic and enticing: perfume, traditional *torroncine*, chocolate covered nougat, almond pastries and a heart shaped box of chocolates. He dug into his case further and pulled out a bottle of prosecco, a pack of De Cecco pasta, small macaroni tubes, a jar of pesto of tomato and olives, and a pack of Miscela D'oro ground coffee. He had even brought a small traditional Bialetti coffee pot to cook the coffee on the stove.

"Good God, I can see you've brought enough provisions to live on while you are here."

"No, Sarah, this is not for me, it is all for you. I want to cook for you, I want to make you coffee, I want us to drink wine together…"

She stared down at the array of goodies piled on the carpet. He picked up the box of perfume and handed it to her. "Open it, I want you to try it."

She unwrapped the box and took out the delicate glass bottle. She sprayed it onto her wrist and inhaled, the smell instantly taking her back to Sicily.

"It's jasmine, Sarah, the smell you love so much, remember?"

She looked up at him, surprised to see tears in his eyes. Her tummy somersaulted again as she looked at him, his blue eyes holding hers, waiting for her to say something. He took her hand and pulled her wrist up to his nose. "Perfect for you." He kissed her wrist.

Pretending not to be affected by this intimacy, she pulled away and walked out to the kitchen. “Well, I suppose I should make you a cup of tea,” she said.

He followed her. “Yes, of course. The famous English tea. Finally in England.”

She filled the kettle and they stood waiting for it to boil.

“You look beautiful, Sarah,” he said.

She had managed to gain some of her weight back and the dark hollows had disappeared from under her eyes. She wasn’t going to tell him he looked beautiful too, but she had to admit to herself that he did. He had taken off his coat and wore jeans and a pale blue cashmere sweater over a shirt. He always looked smart even when he was trying to be casual. Having him here in her sister’s kitchen, in England, it just didn’t seem real.

“So, you’ve booked a hotel right?” she said, taking out two china mugs from the cupboard, feeling her hands shaking.

“Yes, a small hotel in Brighton. This funny little place I heard so much about.”

Sarah remembered telling him about the jazz scene in Brighton, it was one of her favourite towns.

“So, we can go there together, now.” He held out his hand to her.

She laughed. “Oh Tony, you've got to be joking, I don’t think so.”

“Why not? I still love you and I know you love me.”

“Tony, do you really think you can come back into my life, everything forgotten?”

“I didn’t forget anything, Sarah,” he said, and before she could turn away his arms were around her and his kiss locked her into the moment which seemed to last forever.

She packed a few things hurriedly before she thought about what she was doing and changed her mind. She left a note for Lily, beside the roses on the kitchen table.

It was a small boutique hotel, arty and quaint. Their room was tiny, the scent of the pink tiger lilies filling the space which was mostly occupied by a huge bed of white linen, soft feather pillows and duvet. Tony pulled out another parcel from his case: a silky red baby doll. "Let's have a shower and then you can put this on," he said. The mosaic tile and chrome shower was modern and large enough for the two of them. He washed her body carefully with the hotel's tubes of fragrant shower gel and shampoo. She felt dizzy as they kissed under the hot spray. He dried her hair, brushing it till it shone. She twirled in her silk sheath and he carried her the short way to the bed. It was a blissful reunion, more than she could ever have imagined.

When they managed to leave the bed, they ate a late supper by candlelight in a small bistro around the corner from the hotel which was still open. Sarah couldn't eat much, she was too excited, sipping the champagne Tony had ordered, thinking it was all too extravagant and decadent to be real. They ran back to the hotel and Tony spent the night showing Sarah how much he had missed her.

The next morning they ordered breakfast in bed, a tray of coffee, hot buttered wholemeal toast with jam, muesli and yogurt.

"Are we ever going to leave this bed," she laughed, she could hear the seagulls screeching outside.

"No, let's stay here all day," he replied, pulling her back into the snowy depths.

Finally emerging from their room there was a town to discover together and over the next few days they sampled seaside life. The spring sunshine shone, sparkling on the sea, as they crunched over the pebbles hand in hand. They sat on the beach eating fish and chips out of paper bags. Under the arches they wandered along the paved seashore, passing the fishing museum, shops selling local art, knick knacks and postcards, the bars and the boats, and the shell of the pier, a burned out skeleton. They ate burgers, sitting on plastic chairs at plastic tables. Sarah insisted on having a ride on the carousel of painted horses, while Tony waved as she went around and around. She felt like a little girl again, remembering how her father had always taken her to the fair. They strolled along the high street, passing the blocks of hotels and houses facing the sea, turning down to the town inside. They explored the antique shops of the Lanes and visited the Palace. They ate steak at Browns and fish at Englishs. They drank brandy in the Cricketeers, the oldest pub in Brighton, and earl grey tea sitting outside one of the many pavement cafés in the weak sunshine. They listened to the swing jazz band in the street and Tony stood up and sang with them one afternoon. Sarah felt so proud of him, her heart soaring as he sang to her. She was surprised when he pulled her up beside him and they sang together *In a Mellow Tone*. They had a drink with the band after, exchanging cards and promises to keep in touch.

"So, do you like England?" she asked him as they sat drinking coffee at one of the cafés along the seafront.

"I don't think much to their coffee," he laughed. "But yes, of course I like England. I like you more." He kissed the tip of her nose. "Come on, let's go back to the hotel," he said, leaving the money on the table.

Curled up in his arms in their warm white bed, Tony stroked her hair and she wished they could stay like this in Brighton forever more.

"Sarah, I want you to come back with me," he said.

She looked up at him, uncertain.

"I am getting the divorce, Roberto is living with his mother, and we can be together. Just like I said before, do you remember?"

"Yes, I remember."

"And?"

She looked at him and sighed, afraid of what she might say. "I want to Tony, but…"

"Then come."

"I can't just come like that."

"Why not? I want you to be with me, you don't realise how much I suffered without you. I understand why you left, why you thought badly of me. You had every right to. But believe me, I am true to you. I was always true to you, even when you think I was not. I suffered, but I am sorry you suffered more. I want you to be happy, Sarah, happy with me."

"Oh Tony." She wanted to cry. It was too perfect. But still she felt scared. "It's not so easy to come back again. I must leave my family, my job, I must…"

"Sarah, if you live with me you do not need a job. I will take care of you. Better than I did before, I promise."

She snuggled into his shoulder, she wanted to stay in his arms, just like this.

"I could sing again, Tony. We could start again at the bar, like before." She held her breath, wondering how he would react. Singing on the street in Brighton had brought it all back to her, the wonderful career that might have been, that still could be.

"Of course we could."

"Do you mean it, really, do you want to?"

"Of course I do. If that is what you want then I want it too."

She called Lily on her third night away. Tony had gone out to buy cigarettes.

"Sarah! Finally! Talk about a whirlwind romance. I hope you are having a good time. I couldn't believe your note. I had some explaining to do to Mum, not to mention Andy."

Sarah felt momentarily annoyed, she wasn't a child any more but still they treated her like one. "Sorry, Lily," she said. "But it was so unexpected."

"I should say so. He whisked you off your feet by the sounds of it."

"Something like that."

"So, you're all made up now then, I take it?"

"Yes. It's lovely."

"As long as you are happy, Sarah."

"I am. Listen, I want you all to meet him. On my birthday."

"Mum was wanting to do a special meal, remember?"

"Yes, and I want to bring Tony, what do you think?"

"Well, yes, probably a good idea. We are all dying to meet him. Don't worry, I'll talk to Mum."

"Would you? Thanks, Lily. We'll see you on Sunday then."

When they arrived at her mother's, Sarah wasn't sure who was more nervous, her or Tony. He had bought some flowers for her mother and produced another box of chocolates from his case for Lily and a bottle of Sicilian red wine for Andy.

Lunch at her mother's was a different affair to lunch at Carlotta's, she noted. Margaret was full of welcoming smiles, whatever she really thought about Tony: Sarah caught her family whispering in the kitchen.

"Still, he is very good looking isn't he," Lily said, giggling with the champagne Tony had brought them.

"Yes, but that can't make up for the fact he's a bastard." Andy chimed in. "He's a cheating charmer, Mum, don't be taken in."

"Hush, stop this. He's our guest, let's at least be nice to his face."

Not like his own rotten mother, Sarah thought. But it was her birthday and everyone was happy. They raised their glasses to Sarah.

"Quarter of a century! Grown up at last, my baby." Her mother, still all skin and bone, hugged Sarah. She noticed her mother hardly touched the roast beef meal she had cooked with all the trimmings, carrots, peas, beans, parsnips, roast potatoes, mashed potatoes and Yorkshire pudding. Tony was tucking in, helping himself to more.

"I reckon this is probably the first meal you've had without pasta," Andy laughed.

"Actually, no." he said, taking another roast potato from the tray. "I have tried many new things in Brighton."

"Don't do potatoes in your place do they?"

"Yes they do, but it is not something we eat all the time."

"There is even a pasta made of potato, isn't there," Sarah said.

"Gnocchi, very heavy," replied Tony.

"Noky or do you mean nooky?" asked Andy, grinning.

"No, neither, you don't say it like that, it's difficult for the English tongue."

"Too right."

After the meal her mother lit the candles on Sarah's birthday cake and they all sang Happy Birthday to her before she cut into the soft icing and light sponge, her name piped in pink on the white flat surface. Tony left the crust of icing and buttercream which Sarah ate from his plate. "You've left the best bit," she said.

That night they stayed in Lily's house. Sarah took him to her bedroom. She noticed the display of roses in one of Lily's finest crystal vases on the window shelf.

"So, here we are in your lonely bedroom," Tony said, putting his arms around her waist.

"Not so lonely any more," she replied.

He kissed her then pulled away, taking from his pocket a small box. "*Buon Compleanno*, Sarah, *amore mio*."

Inside the box was a silver necklace with a heart shaped locket. When she prised open the small heart she found a tiny picture of her face on one side and Tony's on the other. "When it closes they kiss," he said. "Like this."

Waking up in her sister's house with Tony beside her felt like a dream. She turned to look at him sleeping and stroked his silky hair back from his face. He opened his eyes and smiled up at her. "Let's have breakfast in bed," he said. "First course." He dragged her on top of him and pulled the duvet over them. When they finally got up, Tony cooked them coffee in the small pot he had brought, opening the packet of fresh coffee, the smell filling the kitchen. Sarah made toast and they sat at the kitchen table, kissing crumbs. "Second course," he said.

"Since we are here we may as well go into London," Sarah suggested.

"Yes, good idea." Tony finished his coffee.

"But maybe we should get the train," she added. "Driving and parking in London is somewhat problematic."

Tony smiled, not understanding.

He was silent as they made their way along the railway track to Liverpool Street, looking out at the passing scene of grey urbanity, inside at the people, commuting lives on the treadmill. Rattling along in the tube, Tony covered his ears and poked his tongue out at Sarah.

They walked through Hyde Park, springtime flowers sprouting everywhere, the sun shining brightly. "So big, this place, so green. We have nothing like this back home," he said.

Sarah nodded, feeling proud. "No green spaces in Taormina. No grass. But here, well, we have plenty.

Come on." She took his hand and they started to run across the green expanse until they ran out of breath and collapsed on the damp grass laughing.

They took the open top bus around the city, stopping at all the sights: Buckingham Palace, the Tower of London, the British Museum, Harrods, the Houses of Parliament, Trafalgar Square.

"I feel like a real tourist," he said.

"You are," Sarah laughed, kissing his cold cheek. They sat hand in hand on the bus, the wind whipping through their hair. As she looked at Tony she couldn't have imagined he would ever be here beside her like this.

"It is beautiful, this London," Tony said, his voice full of awe. "I could not have known."

Only the cappuccino disappointed him. "Let us have tea," he said, "while we are in England."

"Fortnum and Mason it is then," Sarah said laughing.

They stayed another night in Lily's house. He cooked for them, using the ingredients he had brought with him, the pasta and pesto. He found fresh tomatoes in the fridge and garlic in the cupboard.

"This is real spag bol, Lily," Sarah warned.

"Hey, you trying to say mine isn't, you cheeky cow." Lily gave Sarah a slap on the arm.

"No, but this is the real thing."

Tony looked at them. "I cook the pasta with this pesto sauce and tomatoes, that is all."

"See, it's not even spag bol," Lily said.

"Ah, but you will see how good it is, believe me," he said.

They opened the bottle of red wine. "A perfect accompaniment to the food," said Sarah, winking at Lily.

Lily ate her plate of pasta and drank the wine. "Blimey, Sarah, I am beginning to see the attraction," she said, rubbing her full belly. "This is definitely the way to a woman's heart."

The next day they drove back to Gatwick, it was the end of his week, time for Tony to go home. They sat with a croissant and cappuccino at one of the many airport cafés. Sarah was trying not to cry.

"My love," he said, wiping the crumbs of croissant from her mouth with his napkin, "let me know soon when you can come. I am waiting for you, Sarah, I would take you with me now."

"Yes, I will think about it." She sipped her coffee, swallowing a sob.

"But not for too long. There is nothing to think about." He kissed the cappuccino froth from her lips.

Returning to the house alone, she washed out the pesto jar with its ceramic face and put it on her bedroom shelf. She fingered her locket and sat on the bed, the bed that didn't seem quite so big and lonely since Tony had shared it with her.

Chapter Ten

She drank tea and ate hot cross buns with her mother on Good Friday, as they always did, thinking of her father who loved hot cross buttered buns. He would always buy her an Easter egg, large and luxurious with chocolates, Suchard, Lindt or Thorntons.

"Sarah, I must say I am not in favour of you going back to that man," her mother said, cutting her bun in half, as if to make it more manageable.

"That's an understatement, Mother." Sarah said, trying to lighten the situation. "But you liked him when you met him."

"Yes I did, what I saw of him, but really I am not happy. Your brother is very disappointed with you, Sarah."

"I can't live my life for Andy, can I?"

"But we are all amazed, after all that man has put you through, you are willing to go back to him."

"It was all a misunderstanding, there was never anything between him and his ex. And he came all the way here to tell me he wanted me back. He realised what he was losing."

"And so he ought to. It's all very well, him being charming and handsome, but he's not the sort of man my daughter should be living with in some strange place."

"Oh Mum, don't be so harsh. You can always come to visit." But as she said it, she knew her mother wasn't well enough to travel. She felt guilty about leaving her again but knew her own selfishness would prevail, despite the guilt. She couldn't believe it had turned out like this.

Ruth was also surprised that Sarah even considered going back to Tony. They met for a coffee in Canary Wharf just before she left. They sat in a bright glossy café sipping huge cups of cappuccino, chocolate sprinkled on top of the froth in the shape of a heart.

"After all that's happened, Sarah, do you really think it's wise going back to him? Isn't it only going to happen again?"

"I certainly hope not, he only ever had one wife." Sarah knew she was being flippant with Ruth, as she had been with her mother, not wanting to hear their warnings, wanting the lovely lightness of Tony's visit to last.

"Yeah, but what else is going to creep out of the woodwork?"

"Nothing, I hope."

"But you never know do you. I mean didn't he lose your trust?"

"Yes, but time has passed and his visit here proved he wants to be with me. It was wonderful." Sarah blushed thinking about the romantic, passionate week they had spent together. "Things will be different there now. Vivienne's gone. Even the son has gone. It will be just me and him now."

"Yeah, but be careful, don't get too sucked in. I've been there, love."

"So, are you over Saro now, really?" She dipped a wafer biscuit into the hot coffee.

"I've had to be, wasn't ever going anywhere, I knew that from the start, but still, it was fun while it lasted."

"Fun?"

"That's all it can ever be, no point getting serious about men."

Sarah didn't agree, but she kept quiet. Ruth always went for the no-hope relationship, somehow avoiding commitment.

"Looks like I shall be on my own now then, love, in my search for the perfect man."

"You'll meet someone soon, you always do."

Taormina. Sarah couldn't believe she was back here again, having thought she would never return. As she sat on the bus driving from the airport up to the town she felt a mixture of excitement and apprehension. Looking out of the window she could feel the change in the atmosphere, but was it really so sinister as she had felt it to be last winter, maybe it had been her own state of mind back then and the damp dark days. She was determined to make a fresh, sunny start. She knew it would be better, Tony had been so different in England, he had changed. So had she.

He was waiting for her at the bus terminal, she insisted he meet her there and not come all the way to the airport. He picked her up and twirled her around as she jumped out of the bus into his arms. He kissed her face and held her tightly. "Sarah, *finalmente*, you have come back to me." He kissed her softly, holding her face between his hands. She looked up at him, dazzled by the love in his blue eyes, reflecting her own.

Going back to the house, however, she entered with trepidation, expecting to see evidence of the lustre and sparkle of Vivienne, expecting to find her under the bed or bleaching the bathroom. Instead she was met by silence and a clutter of plates and papers, Tony living alone in a male mess of loneliness. A raggedy teddy bear sat in the middle of the table amidst the dirty cups and plates. She picked it up.

"I miss him, Sarah, he is my son. I miss him, my heart breaks."

Sarah put her arms around his neck and stood on tiptoe to kiss him.

"Thank God you are here now," he said. "Thank God I did not lose you too." He held onto her.

"Paris is not so far away, you can visit him."

"Yes, we can go together. Soon, eh?"

She could see Tony's monster child running wild in the streets of Sicily, now storming through the streets of Paris. She couldn't help feeling glad he was gone. She found his t-shirts and football shirts folded in Tony's wardrobe, and almost expected to find Vivienne's clothes stacked in a neat pile beside them. But there was no trace of her left behind. They could start again, like he said, just the two of them.

Their reunion was everything she hoped it would be. Bliss in the bedroom, even if it was the cold, damp bedroom. Tony turned on the radiator but it didn't make much difference. "I will be your heater," he said. He pulled the duvet around them and Sarah snuggled as close to him as she could. She felt so glad to be beside him that she didn't mind the cold.

"I feel like we are in a dream, Tony. I never expected this to happen."

"It is *destino*, Sarah. Our destiny."

The next day Tony brought her breakfast in bed: fresh coffee and a small *cornetto*, a croissant filled with jam. He fed her morsels in between sips of the hot coffee.

"This place needs a spring clean," she said with a smile. Tony didn't understand the expression. She looked at him, he never needed a spring clean, he was always immaculate and beautiful. She didn't know how he did it.

Putting on a pair of rubber gloves she found at the back of the cupboard under the sink, she set about scrubbing the house. She could see nothing much had been done since Vivienne had left.

Although it was spring it was still cold, at least in Tony's house it was, surrounded as they were by the tall houses, narrow streets always in the shade, keeping out the sun. But Tony eschewed central heating, preferring to add a jumper than turn up the dial. They were living in a damp sandwich, damp rising from the floor tiles, damp descending from the ceiling. She scrubbed at the white stuff stuck to the tiled floors in their bedroom and looked up at the black mould spreading from the corner of the ceiling down the walls. What with the cold stone of the floors, the height of the ceilings and the heat lost through the old broken windows and doors, this house would never be warm. She sighed and her heart sank as she remembered the winter months. But he would get things fixed, he promised her, when he had the money. She cleaned the house thoroughly, impressing even herself. Tony had gone out, leaving her to it.

After the domestics she lay back in a hot bath feeling content. I'm going to make much more of an effort this time, she thought, I'm going to make it work. Over her comfy grey tracksuit she put on the shapeless green woollen cardigan Tony's grandmother had knitted for him years ago. She made herself a cup of tea, quite sure the teabags were past their sell-by date, and curled up on the sofa with her book.

"Now you look like my grandmother sitting there in all those clothes," he laughed, hugging her when he returned.

"I'm not sure I want to look like your grandmother, but still, I do feel warmer." She waited a moment, expectantly. "Well… are you happy with the service?" she asked.

He didn't understand. She gestured to the polished, de-cluttered table, the worktops and surfaces cleared and clean, the floor hoovered and mopped. He looked around. "Goodness, Sarah, all this you have done while I have been out?"

"Yep. Is my master pleased?" She laughed.

"Wow. *Certo*. Of course." He swung her round and kissed her. "My little Sarah, my little housewife."

"You see, I can be."

"You are glad to be here, this is where you belong now."

She nodded as Tony held her, feeling safe in his arms.

But she couldn't help feeling vulnerable as soon as she stepped outside the house alone. Opening the front door she could step almost directly into the apartment opposite, onto the Russian women with their cheap nylon dressing gowns and brassy dyed hair, constantly hanging out their washing in the narrow street. The proximity was disarming. Above, she could see the woman hanging out her huge knickers on the line outside her window. All around her there was noise. Families shouting, the old man snoring, a toilet flushing, a telephone ringing, a television blaring. There was no silence, no privacy. She had forgotten how close the neighbours were and how much it annoyed her.

But she was domesticating herself, inside the house and out. Visiting the butcher, the baker, the candlestick maker. There were wooden chairs in the butcher's shop so you could sit down while waiting for your meat to be cut fresh from the slaughter, the big hairy butcher in his bloody white apron welding his knife like a cartoon character, his family working beside him, wife, teenage son and daughter who could only be about twelve. She tried to smile as she sat on one of the hard black slated chairs, a square of white padding plonked on top, but she felt uneasy. She couldn't understand the chatter, everyone talking at the same time, crammed into the small shop. They would laugh at her in England if she told them that the highlight of a Saturday night in Taormina was a visit to the *macelleria* for the finest cuts of meat. Tony would telephone the order for her so all she had to do was collect the paper parcels of *involtini*, rolled meat on skewers wrapped in *melanzana* or *cottaletta*, slices of meat beaten flat and covered in breadcrumbs. The meat was always unidentifiable. Tony said it was *agnello*, lamb, or sometimes beef or veal. As she stood up to wait for her order she noticed the tiny red animal set on its side behind the glass counter, hairless and skinless, the eyes and mouth, head and body all intact. She couldn't think what it could be. She asked Tony when she got back home. *Coniglio*, rabbit, he said immediately. But she hadn't noticed the ears, the ears were not long, then she realised the ears were not there at all, they'd been chopped off. The image haunted her. It ought to make her stop eating meat, she thought, but she knew it wouldn't. Tony had quickly fried both sides of the *cottaletta* and they ate it with a bowl of salad, dressed with balsamic vinegar and olive oil, and fresh bread.

"If you think that's bad, they eat *cavallo* in Catania," he said, biting into a crust of bread.

"What?"

"Horse."

"Oh no. That's disgusting." She saw a slab of dark tough horse-meat on the plate.

She would take her trolley to the supermarket, like a granny would in England, she thought, trundling along the cobbled Corso, not resembling the girl on the cardboard wrapper in her bikini wheeling hers to the beach. She had laughed when Tony came home with the new shopping *carello* for her and pointed out the image.

"When did you last see a girl in a bikini with a trolley at the beach?" she said.

"Sex sells everything in Sicily," he replied.

But she didn't feel very sexy as she rattled up the street to the small supermarket. Scouring the shelves full of out-of-date yogurts and packs of slimy carrots more than a month old, she realised it was so much easier in the early days when she had left most of the shopping to Tony. The scowling faces at the deli counter deterred her from ordering a cut of a good piece of *parmiggiano reggiano*, so she chose one from the pre-wrapped display and invariably came home with the wrong piece, too dark and thick at the rind, or cut from an angle and not the centre of the cheese, or worse she may have picked up *grana padano* by mistake, an inferior parmesan altogether, not the matured kind, not the same thing at all, Tony complained. It annoyed her that all the shops still insisted on closing for lunch at one o'clock and not reopening till after four every day. She couldn't understand why this old tradition continued in this day and age in town full of tourists. Her local Tesco was not only 24 hours, she was sure it sold more Italian produce than Taormina.

As her *carello* clattered over the cobbles of the Corso, she passed the bored girls smoking in the doorways of their fancy shops, giving her the once over. She was determined not to look at them, staring straight ahead, steering her vehicle between the sauntering tourists, idling by, licking their huge ice creams while she was in a hurry to get home. On the side streets there were the smaller shops, older hard-faced women selling overpriced goods, clothes, bags and swimwear for unsuspecting tourists. Tony explained the level of prices for everything varied considerably, there wasn't a democratic one price for all, he said, it depends on who you are, who you are related to, who you know, who knows you, your reputation, your associations... and what underwear you choose in the morning, Sarah slipped in, though the irony was lost on Tony.

Pulling her heavy trolley up the crooked streets full of steps and slippery cobbles, designed to make you break your neck, she faced the old women in the small square near home, sitting beside their open front doors, stopping in mid-sentence to look at her, sometimes nodding as they began to recognise her. Above them, bougainvillea and jasmine grew up the walls and pots on balconies dripped with water. Set in recesses in the stone walls were the small shrines shining with light, the protection of the Madonna. The women talked loudly in their spitting, screeching, shot-gun Sicilian. She wondered why the women, young, old and middle-aged, all wore similar expressions of disdain, displeasure and disapproval, as if an invisible smear of shit sat beneath their noses. It amazed her that hardly one of them cracked their faces to smile.

Then there were the many hand gestures and mannerisms like the famous finger wagging accompanied by the shake of the head and dismissive tut. The man in the grocery shop did that silent wag of the index finger, to say no, she couldn't bring the dog in with her and she had turned away, tempted to stick up her own index finger in an unmistakeable direction at the apparent rudeness of his gesture.

But she knew she would have to get used to these things all over again. The neighbours, the noise, the shops, the people, the culture and customs. It was after all a small price to pay to be back here with Tony.

"Are you going to take the dog out for a walk, Sarah? I would but I don't have the time." Tony was getting ready to go out.

"But, Tony, you're not going out again, are you?" she said.

"I won't be long."

"You always say that but still you disappear for half the day."

"I have business to attend to."

"Business? What kind of business?"

"*Niente*, nothing for you to worry about."

"But wouldn't it be nice if we could go for a walk together?"

"Of course. But not today."

Sarah didn't mind taking out Sammy, she needed the exercise too, but she was worried the more she was doing, the more Tony would expect her to do and leave her alone to do it. "You'll have me cooking next," she teased.

"Ah, yes, I was thinking I could show you how to do a simple dish, you must cook pasta, Sarah. If I didn't cook we wouldn't eat."

"Cheek!"

"It's true, we would live on biscuits and crackers and, remind me, what is your other speciality?"

"Toast."

"Of course. Egg on toast."

"Well, my fried eggs are a bit dodgy to be honest," Sarah said.

Tony shook his head. "Your mother didn't teach you to cook, I cannot believe it."

"Aren't we lucky then that your's did."

She dreaded meeting Tony's mother again, expecting to find her even more hostile now that she had come back on the scene, but as they ate an early supper together one evening, Carlotta seemed hardly aware of her presence. Poking at the pasta with her fork, taking small sips of her red wine, and jabbering on to Tony who hardly responded, fixed on his food as he seemed to be, Carlotta seemed older and thinner; her wiry grey hair was clipped back into a severe bun, pulling at her scalp, her face more lined and sad. In black, as always, now also in mourning for the separation from her beloved grandson, Sarah supposed.

Tony put a hand on Sarah's knee under the table and turned to her. "I tell my mother she must come with us when we visit Roberto. It's a good idea, don't you think so?"

Sarah almost choked on her mouthful of pasta but nodded quickly, her eyes wide. "Yes, why not."

Carlotta was shaking her head. "I never leave Taormina. Not now. Not ever. I must wait for Roberto to come back to me." She sighed.

"He will Mamma, don't worry, he will." Tony stabbed his fork at Sarah's leftovers. "You are not hungry?" he asked, not waiting for an answer before he helped himself.

After the food, Carlotta heaved herself up from the table, walked heavily to the kitchen and came back carrying a tray with tiny cups of coffee, just a bitter mouthful inside each cup, the brown sugar stuck at the bottom. It was a grim meal-time, Sarah thought, and she was glad they left soon after.

"Shall we go for a walk, Tony?" she said as they escaped from his mother's.

"Not now, my love, I must go, I have an appointment."

"What kind of appointment?" she asked.

"Nothing important, just a quick meeting before I go to play at the bar." He lit a cigarette and looked away from her.

"Which reminds me, Tony, when shall I be returning there? Do you not want me to sing with you again?"

"Of course I do, I am organising it, don't worry. You will start soon, I promise." He kissed her. "I shall see you later, *va bene*?"

She nodded, it had to be alright, didn't it?

She walked up to the public gardens, standing outside the gates since it was closed although it was only just after six. The scene below seemed surreal, the sea a pale blue, calm and glassy, the diluted sunshine on the flat waves pushing to the shore down below at the seaside town of Giardini, the clouds red beneath, coasting across Etna, hiding the smoking summit. Everything was ghostly on a May evening like this, eerie, pale and daunting. The view never failed to make her feel lonely, she realised. She worried about Tony, wondering if he was drinking and gambling with friends, like so many of the men did here. And she couldn't help feeling he was stalling, not wanting her to sing at the bar again.

She sighed and walked over to the small café where she bought herself an ice cream, *cioccolato* flavour. Licking the creamy cornet, she sat on the wall, looking down below at the grey concrete hotel built in the seventies. Tony said the original plans included cascading flowers everywhere to cover the concrete, but there it was all exposed, grey and ugly, not a flower to be seen.

"It's a great view, isn't it?"

She looked up from her ice cream, not noticing the man standing near her, hands in the pockets of his jeans. He smiled at her. "Yes, but it can get boring," she said.

"Boring?"

"If you see it day in, day out."

"You live here?"

"Yes, I do."

"But you do not look like a Sicilian woman, I would guess you are English." He seemed to be studying her.

"Oh dear, is it that obvious?" she asked, blushing.

"Not in a bad way." He smiled at her again.

She looked at him, at his brown eyes, tanned skin, fair hair. He wore faded jeans, trainers and a white t-shirt that for once was not too tight as was the fashion here. He looked about her own age, maybe older. "You don't look Sicilian either," she said, feeling embarrassed as she licked at her ice cream which was beginning to drip down the cone. "I take it you don't live here?"

"No, I'm visiting, with my mother."

Sarah nodded. "That's nice."

"I have to go now, in fact, she's expecting me," he said, looking down at his watch. "Enjoy your ice cream."

"Bye." She watched him walk away, thinking about her own mother and how nice it would be to have her visit, knowing there was no chance of that.

She realised she did feel lonely, even though she told herself Tony was all she needed.

There was always Roland, however, and they met on the Corso one evening.

"I can't believe you've come back, Sarah, I never expected to see you again." He pulled her close to him in a big bear hug.

"Here I am, back with the spring-time." She smiled up at him. He had put on weight and his cheeks were red which could only mean he had been drinking too much.

"So, you and Tony patched things up, huh, that was something I didn't think you would do." He stood looking at her, as if waiting for an explanation.

"No, it didn't seem possible. But it's going to be different now."

"I sure hope so, for your sake."

"Tony and I are starting again," she said.

“We had better drink to that, don’t you think, and drink to your return, the town wasn’t the same without you, I can tell you.”

“That’s nice of you to say so, you’re being as charming as ever, I see.”

“I will be after a glass of wine. It’s a fine evening so let’s go to the new bar, it has a neat little terrace, bet you don’t know it yet.”

“No, I don’t, I haven’t been going to any bars, well, only if I go to watch Tony at work in the hopes I might join him. But I haven’t seen you there.”

“Nah, I like to ring the changes. And anyway, I was kind of boycotting the place, after what happened to you.”

“Oh, Roland, you needn’t have. That was very sweet of you.”

“Sweet as a jar of honey, that’s me.”

They walked to the bar, down a narrow side street but the terrace spread out facing the view of the sea below them, bougainvillea flowering in those huge terracotta pots so popular in the gardens.

“Here we are again, dear Sarah. Who would have thought. It’s so good to see you.”

Sarah smiled but she felt uneasy. She knew Tony wouldn’t like it. She felt ashamed now of her drunken nights spent with him. “I’ll just have the one, Roland,” she said. “Then I must go.”

“Hey, relax Sarah, we only just got here. You seem kind of uptight. What’s wrong?”

“Nothing. I’m okay.”

“Let’s just enjoy the moment, huh? Now you are here again we can see more of each other. I can tell you all about my latest novel, it's going quite well actually, even if I say so myself."

"That's great."

"Yeah, I'm relieved, I had some block going on, I wasn't getting anywhere. But it's going good now." He took a glug of his wine. "But what will you do, Sarah? Are you going to sing again at the bar? You were good, you know that."

"I hope so."

"Otherwise you will have to work like the locals, in a shop or a bar, or maybe a restaurant or hotel. Hey, maybe a hotel would suit you, they need English speakers."

"Yes, but they need Italian as well."

"You can learn on the job, you must learn anyway now you are here. Not that I have, I must say, just stuck in my own little world, haven't really seen the need." He had almost drunk his glass of wine while Sarah was still sipping on hers. "Don't look so glum. Something will turn up. I'm sure Tony can get you a job somewhere."

"I want to go back to the bar, I want to sing, but I think Tony has other ideas." She knew Tony liked her being domestic, he was happy she spent more time in the house while he was hardly ever in it, but being the domestic dolly wasn't all it was cracked up to be.

"Well, at least Vivvie left, huh, and you came back so you can live happily ever after, right?" Roland said, draining his glass, holding it up to the waiter as a sign he wanted another.

"Something like that. Did you see much of her?"

"Not really, just a couple of times."

"In the bar?"

"No, like I say, I didn't really hang out there." He reached across and put a hand on her shoulder. "Look, Sarah, don't worry. She's gone. But it's great you have come back."

"Yes," she sighed, looking out at the view of the bay down below, the rough waves rolling in.

"You can be suspicious and mistrust him or you can put your arms around him and just love him," said Roland.

"That's very romantic coming from you. You were the one who told me he still loved her, remember?"

"I didn't mean it. I was trying to protect you, that's all. Besides, you seem more balanced, not to mention more beautiful now."

She laughed. "Oh, really? I'm not sure I feel it at the moment. I'm more like the village housewife."

"Nonsense, you are a trolley dolly, queen of the *carello*s."

"Don't say you have seen me cruising up and down the Corso with that contraption?" she said, feeling embarrassed.

"I sure have. I yelled out to you once but you were rolling on and didn't hear me. Guess you are the real home-maker now."

"Such fulfilling activities, I just love folding the washing."

"Piece of cake, all that stuff. Not that I indulge in it much, you've seen my place, right."

"Yes, I remember it well. You need a cleaner."

Roland held up his glass and stopped. "Hey, now you're onto something."

"What?"

"How about it?"

"What?"

"I need a cleaner. You need a job."

"Not quite the kind of job I had in mind."

"Don't turn your nose up young lady, think about it. I'd pay you, what five euro, hell, no, that's too low, ten euro an hour, for… well, however many hours it takes. And a free glass of wine after the effort!" He thumped the table with his fist. "Bet you can't get better than that!"

"Well, now I am tempted."

"There, you see, I've given you your first real job in Taormina. When can you start?"

Chapter Eleven

"I do not want you to go to this man's house to clean. You do not need to do this, Sarah."

"But why, it's not as if he's a stranger, he's Roland."

"Even worse. Still, I don't care who he is, you cannot go there."

"We need the money, Tony."

"No, we don't, I have enough for us. I have never asked you to work."

"But I want to work, Tony, you know that, I want to sing at the bar."

"Okay, but we don't need the money."

"Oh no? You are gambling, Tony, I know you are." The challenge blurted out of her and she stared at him across the table, defying him to deny it.

"Sometimes." Tony looked away, down at his coffee cup.

"More than sometimes. Don't think I don't know. That's why we don't have enough money."

"We have enough. Don't worry. Anyway, I am changing jobs soon."

"What?"

"That's why there is no point you starting to sing there again. I don't like it at the bar any more, there is a new owner now and he will make changes. I am leaving there. So I will earn more."

"Where, do you have another job lined up?"

"No, but I shall find one easily, don't worry."

"Even more reason I should take this cleaning job then."

"No. You do not need to work, Sarah, I do not want you to work, can you not understand that?"

"But this money will be mine, so I don't have to ask you every time I want to buy a packet of biscuits, a lipstick or a bottle of wine."

"You know I don't like you to drink, biscuits will make you fat and you don't need lipstick." He smiled at her.

"Don't try to be clever, Tony, this isn't funny."

"But you must stop worrying, you don't need a job. How many times must I say it?" He sighed.

"Let's call it my pocket money," she said.

"Your what?"

"Money for my pocket." She patted the pocket on her dressing gown.

"But I can give you money for your pocket. I do not want you to go to his home."

"It's not a pleasure visit, I promise. It's work."

"You call that a real job? I don't." He took a bite of his toast, thick with butter and the marmalade his mother made from the plentiful supply of oranges growing on the island. She had managed to introduce the idea of breakfast which Tony seemed never to have entertained before he came to England. Missing her morning tea and toast, she realised she could still have toast even with coffee and started to buy the cellophaned loaves of bread from the supermarket: *integrale*, wholemeal or *cereali*, with grains or *pane bianco*, plain white bread. Once he got into it he would pop three or four of the tiny slices into the shiny new toaster Sarah had made him buy. Sitting at the table, he would spill the coffee from the pot and spray the toast crumbs everywhere, oblivious to the mess he was making.

Sarah chewed thoughtfully on her wholemeal slice, annoyed that Tony had kept it from her, his intention to leave the bar, realising he never intended that she should join him again there. That decided it, she would clean Roland's house, whether he liked it or not.

It took her five hours. Layers of dust, sticky, greasy surfaces and crumbs in every corner: it was far worse than she had remembered.

"I can let you do my washing and ironing next time," said Roland, handing her a glass of cold white wine.

"Thanks, I can't wait." Sarah flopped on the sofa, feeling exhausted.

"Well, look, all I am saying is there will always be hours of work for you. More work, more money. And more vino after."

She drank the wine gratefully. "I don't get money or vino after I clean our own place."

"Well, maybe you should. Get Tony to pay you, hey, that's an idea!"

"Very funny."

"Cheers, Sarah, here's to your first pay packet!"

Walking back up the hill from Roland's house, she bumped into Carlotta standing outside a small church. She was wearing a black cotton dress with a stiff black handbag over her arm.

"Ah, Sarah, *bene*, you are in time, *vieni*, come, come here with me."

"What?"

"Inside, yes, you must, you are here, no?"

"But I'm not really religious." She didn't feel like being dragged into church, she wanted to go home and have a hot bath.

"No?"

"Not really, no. Never been baptised."

Carlotta shook her head and linked her arm through Sarah's. "Come. Is a *festa*. San Antonio. Antonio, *mio*." She pulled her, leaning heavily on Sarah as they climbed the few steps.

Inside women sat scattered in the darkness. Dagger looks were darted in her direction as some of the women turned to see who was entering their sacred place, old women in cardigans, fake candles illuminating their faces, plastic flowers at the altar. She noticed there were no men in the church. Sarah sat on the hard shiny wooden pew and looking up at the dark paintings surrounding her she remembered how Tony had told her about this church with its paintings in need of conservation and its shiny granite floor which had replaced the original stone and the red and grey Taormina marble which had been stolen from the church. She must have passed it so many times on the way to the grocery shop but realised she had never really looked at it, let alone gone inside.

"I cannot stay," she whispered to Carlotta who immediately frowned, a finger to her lips to hush her. The mass had begun.

It seemed to go on forever but Sarah dozed, though she could still hear the priest droning, maybe it was that which sent her off, that and the glass of wine after all that exertion. She woke with a start, her head bobbing, fearing Carlotta would have noticed, but looking at her from the corner of her eye she could see Carlotta was absorbed, sitting slightly apart from Sarah as if in her own world, the black rosary beads in her hands.

Emerging into the evening darkness, Sarah helped Carlotta down the steps. Outside the church, stalls were stacked with sweet peanuts and almonds, candy and plastic toys sold by rough-looking men.

"Let's have some sweets, shall we?" Sarah suggested.

Carlotta shook her head, not understanding.

"Look, here, let's have some almonds." Sarah went to the stall with its mountains of almonds, pistachios, peanuts, nougat and sweets. "*Mandorle*?" she asked Carlotta.

"Oh no, no," she shook her head, as if offended.

Don't suppose she has the teeth for them, Sarah thought as she bought a bag of sticky sweet almonds. Not sure I have either, she considered as she dubiously chewed on one.

"*Vado a casa*," said Carlotta.

"Yes, you go home, me too," she said.

"*Io sono stanca*." Carlotta spoke slowly as if to make Sarah understand.

"Yes, I'm tired too, very tired." Sarah yawned and smiled.

Carlotta kissed Sarah's cheeks but she didn't smile. "*Buona sera*, Sarah," she said formally. Her handbag still over her wrist, she walked away stiffly into the darkness up the Corso towards her apartment over the ceramic shop. That's the friendliest she has ever been to me, Sarah thought.

When she arrived home Tony was pacing the sitting room, smoking.

"Finally, you return. So, you clean for hours, eh?" He stood close to her, seething with anger, his blue eyes contained a look she hadn't seen before. "Just as I thought, you have been drinking, I can smell it."

"Tony, what are you going on about," Sarah stepped back, alarmed.

"All these hours to clean one small apartment. No, I don't think so."

"No, I wasn't. If you must know, your mother invited me into the church, I thought you might be pleased. Your bloody *festa*. Here, have a sugared almond," she thrust the bag at him. "Saint Antonio that you are."

His ash dropped to the floor, along with the bag of almonds. "Don't lie to me, Sarah."

"I'm not lying, I sat in that church for hours. Ask your mother if you don't believe me."

"You, in church, no, I don't believe you."

"I might have gone to say a prayer."

"They don't serve wine in church unless you took communion. You were with him, with Roland, drinking at his house. Just like before. I knew this would happen, I should never have let you go."

"Look, he gave me one glass after the cleaning."

"Yes, now it comes out, the truth."

"One small glass, that's all, then I left. I was walking home when I met your mother."

"Stop it, Sarah, stop the lies I say."

The slap came suddenly, hard across her face. For a moment they looked at each other, as if they were both stunned. Her hand reached up to her cheek. She felt strangely calm, as if it had happened to someone else, as if it was not her own face stinging.

"All this with him, it's not right."

"Not right? How dare you. What you have just done is not right." Tears fell from her eyes.

"I'm sorry, Sarah."

"I am shocked at you, Tony, I really am." She said this quietly, looking into his eyes.

"But, is it true? I cannot bear to think…"

"Is what true?"

"I'm sorry, I didn't mean to hurt you."

She was silent, still looking at him.

"I just got so angry, waiting for you. I didn't want you to go there in the first place."

"But you don't believe me. Call your mother, now, this minute."

"What?"

"Do it." She took the phone and handed it to him. "Call her."

He dialled her number. "*Mamma? Ah si...in chiesa, con Sarah, si, lo so…*"

Sarah turned away, she went to the bathroom to examine her cheek: a flush of red, like blusher in the wrong place. He soon followed her, attempting to come close to her.

"Satisfied?" she said.

"Sarah, I'm sorry, I am a fool. I don't deserve you."

"No, you don't, not if you are going to behave like that. And I thought I was the jealous one."

"Sarah, please forgive me. I don't know why I did it."

"No, but you will never do it again."

He looked at her, a pleading pathetic look in his eyes that she couldn't bear to see. She pushed him out of the bathroom and shut the door.

She lay back in the bath, the bubbles frothing around her, softening and soothing, thinking about what had happened. This wasn't the Tony she knew or wanted to know.

She refused to eat dinner with him, even though he tried to coax her with fresh pasta and a pesto sauce he made from scratch, leaving a mess of pots and pans in the kitchen and parmesan shavings all over the table. Locking the door to their bedroom, she went to bed and waited for Tony to leave for work. She couldn't stay alone festering so she got up, dressed quickly and called Roland.

"Hello, again," she said, trying to sound bright.

"Hey, Sarah, you okay after all that hard work?"

"Course I am," she hesitated. "Look, Roland, can I come and see you just for an hour, I need some company, would that be okay with you?"

"Sure you can, come right away."

When she arrived she noticed Roland looked scrubbed as if he had recently emerged from his now clean bathroom. He was wearing checked pyjamas and a dressing gown.

"Sorry, Roland, were you in bed?" she asked.

"Hell, no, it's way too early for bed. I stay up writing till the small hours, you know that, just me and the vino waiting for the muse to arrive." He grinned.

She looked at his computer, at the shiny keys and screen, remembering how greasy it had been, full of crumbs.

"Your work has made a hell of a difference, I can tell you. But, hey, sit down, you look terrible. What on earth has happened?"

"Me and Tony had an argument, just a tiff, nothing really." She tried to sound light.

"Oh yeah and what the hell is that on your cheek?"

Sarah had brushed her face with powder, it was only slightly red, but her eyes were puffy from crying. "It's nothing."

Roland shook his head. "I don't like this, Sarah, I don't know what's going on and maybe it's none of my business, but if I can, I want to help."

"You can help by getting me a drink."

"Sure, but are you going to tell me why Tony has hit you or did you just fall down the stairs?" He stood looking at her, his arms folded.

"Look, I shouldn't really be here, Roland, I'll just stay for a drink and go back home."

"You don't have to go back home, you can stay here. The couch is clean, you just hoovered it."

She smiled. "No, really, there's no need, I'll be fine. I think I've exaggerated. I feel better now."

"Well, maybe it will help to talk about it?"

"No, I just needed some company, that's all."

"If that's how you want it, Sarah, okay, no more questions asked." He went out to the kitchen and came back with two glasses of red wine.

She let herself into an empty house and went straight to bed. She lay awake, finally dozing fitfully, aware of the empty space beside her. Tony didn't come home till the next morning, looking for the first time unshaven and ill-kempt, as if he had slept on someone's sofa, or not slept at all. Sarah had made herself some tea, trying to think about what to do.

"What's happening, Tony?" she asked. "Where have you been all night?"

He remained silent, rinsing out the coffee pot, packing the filter with fresh coffee, filling the water chamber, lighting the gas ring, going through the ritual automatically, without thinking. He turned to her, lighting a cigarette, a question mark hovering in the air between them.

"Sarah… what I did… the feelings I had… I have never done such a thing." He ran his hand through his hair.

"That's good to know." Sarah sipped her tea.

"Even provoked as I have been many times by Vivienne, you can imagine."

"I'm sure."

"She would spit and throw things at me. But I never retaliated. Never. I walked away."

"Great, never touched her, but me, wham."

"I am more jealous of you."

"Am I supposed to be flattered by that?"

"No. But with her I didn't care so much. I gave up caring. She did what she wanted most of the time. Oh, Sarah, please, I am so sorry." He sat down, then stood up again, checking the coffee. He took out two cups.

"Not for me, I have tea," she said. Good old British tea. Maybe she would have to go back to Britain. Again. But she couldn't bear the thought, she felt too ashamed.

"Sarah, listen to me. I am shocked at myself. I am afraid." His hand was shaking as he spooned in two heaped sugars, stirring the mixture over and over as if in a trance.

"Well, I'm not afraid, Tony. Not of you. I am sad, that's all. Shocked and sad. I don't think I want to be with you any more."

He sat down beside her at the table, sipping the coffee in between puffs of his cigarette. He put his hand on top of hers on the table, but she pulled it away.

"Sarah, please, don't leave me, I beg you. Please. Let me make it up to you." There were tears in his eyes.

"I don't see how you can."

"Just let me show you. We are going to Paris." He pulled out the tickets from his pocket and placed them on the table.

Chapter Twelve

It was a beautiful hotel in the St Germain quarter.

"We can go to jazz bars, we can have fine French food, and more..." he turned her to face the bed, a romantic four poster, with voile and silk drapes everywhere. She had never stayed anywhere so luxurious. She wondered, fleetingly, how he had managed to pay for this extravagant weekend. Not to mention how he had managed to persuade her to go there with him. He ordered room service, champagne and oysters. She had never eaten oysters before and choked after the first gulp, drinking more of the champagne, glass after glass until the room was spinning.

They took a midnight walk through the city where romance seemed to ooze from the pavements. She was floating beside Tony as if in a dream.

"I love you, Sarah, believe me and what happened will never happen again, I swear." He kissed her before she could reply. "I want to show you how precious you are to me. That's why we're here." Taking her back to their splendid silk-sheeted bed, he spent the night showing her.

They slept late and ate breakfast in bed on heavy wooden trays, soft warm croissants with jam, hot coffee and freshly squeezed orange juice. As the rays of sunlight shone into the room, highlighting the thick soft carpet and the tasteful expensive furnishings, all in shades of cream and brown, Sarah wondered how they would spend the day, thinking of the many museums and galleries, the Notre Dame, the Champs Elysées, the Seine, the jazz and café society of the city.

"So, what shall we do, explore the city?" she said.

"We are going to see Vivienne and Roberto."

"What?" She almost dropped her coffee cup.

"Yes, I called them before we left Taormina."

"You did what?"

"We are here, in Paris, no? I must see my son."

"But I thought…"

"Besides, there are papers to sign. We have a divorce going on, Sarah, remember?"

"But this was supposed to be a trip for us." She couldn't believe it.

"And it is. You will see." He kissed her. "Now come on, let's get dressed, I have to collect the car."

As they drove through Paris, leaving the city centre behind, Sarah's disappointment increased. "You were supposed to be making it up to me, Tony, remember?" she said. "And not just in bed."

"Of course, Sarah, I am. You will see."

They arrived at Nanterre by midday. Tony parked the car down a side street, the apartment was on the busy main road, a small shabby block with a lift up to the sixth floor.

"*Bonjour*, here you are, *alors*." Vivienne kissed Tony. "And Sarah, of course, you are here too." She air-kissed Sarah's cheeks, lips not quite touching skin, and studied her for what felt like a long time, making her feel self-conscious. Having made an effort to compete with Vivienne as she dressed and applied her make-up that morning, feeling sick at the thought of having to see her again, Sarah realised she needn't have worried. Vivienne looked tired, a shadow of her former dazzling self, her golden hair was dark at the roots, her face dry and bare of make-up, and there were dark circles under her eyes.

"I have bronchitis," she said, coughing in between puffs of her cigarette. "The antibiotics do not work," she said flatly.

The apartment was small, the sitting room was cluttered, a sofa, table and chairs, computer desk and shelving all crammed into the room, the floor littered with toys and books. Vivienne returned to her computer card game, sitting huddled in a thick black cable cardigan, cigarette in her hand, glass of red wine by her side, while Tony went straight to his son's bedroom with his gifts, a set of toy cars and boxes of sweets and chocolates. Sarah was shocked at how prepared for this visit Tony had been, while keeping her in the dark. She sat on the sofa trying not to feel mortified, wondering how long she would have to endure this uncomfortable silence. Vivienne wasn't making much of an effort but eventually she thawed with the red wine, turning to Sarah to offer her a glass as she refilled her own.

"I lost my job, you know," Vivienne said as she poured the wine.

"Oh dear, I'm sorry." Sarah sipped her wine, thinking how she always managed to sound polite even when she didn't want to be.

Vivienne shrugged. "Problems with my boss, too many problems. I was forced to leave."

"And now?"

"I wait. I will find something better." She lit another cigarette and started coughing.

"Do you need some water?" Sarah asked.

Vivienne waved her away. "No, I have the wine, it's okay," she said, taking a gulp from her glass.

Emerging from the bedroom, Tony announced he and Roberto would go for a walk, the boy was kitted out in his duffle coat, woollen scarf, hat and mittens. "Say hello to Sarah," Tony said to the boy. Roberto grunted from beneath his scarf. She kissed his chubby cheeks after which he wiped his face with a mitten.

"Tony, it isn't that cold, why have you got him wrapped up like that, you will smother him," Sarah said.

"It's much colder here than back at home, better to be careful," Tony replied. "Now, come on, Roberto, *andiamo*." He pulled him by the scarf and Roberto laughed, following his father out of the door.

"Antonio came to Paris only to be with you, I think," Vivienne said, once they had left, pouring herself more wine.

"Well, I thought that too. But of course he has come to see his son," Sarah replied, trying not to sound bitter. Her cheeks felt hot, flushed by the French wine which she had drunk too quickly.

"I thought Antonio would come alone and stay here with us, not in a hotel, but of course you want to see Paris, the charming city of love, no?" Vivienne shrugged.

"I don't understand," Sarah said feeling confused.

"It doesn't matter." Vivienne put out her cigarette.

"And the divorce?"

"The divorce?" Vivienne laughed. "What a farce."

"Surely it's better to have everything legal?"

"Indeed." Vivienne looked at her as she lit another cigarette.

Tony came back bringing baguettes from the *boulangerie* down the road. Sarah hadn't realised they were staying for lunch. They ate a thin mustard coloured soup Vivienne had made. Roberto slurped his, dribbling the thin liquid down his chin. After they were served meat from the bone with chunks of carrots taken out from the soup. Sarah ate her hunk of crusty bread and accepted another glass of the red wine, though Tony tried to decline for her she needed more to get her through this unexpected and unwanted meeting.

After lunch, Roberto thought it clever to climb up the door of the sitting room and swing on the top, to fall down and then stand on his head and generally perform for the doting proud parents. Sarah noticed the sweets Tony had brought were already discarded on the floor, scattered and crunched underfoot. Vivienne asked Tony to fix the television connection and look at the tap in the kitchen, making the most of having a man about the house, though Sarah was sure she wasn't short of one or two, remembering what Vivienne had told her about the besotted neighbour. Tony put Roberto to bed for his afternoon nap, staying with him to read a story.

"It is hard alone. It is hard for me to cope with Roberto. He is difficult sometimes." Vivienne said.

"But isn't this what you wanted?" Sarah asked her.

"Yes, of course it is, but it is not easy. I have no family here to help me." Vivienne lit another cigarette and poured herself a cognac. "For you?" she asked.

"No, thanks." Sarah was still nursing her wine. "Surely he is happy to be here with you?"

"He is. He goes to a good school, he has made friends already. I think he is fine but of course he does miss Antonio and his grandmother." Vivienne sighed and looked at Sarah. “And you, I suppose you want to have kids with him?”

Sarah was caught off-guard. “I don’t know. Perhaps I do. One day.”

“You are young, you have plenty of time. But don’t be in such a hurry.”

Sarah had felt it occasionally, in her domestic moments she thought it might be the answer, the thing that sometimes seemed to be missing, but having a child with Tony would not be a simple affair, not when he had one already. He often joked one was enough. She didn’t know if he really meant it.

Finally they left, not too soon for Sarah who had been dying to get away. “You’ve got some explaining to do, Tony,” she said as they got into the car. “Vivienne thought you were coming here alone. She wanted you to stay there in her apartment with her and your son. She didn’t even know I was coming. You see, it’s all happening again.”

“Don’t be ridiculous. It’s not true. Nothing is happening.”

“Well, you’ve managed to misguide both of us then.”

“What?”

“I should never have come,” she said, turning her face to the window as they drove through the outskirts to the centre of Paris. She wanted to cry, to scream, to jump out of the car and run into a bar and meet a man she didn’t know. Something shocking to get through to him. Instead she seethed in silence as they drove along the glamorous, dazzling avenue, the Champs Elysées, passing shops, banks, cinemas and restaurants.

"She wants something from you, Tony, I don't trust her," Sarah continued. "She won't let you go. It's always going to be like this."

"Nonsense, she agreed to the divorce, we are signing the final papers. Tomorrow we go to court."

"What? You go to court? Tomorrow?"

"Yes. This is why we are here."

"What?" She couldn't believe what she was hearing.

"I am doing this for us, Sarah. It has to be legal. There is Roberto involved too."

"Why didn't you tell me all this before?" She shook her head. "Why have you kept it from me, Tony, how could you?"

"You must support me, Sarah, I cannot go through this alone."

"But I cannot go to court, what do you want me to do?"

"Nothing. You just have to be there for me. Please, try to understand."

"I am trying." She sighed. "So, let's get this straight, you have to appear in court tomorrow?"

"Yes, we go tomorrow morning. And that is it. Once we are divorced everything will be finished. We can put all this behind us. You just have to come with me, my love, that's all I ask. Tomorrow night we can celebrate, dinner and a jazz bar, it will be wonderful. I have plans for us. Just us. You will see."

She was silent as they drove through Paris, the late afternoon sunlight twinkling through the trees lining the long avenue.

"It's romantic, eh?" he said, his hand on her thigh. "Let's go back to our beautiful bed."

It was always in bed that he convinced her everything would be alright. Everything there was alright, more than alright, it was the one place where everything was perfect, and this is what she held on to. No one had made her feel this way and she realised how addictive it was, this physical closeness, this intimate world, like a dream that was nothing to do with reality.

But that night, after all the tenderness, loving and reassurance, she couldn't sleep.

The next morning they woke early. She stood at the window looking out at the street below, at the Tabac across the way, people buying papers and cigarettes, hurrying, going to work. Turning back to Tony she could see he was tense, chain-smoking as he studied all the legal papers, his reading glasses on the end of his nose. Breakfast in their room was more of a formality. She sat at the table, drinking the coffee and crumbling the croissant on her plate. Tony didn't eat anything. He gulped his coffee while checking the map to make sure he knew the way to the courts of justice. She didn't want to go, didn't want to be a part of this. She would rather wait in Paris, visiting a gallery, pretending she was a normal tourist, that none of this was happening. Although she wanted Tony to be free, she wondered what the price would be, what Vivienne would make him pay. And the boy, who would keep the boy, his mother surely, but would Tony fight for him? It was possible Roberto would come back and live with them in Taormina. She dressed in black trousers and a black wool sweater, feeling as if she was about to be put on trial. Ridiculous, she told herself, but still she felt a gnawing apprehension.

They arrived early at the modern district of glass and technology, riding the roundabout several times before they found the palaces of justice, a building of glass and concrete that offended Tony's ideas of aesthetic architecture, though how he could think of such abstractions at a time like this puzzled Sarah.

"Come on, Sarah, let's get this done." He kissed her forehead before they got out of the car and squeezed her hand.

Inside, they stood holding hands, looking out from the glass walls, waiting to be summonsed. Vivienne arrived. Sarah noticed she'd curled her hair and got rid of the dark roots, but still her face was pinched and pale and without make-up. Was this her new look as mother, Sarah wondered, noticing her grey suit looked slightly shabby.

"You come together?" she said, glancing at Sarah, a contemptuous look. "I think you come here alone, Antonio, this is between you and me."

"I want Sarah to be here with me."

"I see." Vivienne shrugged.

"Don't worry, I'm not coming into the court-room with you, if that's what you think," Sarah replied, wishing she had stayed in Paris.

Vivienne tutted and shook her head. Just then they were called in. Sarah sat waiting on the cold uncomfortable bench while Tony and Vivienne disappeared to discuss their future in a small room with the judge.

After an hour they emerged, Vivienne with a grim face.

"Well?" Sarah asked.

"We can discuss this later," replied Tony. "Now, come on, let's all go and have some lunch, I'm starving."

"Lunch?" Sarah couldn't believe they were going to have lunch together. "I don't want any lunch, I'm not hungry," she said.

"Come on, you must eat, something light. Vivienne?"

"I don't have long, I must collect Roberto from school, our son, remember?" She lit a cigarette.

"We'll collect him together, don't worry."

Sarah sighed inwardly.

They went to a nearby café and Tony ordered the same for the three of them, goats cheese on toast with salad. Vivienne turned up her nose. "This is not so good," she said, leaving most of it on the plate. Tony and Vivienne talked in French, while Sarah sat between them wondering how they could be so civil to each other while she felt virtually ignored. She sipped her glass of dry white wine and got the chewy cheese stuck around her teeth.

Back at Vivienne's apartment, waiting for them while they collected Roberto from school, she felt trapped; trapped in someone else's apartment, trapped in other peoples lives. She wanted to be in Paris, walking the streets, visiting museums, looking in shop windows, sipping expensive coffee in café windows. She wanted lightness and love, not this heaviness, not ex-wives and sons and battles with money. Unable to bear it any longer, she left a note and took off, she would find the Metro and her way back to Paris.

Walking through the streets of St Germain, her feet throbbing in her high-heeled boots, having tramped through the halls of the Musée d'Orsay, Sarah tore off chunks of the French baguette, the sesame seeds falling and sticking to her sweater. The woman serving in the *boulangerie* was very pleasant, calling her Madame, while Sarah ummed and arred, pointed and smiled and forgot her French but managed *merci* and *au revoir*, leaving the shop feeling stupid.

The museum had been uplifting even if she had worn the wrong shoes. It was liberating to stroll around the halls and stand in front of the paintings. A much better way to spend the afternoon, preferable to watching the boy do gymnastics from the door frames and drinking red wine with the depressed Vivienne. Obviously life wasn't shaping up as she had expected it to when she left Taormina again with her son.

Tearing off more of the French loaf and trying to forget about her aching feet, she walked and walked, a different feeling now she was on foot instead of passing through in the car. It felt more real to be walking the streets, passing other people who were living here, working here, or visiting like her. The busy streets, the city smell, it thrilled her to be here, a part of it. That's what she missed in Taormina. There were no streets to walk along, only the Corso and she got sick of that. She wandered through a small market, wooden stalls, colourful bags, candles, smells of spices, music playing somewhere. She passed a small bar announcing jazz every evening, tonight bass and piano at 9.30. She knew they wouldn't go to the jazz even though Tony had promised they would. No doubt he would want to see his son and ex-wife yet again. At least she really was his ex-wife now, she thought. She decided she would spend her last night in Paris, alone if she had to. She wouldn't be playing happy families. Her mobile rang and delving into her bag she checked to see if it was Tony before answering.

"Where are you, Sarah? How could you leave like that?" He sounded angry.

"I left a note, didn't you see it?"

"Yes, but why could you not wait for us?"

"I wanted to see something of Paris, we haven't seen much of it so far. Time is running out, Tony," she said.

"Alright. I'm coming back, I'll see you in about half an hour."

She smiled to herself, surprised, guilty and glad all at the same time. "Okay, I shall wait for you in the Café Metro near the hotel."

She sat alone watching for him at the window of the café with her hot cup of milky coffee, wondering if he would arrive happy or annoyed with her. She looked up and suddenly saw him walking towards her across the street; she looked away and then back again at his tall, handsome figure striding to the café. He smiled at her and waved. Then he was there inside, beside her, his words rushing in with the draught from the door.

"The traffic was terrible. I never thought I would reach here. I wasn't sure you would wait. You gave me a fright, Sarah, running away like that." He kissed her cheek, sat down and put his hand on hers on the table. "I was worried."

"There was no need to be," Sarah replied coolly.

He ordered an espresso. He kissed her cheek again.

"So," she said, "are you going to tell me how it went?"

"*Allora*. It is official. We are divorced. Roberto will live with Vivienne, but he will visit so many times a year. I must send money of course."

"I see."

"So, we can celebrate tonight, just us. We have plans, remember?" He took her hand and kissed it.

Feet still throbbing, they walked back to the hotel hand in hand.

"Let's start celebrating here, now." He took her in his arms and kissed her softly. "Are you happy now, Sarah?"

She looked up at him. "I suppose so."

"Well, you should be. Don't you see, now I am divorced, we can be married."

"What? Are you serious?"

"Of course I am. When we get home I want you to wear your ring. We are engaged now. You are my *fidanzata*."

"Oh, Tony!" She looked at him, stunned.

He kissed her again. "Wait, I have something for you," he said. From his jacket pocket he pulled out a small parcel.

Quickly she unwrapped it to reveal a white nightdress of satin and lace. "Tony! It's beautiful."

"Now try it on. So I can take it off you."

They ate at an expensive restaurant, crowded and noisy, buzzing and blazing with lights. They drank light red wine and ate rich veal with cream and mushrooms and a baked baguette. He raised his glass to hers. "Here's to our future, Sarah," he said. "To us and our new beginning." They kissed across the table.

Leaving the restaurant, feeling tipsy and happy, Sarah leaned on Tony as they walked the streets of St Germain in search of a jazz bar. They didn't search long, music was wafting up from a basement bar and they stumbled down the stairs to the dark, intimate, smoky space, drinking champagne till the early hours of the morning.

She wore her satin nightdress for their last romantic night in the four poster bed and put it back on for their last breakfast the next morning. They kissed and canoodled and when a drop of the *confiture de framboises* fell from her crumbling croissant, he stroked the satin and kissed the jam from her leg.

After breakfast they drove to Nanterre to say their goodbyes. Roberto seemed oblivious while Vivienne wore her couldn't care less look, smoking as they stood in the street together, back in her black cardigan.

"So, I hope you like Paris, eh, Sarah?" Vivienne said.

Sarah nodded. "What I saw of it."

"Maybe you come again?"

"Yes, of course we shall come," said Tony.

"Maybe you can stay here with us next time, it's better, no, if you are here, Antonio, with your son?" Vivienne looked at him, her eyebrows raised.

"*Certo*."

Kisses and hugs goodbye. She could see Tony was reluctant to let his son go, but she was relieved it was all over.

On the flight back to Catania, Tony was silent, looking out of the window at the clouds. Sarah wasn't sure how he was feeling. She took his hand. He looked at her absently and then back out of the window.

Chapter Thirteen

Sarah sat in her damp dank sandwich of a bedroom and momentarily wondered what she was doing there, wishing she was still in their beautiful room in Paris. Taking her ring from its box in the bedside cabinet she slipped it onto her finger. She couldn’t believe Tony had proposed to her on the day of his divorce. Well, kind of proposed. Shouldn't she feel happy now? The link between Tony and Vivienne was finally broken, wasn’t it. Of course they would always be connected through their son. She worried they might even return to Taormina, that all was not so perfect in Paris, that Vivienne was running out of money and hadn’t got another job, despite her former appearance as a super efficient sexy business woman.

Tony had got another job. Having told the Stella Luna he wouldn’t be going back there before they went away, he had managed to find work immediately after their return, as easily as he said he would, playing in the bar of one of the poshest hotels in town, not just singing sets on his own, but part of a quartet. More upmarket on the surface but he didn’t get paid any more, or if he did Sarah didn’t know about it. They had enough to live on but there didn’t seem to be much around for luxuries, and Tony seemed to regard shampoo as a luxury, refusing to pay an extra euro for a better brand.

She asked him if she could sing with him at the hotel, but he dismissed the idea. “Don't start, Sarah, please. Who knows, maybe later. But not now, give me a chance, eh, I have to prove myself, I cannot think about you too.”

She wouldn't be going to clean Roland's house again either, that was for sure. She met him for coffee one afternoon to explain. They sat outside a café in the warm June sunshine, clusters of tourists milling in the square opposite, looking out over the view, old men sitting on the benches lining the square.

"I don't understand, Sarah. Once was enough, huh, was it that bad?"

"No, of course not. It's just not my cup of tea."

"But I wasn't offering you tea, godamnit, you got good Sicilian wine after your first stint."

"Very good, but…"

"Not good enough, eh?" Roland shook his head sipping his caffè latte. "I am disappointed, Sarah, got to say it."

"Me too."

"Yeah, but it's your decision."

"Well, yes, but…"

"Oh, don't tell me, I get it. It's that great guy of yours."

"Roland…"

"Well, is it his decision or yours?"

"He doesn't want me to clean houses."

"You mean he doesn't want you to clean my house."

"No."

"Is that why he slapped you?"

Sarah was silent.

"It is, isn't it? Jesus, Sarah, why on earth didn't you tell me that night?"

She shook her head. The trip to Paris had put all that out of her mind, at least while she had been away.

"These jealous Sicilians, got to hand it to them. Worse than Arabs they are. Do you know some of these guys even take away their woman's passport, especially if they are foreign, like you? You might escape, couldn't be having that, huh."

"Tony doesn't do that."

"No? Wouldn't put it past him. And not so long ago you know, it was quite okay for a man to murder his wife if he caught her with another man. *Delitto d'onore.*"

"What?"

"Crime of honour. In the fifties it was legal to murder your wife."

"Good God!"

"I'm warning you, these fellas don't joke."

"Sounds like I'm in danger just by being with you. Better that I won't be cleaning your house again, then."

"I'm just saying, for these guys it's all about honour, it's their honour at stake. You better watch out. I mean, it's started already, hasn't it."

"That was a one-off, it won't happen again."

"Well, look, it's not until women are involved that you get to know a guy, his true colours emerge. Say, I've had enough of this coffee, I'm ordering a glass of wine."

Sarah laughed. "Poor Roland, I've driven you to drink."

"Sure thing." He called to the waiter and ordered a glass of chardonnay.

"It's simple really. Tony just doesn't want me to work. He never did. He's old fashioned. It's nice in a way."

"Nice? If you agree. But you said you needed the money, so is he coughing up now?"

"He supports me, of course he does. And we're not even married. Yet. Though we will be."

"What?"

"He's divorced Vivienne and proposed to me."

"You gotta be kidding me? When did all this happen?"

"Just now, in Paris."

"Doesn't waste any time does he? He may be a free man, but nothing comes free. He'll be paying out if there's been a divorce settlement."

"Yes, that's why we were there."

"Guess it was business and not all pleasure. So, you got to see Viv again and the kid?"

"Yes, unfortunately."

"How's the boy?"

"Fine. Bit of wild child, isn't he."

"I got kind of used to seeing him running around town with all the other kids. He was a cutie." He drank half the glass in one mouthful. "And Vivvie?"

"Not so vampish. She wasn't well."

"Oh?"

"Bronchitis, but that didn't stop her smoking heavily."

Roland laughed. "That's Vivvie alright, strong and stubborn."

"And stupid, that's her health down the drain. And she has the boy to look after. And no job."

"She's out of work too, like you?" Roland smiled.

"Yes."

"But I thought she had a great job."

"I never actually did find out what her work was."

"I'm not sure either, high-powered stuff, sales and advertising, that kind of thing. Travelled all over."

"She made it sound so glamorous."

"And now?"

"She left. But she hasn't got another job yet."

"You sound worried."

"Well, she has her son to consider."

"But Tony will pay out now to her and the kid."

"For Roberto certainly, but I don't know, I didn't think to ask if he must give money to Vivienne."

"Ex-wives usually do get a sum of money. I got out of all that shit, wasn't paying that bitch a dime."

"You're right, a man's character certainly does come out when it comes to women." Sarah laughed.

"Yeah, well, my wife was a bitch alright, she took my two kids away from me. Set up with a guy from Texas, some big oil tycoon, hell, she didn't even need my money."

"You didn't tell me that bit before."

"No, well, didn't want you feeling sorry for me."

"Oh Roland, as if I would do that." Sarah rubbed his arm.

"Do you want to order a real drink?" he asked as she finished her cappuccino.

"No, thanks, I'd better not." She wouldn't make the mistake of staying out drinking with Roland. Tony would find out, someone would be sure to tell him.

They could hear music approaching, a band parading along the Corso, trumpets blasting, drums banging.

"Another festa, another Saint, doesn't it always sound the same to you, the music these bands play?" said Roland.

Sarah looked at the men and women dressed in white shirts and black waistcoats, walking along as they played their instruments. "It's traditional, I suppose," she said.

"Bands and fireworks and processions, they love all that stuff. I'm telling you, it's Disneyland every day here."

She woke to the sound of the mass, direct from Rome, the Sunday sermon, complete with singing. It droned from the tv in the house above, opposite them, wafting in through the open window. Sarah visualised the old lady in front of the tv on her knees, the yapping dogs at her feet. She sighed and rolled over to Tony, only he wasn't there. She hadn't heard him rise. Come to think of it she hadn't heard him come to bed. She sat up and looked at his undented pillow. After the divorce everything should have been perfect, but since they had returned from Paris she felt he was spending more time away from her. And he hadn't mentioned anything more about them getting married.

"Where have you been, Tony?" she asked him when he finally returned. "I thought you'd got up early this morning but you haven't been home at all. Am I supposed to be grateful to see you at last?" She was sitting at the kitchen table with a cup of tea, fretting.

"Don't start on me, Sarah," Tony said. He sat down and lit a cigarette.

"Don't start? But where the hell have you been?"

"You know after the late session at the hotel me and the boys play together, we relax, we jam as you call it, no?"

"What, all night?"

"Well…"

"Were you doing more than that, Tony?"

"Like what? What could I be doing?"

"Is there a woman?"

He laughed.

"Well, is there?" she asked.

He laughed again. "A woman? No. There is not."

She looked at him. "A man, then?"

"What?"

"Well, I know how much you love the company of all your male friends, very close you are." She remembered the dreadful story Ruth had once told her about Sicilian men being bum boys on the quiet. The thought of Tony being with a woman was bad enough but being with a man was just unthinkable.

He looked at her as if perplexed. "What are you talking about, Sarah?"

"It doesn't matter." She took a sip from her mug of tea. "But the fact is, I just don't believe you, I want to know what you've been up to."

"Look. This will explain everything." He took from his pocket a wad of notes, all five hundred euro notes.

"What on earth is this?" Sarah began.

"I won it. You see, sometimes I win." He smiled as he spread out the notes in a fan on the table.

"My God!"

"This is what I having been doing all the night."

"But how could you win all this?"

"I got lucky. Now, I want you to put this into the bank, Sarah. I don't want to lose it. We can save, no?"

"Yes. We should, but…"

"For our future."

"Our future?"

"You and me and…" He trailed off.

Sarah thought about what he said as she took the pull off ticket at one of the few banks in town. The ticket system had to be introduced because the locals didn't go in for queuing so it was the only way to get served. You took your ticket and waited for the red digital number to click up with a ping, though the number was always wrong and the wait was always long. The dour man grunted at her as she handed over the notes and the paying-in form. In England you could go to the bank on a Saturday afternoon and have a cup of tea, she thought. Here, never mind opening on a Saturday, they didn't even open all day, closing halfway through the afternoon for an extended lunch. As she stood at the counter, while the miserable man took his time, she wondered whether Tony was referring to a future which included marriage and kids… a child of their own. She wasn't sure what he meant and hadn't asked, being too shocked at seeing all that money on the table, gambling money. But she was beginning to wonder if the thing niggling her was the idea of having a child, Vivienne having raised the issue in Paris. Perhaps a child with Tony would make everything alright. She had thought he would want to have more children, that for Italians one was never enough, but whenever she tried to talk about it he always skirted the subject. And he always checked she was taking her pill.

"Don't think it's so easy, Sarah, to have a child, they bring problems too, you don't understand," he said to her the next morning when she broached the subject, swallowing her pill pointedly with her orange juice.

"Yes, I know that, but together we could do it. I thought that's what you meant yesterday?"

"What?"

"That we could have a child. Isn't that what you meant?"

"But it isn't how you think it should be, it never is. You don't realise these things. You are still a child, Sarah."

"You always say that, Tony, but I'm not."

"Think about it. I am much older than you. You could be my child."

"Don't be so ridiculous. Is that how you see me, as your child?"

"No, of course not, but, well, it's not right."

"What isn't right?"

"Look, I don't want to talk about this now, I must go, I have to see my mother."

"God, if it isn't your bloody friends, it's your mother, is it so hard to stick around me for a while?"

"Sarah, stop." He held her and though she tried to pull away from him it was half-hearted. "Come on, come to the hotel tonight, you can have a sip of something and watch me at work, eh?"

"Sit on my own, like a groupie you mean?"

"What?"

"I don't like sitting alone."

"So, you should make some friends here."

"Don't make me laugh, friends, here? I don't think so."

"Why not?"

"Where would I meet them? In the supermarket? On the Corso? Or should I put an ad in the local paper?"

"Sarah, by now you must be meeting people."

"No, I do not. And what I have seen so far of women here I don't want to either."

"Why must you be so unfriendly?"

"Me? Take a look around, Tony, have you seen any friendly women here? Actually don't answer that, I am sure they are more than friendly to you, they probably throw themselves at you."

"Who?"

"All those women at that posh hotel of yours."

"Nonsense. Now listen to me, I want you to come tonight, so you can see it for yourself. Will you try?" He stroked the hair from her face. She looked up at him and nodded. He kissed her forehead and left.

Maybe she was his child, maybe that's how he wanted it, she thought, and maybe in him she was finding the father she had lost.

It was a hot sunny morning so she took Sammy and walked down the steps to Isola Bella. He tugged at the lead, nearly pulling her down the uneven broken steps, curving levels full of fallen leaves, flowers and clouds of mosquitoes. Dogs barked from the houses along the way, cats curled on paved yards, the construction of hotels and houses continued or were left half done. At the bottom of the steps they crossed the busy road and took the further steps down to the pebbled beach. She sat on the pebbles, leaving Sammy to roam free, sniffing around where he liked. The sound of the pull of the waves over the pebbles soothed her. Looking at the paleness of the sea, almost flat, and the grottos further out, waiting to be explored, the scene stirred something inside her, she felt a nameless yearning. Tony said he would take her out to the grottos but so far it hadn't happened. She looked in the direction of the little restaurant where they had once sat with a glass of wine and plate of spaghetti. One of their early dates, only last summer, but it felt like years ago.

Slowly she walked back up the steps stopping along the way to catch her breath, tying her cotton cardigan around her waist. She noticed the steps were littered with dog shit and used condoms. As she turned up to another set of steps she walked into a man doing up his trousers, a magazine lying open on the step in front of him. He leered at her as she passed, red-faced and shabby. She looked away, quickening her pace until she reached the next level, turning around, fearing he was following her but it was someone else, she saw with relief.

"Hey, are you okay? I was behind you and saw that creep down there, I told him to get lost." The man was out of breath since he had sprinted up to catch her.

"Yes, thanks, I'm fine but he did look kind of creepy, these steps are not so safe any more."

He looked at her. "I've seen you before," he said.

"Have you?" His brown eyes looked familiar. The brown eyes, the fair hair, the jeans and trainers. "Oh yes, I remember, I was eating the ice cream, outside the gardens."

"That's it, I knew I'd seen you somewhere." He smiled at her.

"It happens in a town this size, can't escape anyone," she said. "Not that I meant you." She could feel herself going red.

He laughed. "No, but let's hope you don't bump into that pervert again."

They reached the top, the lookout point facing Isola Bella. "You're safe now," he said. "Though your dog might have bitten his ankle?" He bent down to ruffle Sammy's head.

"He's too lazy to bite anyone, aren't you Sammy?"

"Nice dog. Anyway, I have to run, see you around, then."

"Thanks," she said, as he waved and jogged up the road.

She decided she would go to the hotel bar. It would be good for her to assess the situation there. She didn't see why she couldn't sing there sometimes, if Tony put her forward. She was longing to sing again and was going to fight Tony for this, though she was afraid it might be futile. She dressed herself up a bit, feeling she had been playing the plain housewife for too long, her face permanently bare of make-up, her hair scraped back from her face, in her uniform of jeans and t-shirt. Tonight she decided she would remind Tony of what she was really made. But her make-up went wrong. As she studied her face in the mirror, the eye-shadow looked too dark and she began to look like a clown. She rubbed it all off with some Vaseline and started again. Just a black line around her upper eyelid would suffice and mascara. The wine red lipstick was too strong so she tried a paler more orange colour which made her teeth look yellow. She scrubbed that and coated on a gloss with a faint hint of pink. Being the painted dolly was not her forté. She left that to Vivienne. The image of her still haunted Sarah, even though last time she looked nothing like her image. She knew they would visit Taormina soon, during Roberto's school holidays. That was inevitable. She pushed the thought away.

She wore a black silk skirt and thin camisole top with a shawl around her shoulders. The evenings were still chilly, but she was determined to be glamorous. She managed to take tiny steps up the path to the hotel, looking up at the lights twinkling in the trees as she trod carefully, the high heels of her sandals liable to let her down at any moment. The music had started and Tony didn't see her come in. She sat up at the marble-topped bar, an array of bottles stacked behind the uniformed bartender, and ordered a Campari with fresh orange juice. She stirred her drink with the cocktail stick and felt very sophisticated as she crossed her legs and turned to face the music. The plush surroundings were impressive and she imagined living this kind of life, staying here in this posh hotel, sipping drinks at the bar before dinner, visiting the sites of the town before flying home, where would home be, she wondered, lost in her fantasy, until she realised someone was standing beside her, addressing her.

"Hey, you were right, you can't escape anyone in this town."

She looked up to see the boy in the jeans from the afternoon, except now he was wearing a very smart suit, white shirt, black tie and shiny black leather shoes instead of trainers. He looked older, and she realised he wasn't a boy at all.

"Hello again. I told you it's a small world here." She looked at the elderly lady standing beside him, elegant and stately in an evening dress, her arm looped through his.

"This is my mother." They nodded to each other. "We are just going for dinner."

"Here?" she asked.

"No, we're staying here but we thought we would venture out for some food."

"Lucky you." She smiled.

"See you again then, I'm sure."

She watched them leave and wondered where he was from as he didn't sound or look Italian. She sipped her Campari and looked up to find Tony staring at her. He didn't look very happy.

At the break he came straight over to her.

"Aren't you pleased to see me, Tony, you told me to come, remember?"

"Of course I am, Sarah. You look beautiful." He kissed her cheek and stroked her shiny dark hair. "Too beautiful."

"Thank you." She looked up at him.

"Who was that man?" he asked.

"What?"

"That man, who was he? I saw him talking to you."

"I bumped into him today walking back up from the beach."

"Oh, did you? Who is he?"

"I don't know who he is but he's staying here with his mother."

"It is obviously not safe for you to sit here alone at the bar." She could tell he was angry with her.

"Look, Tony, you were the one who told me to come but next time I won't bloody well bother." She struggled to step down from the stool and slipped into his arms.

"See, you are not stable. How many drinks have you had?"

"Oh, Tony, stop it, this is my first."

"But these drinks are strong, you are not used to it, you are too frail."

"Right, I shall go home now and go to bed, will that make you happy?"

"No, Sarah, stay, please, but watch out, be careful who you talk to."

"I won't talk to a soul, I shall sit here and be a very good girl, I promise." She shook her head and sighed. There still existed the idea of the good and bad girl here. The girls who were glam and sent out the vibes 'here I am guys, come and get me' and the more gentle girls, demure and shy; the Madonna and Whore syndrome, one was for fucking, the other for family. What was she, she wondered. She sipped her drink and suddenly had an idea. "In fact, why don't I sing with you?"

"Now?"

"Yes, why not? Go on, Tony, please, just one song. Like the first night I sang with you, remember?"

"That was different."

"Come on, just one." She walked over to the group and reluctantly, he introduced them to her. They agreed to play *Love Me or Leave Me* and she sang well, having been belting out her heart every day at home when she got bored with cleaning the house. The guests sipping their cocktails clapped politely. She pushed her luck and asked for one more, knowing Tony couldn't refuse. She smouldered and smooched, enjoying every moment.

They walked home together, his arm around her and they stood looking out at the bay, all the lights of the towns below blinking before them.

"Wasn't that fun, Tony," she said, still thrilled by her spontaneous performance. She sighed. "It's so romantic."

"Of course it is. This land must capture your heart, Sarah, as much as it does mine, as much as you have captured my heart," he said, putting his arms around her. "You belong here now, just as you belong to me."

She pushed her face into his neck. He smelt of the cologne she had brought him months ago, duty free at Gatwick, Chanel for Men.

She wore her black lacy baby doll, deciding she didn't want to be the Madonna tonight. Very gently he held her, caressing her like she was a doll and promptly fell asleep on her shoulder. His head became heavy so she pushed him off and pulling on her dressing gown she went to sit in the kitchen. She stole one of the cigarettes from his jacket pocket and sat in the darkness watching the smoking cylinder burn down to nothing. Sighing, she went back to bed to hear Tony still snoring. She crept in beside him and tried to sleep.

Chapter Fourteen

"You fell asleep so quickly last night." She couldn't help bringing it up the next morning. "I shall start to think you are going off me." She laughed, wanting to tease him but he didn't reply, he was obviously without humour this morning. "I expect you're working too hard."

He shrugged.

"Wasn't it good to sing together again, did you enjoy as much as I did?" she continued, ignoring his bad mood.

"Of course, but don't think this can be a regular thing, Sarah. They are strict at the hotel, you cannot just get up and sing when you want to."

"But can't you ask them if I could perhaps do a few nights with you?"

He sighed. "Sarah, must you persist with this?"

"Yes, I must. What happened to our marvellous career?"

"I told you, it isn't for you."

"You mean it isn't what you want for me."

"It isn't like that, Sarah. I will try to talk to them, I promise, okay?"

"I won't hold my breath," she said, looking at him. She noticed he was wearing another new shirt and couldn't help wondering once again where the money was coming from for all these expensive clothes. The hotel was either paying him more after all or he was constantly winning at the gambling tables.

"It's bad to gamble, Tony," she said.

"What?"

"It gets addictive, doesn't it?"

"Come on, Sarah, it's just a game."

"But what if you lose, you won't always win, gambling is a loser's game, you must know that."

"I am careful."

"Careful? If you lose, you lose, you cannot prevent that."

"There are ways."

"Ways?"

"I am not losing, so don't worry."

But as the weeks passed Sarah continued to worry, feeling something wasn't right, things were changing too quickly. Life was suddenly becoming more glamorous. Tony was no longer mean about buying shampoo. On the contrary, he wanted her to have the best of everything. Face creams, make-up, body lotions. He made her appointments at the hairdresser and beauty salon, for manicures, pedicures, facials and leg waxing. She was overwhelmed at the sudden change in him.

He was buying her new clothes too, designer dresses and impossibly high shoes.

"But where will I wear all these clothes, Tony? I am not even allowed to sing with you any more though I would look perfect if I did."

"When we go out, of course. I have some business dinners and you must come."

"What sort of business dinners?"

"You will soon find out."

And he never fell asleep on her again as he had that night. "You are my queen," he told her. "And you will live like a queen."

And so they started to go out for fancy dinners with friends of Tony, people she didn't know, from out of town. She never understood anything they were talking about but all Tony seemed to require of her was that she sit beside him looking pretty. She would nibble at her food feeling self-conscious and bored, waiting for her glass to be topped up to obliterate some of her feelings or at least make the company appear more pleasant. She didn't like the other women, haughty and hard, most of them with over-made up faces and she kept herself apart, hardly speaking to them. She didn't like the men either, dressed like gangsters in shiny suits with faces of criminals. She couldn't help wondering if Tony was involved in something. Something illegal. They were after all in the land of the unmentionable mafia.

"Tony, who are these men and what do they do?" she asked, one night, having eaten at an expensive restaurant in the country, up winding roads into the mountains, places that looked desolate and closed up, the ghost towns of Sicily, she called them. Inside the cosy restaurant they were served with plate after plate of home made country food: mushrooms, fried cheese, hams and salads, fresh pasta with rich sauces, and meat of every description, sausages, *involtini*, cutlets, meatballs, as well as endless jugs of local red wine. After the meal there was limoncello and grappa with coffee. She felt it just amounted to greed and waste since they weren't even allowed to take any of it home, the idea of the doggy bag being unheard of or frowned upon in these parts.

"They are business men, political and otherwise," Tony replied, taking off his tie.

"What do you mean, otherwise?"

"They have influence, these men."

"What kind of influence?"

He shrugged. “The right kind of influence. Which is what you need here, of course, if you want to get on. People are only in their positions in finance and politics because of who they know. They are the son of this one, a cousin of that one. They don’t get on because they deserve to or they work hard. Everything here is fake. It’s complicated. Sicily is complicated, haven’t you learned that much by now?”

“Yes, I have, but I try to keep my head in the sand, I don’t want to know, it will only scare me.”

“Keep your head where?”

“It’s an expression, if you keep your head in the sand then you don’t know what is going on, get it?”

“Better not to know, you mean?”

“Exactly.”

“But there is nothing to fear, my love, I will keep you safe.” He put his arms around her.

“Are you becoming political then, Tony, do you want to become part of the *sindaco* or whatever it’s called? Is that what all this is about?” she asked, pulling away from him.

“Possibly.”

“But it's just a minefield here, corrupt and incorrigible, surely?” Of course she knew that in this society nothing is what it seems, the truth was not something attainable, hidden under so many layers. There were no straight questions and no straight answers. Sometimes it just amounted to something like a secret society, friends of the friends, favours and the return of favours. But this other layer covering everything was indefinable and intangible yet the implications were real and sometimes horrifying. She knew this. She heard the stories. She looked at Tony, wondering, as she pulled off her tight-fitting dress and stepped out of her high shoes.

"You know at the end of the month my son will be here, don't you?" Tony said, changing the subject.

"No, I didn't know he was coming so soon. You didn't tell me."

"Yes, he's coming with Vivienne, of course."

"For how long?"

"Just for a month."

"A whole month!"

"It's not long, Sarah."

"It sounds like a long time to me."

"He is my son, I want to see him for as long as I can. He will be here for his eighth birthday."

"Sorry, I didn't mean to sound harsh, but it's a long time for your ex to be here."

"It doesn't have to be a problem, unless you make it one."

"No, it's always my problem, isn't it?" she snapped.

"Sarah, please don't start, not tonight, we had a good evening, now let's go to bed. You are drunk anyway, all that red wine and limoncello."

"You drank more than me."

"I should think so too. You cannot drink like a man." He picked her up. She was in her lacy bra and thong. He stroked the smooth skin of her bottom and carried her to bed.

It was suddenly summer once more. Tony's house was better in the summer, the dampness and the coolness of the stone a welcome relief from the hot sun. But the courtyard didn't see much of the sunshine so she had to go out to the public gardens to sit on a bench. She would take her book and bat away the flies. Sometimes they went together, taking Sammy for a walk.

"Imagine living somewhere spectacular like this and not having a view," she said as they took one of these walks one afternoon. "It's a contradiction, it's ironic, you might as well be anywhere since you cannot see anything, the sea and the volcano, all of it denied access because of the height of everyone else around you, it's absurd. We are down in the dungeon while everyone else is up on high.".

"You don't have to tell me this, Sarah, I know very well how it is."

"Then let's move, Tony, please. Let's rent somewhere else," she begged, slipping her arm through his as they continued to walk.

"Renting here is expensive, don't you realise that?"

"But if we could find somewhere with a view then you could sell your house."

"Sell it? But I can't do that, this house belongs to my family."

"Yes, but it's old and it's damp. Couldn't you rent out the house if you don't want to sell it and that way we could rent something better?"

"It's not as easy as you think."

"Nothing ever is here. Can't you at least think about it?" But she knew he wouldn't. Family blood runs deep, she thought, but at least his mother didn't live with them, she had almost expected her to move in when Vivienne had left with Roberto.

"Sarah, I have to go now, I'm playing tennis with Mario, okay." He kissed her and ran off to the other side of the gardens, to the red clay tennis courts.

She couldn't help feeling she was always getting on to Tony about something. The house, the business or politics he was involved in, his son, her singing... she didn't feel a part of anything, she felt as if it was all happening to her, that she had no control over her life. Tony controlled everything, including her.

She continued to walk with Sammy, up into the maze of small streets. People always stopped to admire him, it was all part of the afternoon dog show… roll up, roll up… as if these people have never seen dogs before, she thought. She stood outside the *panificio* while Sammy lay on the road panting, refusing to move. A tour guide stood in the street above them, dressed all in white, her ID badge laced around her neck. Having shown her group the site of the ancient amphitheatre up the road, she looked down to show them another sight of more contemporary interest. "Look, see, he is tired this dog, *stanco*, the poor… he needs water."

Sarah looked up, finding herself, or rather Sammy, the centre of attention.

"Do you know this dog?" the woman in white continued. "Is a beagle. A beagle dog."

Sarah looked up again at the woman and the tour pack. No one spoke. Sarah wanted to poke out her tongue but smiled instead, the sunlight flickering into her eyes. I'll give you *stanco*, you fat lazy dog, she thought, pulling Sammy up the road, passing two of the Bangladeshi rose sellers carrying huge bunches of cellophaned roses weighing heavy in their hands. These were tonight's offerings to be thrust in the faces of couples strolling the Corso. As well as the Indians proffering roses under the tourists' noses, there were the Senegalese selling sunglasses, their wares laid out on white sheets along the Corso. If they needed to evade the approaching police, all they had to do was gather everything into the white sheet and run. One particular friendly African always accosted Sarah, putting his arm around her with a *Ciao Bella*, leaving a wet kiss imprinted on her cheek. She yanked at Sammy's lead as once again he stopped to wee up the walls of the shops, scratching his nails on the road. Sarah scolded him, jerking him away from the doorways and the tutting women inside.

The Sicilian summer. Dusty streets, humid heat and persistent *zanzare*, those bloody mozzies that no amount of spray and plug-ins would get rid of. Her legs were bitten and she was reluctant to go to the beach covered in red swellings. Tony liked to go for a swim and a sunbathe in the afternoons, often he went without her, meeting up with friends at the beach bars. Sicilians loved the sun, soaking it up, turning a deep golden brown, some looking almost baked. She had always been careful in the sun, not that there was much of it in her part of England and her family had never been one for holidays abroad. Maybe that was why she was so attracted to Sicily when she first came. More likely, she admitted to herself, she was so attracted to Sicily because of Tony…

Like last year, there were the two pale orange hibiscus flowers outside their bedroom window.

"Have you seen them?" he asked her. "They are facing each other, ready for a kiss, facing each other in love. Look, Sarah, come here."

"How romantic you are, Tony," she said, standing beside him at the window.

He took her hand. "They are a symbol of our love. See." They faced each other and he kissed her.

The two flowers were still alive the next morning, lasting longer than the average hibiscus flower, Sarah noticed. But by the evening one closed and fell, a life surrendered, while the other was closing but still hanging on. She stood at the window and sighed.

The blot on her horizon was the end of the month: she was dreading the arrival of mother and son, feeling as if she had just seen them, the trip to Paris was not far enough away. But she knew she would have to grin and bear it, what else could she do.

Tony's mother was happy, of course. At least they would be staying with her, Sarah thought, when they went to collect Carlotta before they drove to the airport to wait for the arrivals.

"Your mother laments the thin English girl who cannot cook, who cannot be the strong wife in the home. Not like her Vivvie." Sarah looked at the photo collages of Tony with his wife and child plastered on his mother's walls. She hated seeing them, in her face like that, she stepped back, irrationally offended. Pictures of Tony's past, a past that was forever present it seemed. Tony ignored her or pretended not to hear. He helped his mother put on her coat and off they went.

It was a tearful reunion when Vivienne and Roberto appeared through the arrival gates: Carlotta was overwhelmed at seeing her beloved grandson again and there was a confusion of kisses, hugs and fussing and talking all at once. Vivienne looked much better, Sarah noticed immediately, more her glamorous self. By the end of the first hour together, Sarah's upper lip was so stiff she couldn't smile any more. Carlotta cooked lunch for them all: fresh pasta and her special home made sauce with olives, anchovies and capers. Vivienne had brought wine and cheeses from France for them to try. After lunch they left Carlotta alone to have her afternoon nap and took a walk on the Corso. Tony ran off with his son to show him a new play area set up in the public gardens.

Vivienne lit a cigarette. "Look, Sarah, all that stuff that happened here last year, you needn't worry, we are divorced now, so you are safe, okay. We can be friends, I think, not enemies."

Sarah was silent, not sure how to reply.

"Friends, yes?" Vivienne said.

"I suppose so," Sarah replied. "But you didn't seem very friendly when we visited you in Paris."

"I was not so well then and it was the divorce. It was not such a good time for me."

"You are looking better now."

"And I must say you are looking well too."

"Am I?" Sarah was shocked at anything like a compliment coming from Vivienne.

"Very stylish. I like your hair."

Tony had suggested Sarah cut her hair shorter, hanging lighter around her face in layers. Once again he had managed to prise her out of the jeans she favoured and so she would wear the pretty skirts and dresses he bought for her. Her bites had healed leaving faint scars and she remembered to spray them more often so that she wouldn't keep getting bitten. She knew she looked more sophisticated, not so girlish now.

"Tony is looking after you I think, no?" Vivienne said.

"Isn't Tony looking after all of us?" she replied.

"Of course, you are right, so he is. And you are happy with him?"

"Yes, I am. And you, are you happy?" she asked.

"Happy being alone, I guess." Vivienne laughed bitterly. "It's difficult to meet a serious man when you have a child."

"Is it? Surely men are in this position too, especially in a city like Paris."

Vivienne shrugged. "I do not meet the right ones. This is the problem."

"But you have a new job?"

"Yes, but I am limited now, I cannot travel like I did, I cannot work the long hours I was working before. I must adapt. I have my son to consider."

"I imagine you have by now, adapted, I mean?"

"I try. The job is okay, it's not the level I am used to, I have come down, but it's not so bad."

"It must be worth it, to have Roberto with you."

Vivienne smiled. "Maybe you will know one day how it is to have a child."

Sarah was silent.

"So, you must come to Paris again, you and Tony, eh?"

"I am sure we will," Sarah replied, though she wasn't in a hurry to go back.

Roberto's birthday lunch was held at the beach, at the Sole Mare, a restaurant set back with a view of the sea. Carlotta had come down especially and sat with her plate of calamari. Roberto and his friends, four boys all around the same age, had huge plates of pasta with *pomodori*, while Vivienne ate a seafood salad of squid and prawns, the olive oil running down her chin. Tony ordered spaghetti *con vongole* for him and Sarah but only one dish arrived so they shared it, Tony feeding her forkfuls from his plate. There was a birthday cake to follow, cream and fruit and sponge, with eight candles which Roberto blew out in one gust of breath. His friends cheered and they all ate a huge lump of the cake, smearing cream around their mouths.

After the meal there was an argument. It seemed to come from nowhere. Sarah couldn't understand what was being said but it was obvious Vivienne was angry with Tony: she stood up tying her sarong around her blue shimmering bikini, leaving the table in tears.

"What's going on, Tony?" Sarah asked.

"She wants more money," Tony shrugged. "*Andiamo ragazzi*," he shouted to the boys and they all ran off, down to the sea.

Carlotta sat shaking her head, dabbing a handkerchief to her eyes.

Sarah followed Vivienne, catching up with her on the beach. "Vivienne, stop, what's wrong, what's going on?" she asked, catching her breath.

"Look, don't get involved, it's better if you don't."

"But you have just involved us all at the table, what was it all about?"

"Tony isn't paying up."

"What? What do you mean?"

"The money to me and Roberto. He is not always sending me the money, every month I mean."

"But he has to, it's legal, all arranged by the court. You agreed with me that he is looking after us all."

"Yes, I know that."

"So?"

"I am angry with him, he wants to pay me less. And spend more on himself." She looked at Sarah.

"And me, you mean?"

Vivienne looked away. "He must pay for Roberto, but maybe he doesn't want to give money to me."

"I see."

"Especially now I am working again." Vivienne sighed. "But I am just not managing so well. I used to have so much money, now I cannot get used to having less."

Sarah didn't know what to say.

"I need to meet a rich man," Vivienne said, lighting a cigarette.

"But maybe not here?"

"Another Sicilian man? Oh no, never again." Vivienne laughed. "Ferraris, football and fucking, that's all Italian men care about."

"Corrupting cheating charmers my brother calls them," Sarah replied. They laughed together.

"I remember your brother, he is right. And never forget, Sicilians are worse than Italians."

"So I gather."

"In Taormina especially they are spoilt. Spoilt and lazy."

"How do you mean, spoilt?"

"They think they have everything, they think they are better than everyone else and so it spoils them. They are spoilt so they think they need do nothing, so they are lazy. But they cannot survive anywhere else. This is all they know, this all they can cope with."

Sarah was silent.

"Sicily is seasonal, the place and the men," Vivienne said. "It's not the kind of place you want to be all year round. Summer is too hot, too crowded. And winter is too damp, too deserted."

"When would you want to be here, then?"

Vivienne looked at her and shrugged, throwing her cigarette on the sand. "What do you think?"

They went back to Carlotta at the beach bar and drank *caffè freddo*, shot glasses of sweet cold coffee. Then they took the bus back up to Taormina. Tony stayed at the beach with Roberto and his friends.

"Are you going to tell me what's going on?" she asked Tony when he came back home in the early evening.

"What are you talking about now?"

"With Vivienne. She said you don't want to pay her."

"Look, I pay her too much. I resent this."

"But Tony, you have more money coming in now, surely you can afford it?"

"For my son, yes, but why should I spend my money on her? Come on, think about it, Sarah. Do you want me to give the money to her or to you?" He stood looking at her as if she was stupid.

"I didn't think of it like that, I suppose you are right." Sarah felt lost for words, wondering why she was defending Vivienne.

"Thank you. Now I will take a shower." He turned away from her and left the room.

Tony had brought Roberto back to the house. She found him sitting in front of the television, zapping channels to find cartoons, his new birthday gun and bullets scattered on the floor. She sat on the sofa next to him but he moved to sit on the rug, closer to the tv. There was a knock at the door.

"Ah, there he is," said Vivienne, seeing her son sitting on the floor.

"Come in," Sarah said.

"I am in a hurry, I cannot stay, but I want to ask you something. Roberto can stay here, no, this evening?"

"I suppose so," she replied.

Vivienne hesitated. "I am going out."

"Oh, I see." She wondered how Vivienne could think of going out when it was her son's birthday.

"So, I thought Roberto could stay with his father."

"Tony is going to the hotel at nine."

"But you can have dinner together and then take him to his grandmother to sleep?"

"Yes, of course we can."

"Good." She kissed Roberto and left.

"But I am going out, Sarah." Tony was dressed in yet another smart suit.

"What do you mean, you are going out, you're not due at work till nine and it's your son's birthday."

"Yes, but I was meeting Franco before."

"And eating with him?"

"Just a bite at the hotel."

"Why don't we come with you, then?"

Tony didn't seem impressed with the idea. "Why can't Roberto eat at my mother's?" he said.

"I find it very odd that neither mother or father want to be with their son on his birthday."

"But we all ate together at the beach."

"And?" she said, looking at him.

He sighed. "Come on, then, get ready."

Showered and powdered, in a change of clothes Sarah had found in the cupboard, Roberto was all set to go with his father. Sarah wore an elegant pale blue silk dress, long silver ear-rings and high silver shoes.

"Oh, Sarah, that's too much," Tony said, looking at her.

"What's too much?"

"Don't exaggerate. You're not going to a party."

"We are going to your very posh hotel, I want to look nice."

Tony sighed. "Okay, *andiamo*."

She held out her hand to Roberto but he took his father's instead.

They ate ham and cheese panini in the hotel kitchen. Not quite what Sarah had envisaged. She thought they would be on the other side, in the rather plush restaurant. Tony had a huge napkin tucked like a bib into his shirt collar.

"You look ridiculous like that, Tony, you're only eating a sandwich not a plate of spaghetti," Sarah said.

"You never know, I don't want to spill anything," he replied.

He and Franco were talking and eating so quickly, both at the same time, while she took small bites of her panino wrapped in its napkin, watching Roberto who was focusing on his food, his hand in the bowl of chips, swallowing almost without chewing.

"We can stay for a while, Tony, listen to you for a bit and then I can take Roberto back to your mother's," Sarah suggested.

"I suppose," he said, though she sensed he seemed reluctant.

"I can have a drink from the bar," she said.

"Only one," he replied.

Feeling like a part of the staff she left and walked out to the bar. This is more where I belong, she thought, not liking the idea of them being shunted into the kitchen. She thought wistfully about the boy in the jeans and his mother being rich enough to stay here. Tony cleaned up Roberto's hands and mouth and they all sat down together in the bar lounge, set up with elegant low tables and easy chairs. Tony explained to Roberto that he must work but they could stay for a while and Sarah would take him back to his grandmother, his *nonna*. Roberto shook his head at first but Tony promised him a glass of coca cola and so he shut up.

Sarah smiled at him as they settled down with their drinks, but Roberto looked away from her, crunching his ice from the glass. She sipped her prosecco. "Happy Birthday, Roberto," she said, raising her glass to him. He looked at her, poked out his tongue and then looked back to his father seated at the piano. Putting down her glass suddenly, she got up and ran over to Tony, whispering something. The band struck up the chords of Happy Birthday to You and Sarah sang to Roberto, in Italian. *Tanti Auguri a Te*. Everyone clapped and Sarah sat down, finishing the rest of her prosecco. Roberto managed to smile at her and she smiled back.

As the quartet played a sad Sicilian song, Sarah looked up to see Vivienne walk to the bar with Roland beside her. She looked very glamorous in a low-cut short backless black dress, her legs long and brown, her hair much blonder, perhaps from the sun, or the bottle, Sarah couldn't be sure.

"Mamma," Roberto rushed up to his mother, his arms around her legs.

Vivienne was shocked. "*Mon Dieu*, Robbie, what are you doing here?"

"Papa, papa, *qui*."

"What?" Vivienne looked up to see Roberto pointing to Tony. "*Merde*!"

Sarah stood up, she could see Roland looking confused and his face was turning redder as he spotted her. She went up to them to explain. "We thought we would sit here for a while and then I planned to take him home to his grandmother."

"I don't want my son to be here in this kind of place," Vivienne said.

"What?"

"This is not for kids."

"But Tony is here, we ate together."

"He should be in bed."

"It's not late."

"It's after nine."

"Well, we were going after this one drink."

"What drink? What did you give him?"

"A cola, that's all."

"Hey, calm down, Vivvie, it's okay." Roland put his hand on her bare back. "How you doing Robbie, heard you got a birthday today." He bent down and ruffled Roberto's hair. The boy nodded, smiling up at Roland.

Sarah looked over at Tony who was trying not to look at them but concentrate on his performance.

"Roland, let's go," Vivienne said.

"If that's what you want, then sure."

"Is there a problem here?" Sarah asked, feeling annoyed.

"No, let's go, I want to go, that's all. I cannot go out for one night in private."

"But what do you mean, you have come here where Tony works, what did you expect?"

Vivienne blushed. "I didn't realise this was the hotel, I thought it was the other posh one."

"Look, it doesn't really matter, does it?" Roland said. "Why don't we all just sit down and have a drink together, hmm?"

"Dear Rollie, that is your answer to everything," Vivienne said, slapping his arm playfully.

Sarah could see Roland had made an effort to look more attractive, clean jeans, a blue shirt and panama hat. Was this a date, she wondered vaguely, or just a drink with an old flame?

"Well, it's a good idea, isn't it, since we are here?" he laughed.

Vivienne shrugged. "*Va bene*."

"Okay then." Roland ordered them a bottle of prosecco and Roberto had another cola.

"*Grazie, zio* Rollie," Roberto said, looking up at him, smiling shyly. Sarah hadn't realised the boy was so familiar with Roland.

"And now, you will never sleep," Vivienne scolded him, smoothing his fine blond hair back from his sweaty forehead.

Poor Tony, Sarah thought, he would be wondering what on earth was going on. She could feel an awkwardness as they sat listening to the music, sipping their long flutes of sparking wine, Roberto playing with the ice in his glass, sucking a cube into his mouth, then spitting it back into his drink.

"Look, you two have another drink and I shall take your son home," Sarah said, standing up and holding out her hand to Roberto.

"No, I cannot allow that, of course not," Vivienne said. Roberto was shaking his head. "He won't go without me, anyway." She kissed his cheek. "You both stay and I shall go," she said.

"Now Vivvie, that's absurd, we were going for dinner..." Roland stopped.

"Another time, Rollie, another time," Vivienne said, getting up and leaving them without saying goodbye. Roberto, holding his mother's hand, turned back to wave at Roland.

Sarah sat with Roland, watching Tony who was watching them.

In his break he came over to them. He looked cross. "Well, isn't this cosy?" he said.

"Hi there, Tony, looks like me and Viv were gate-crashing the party," said Roland, laughing.

"What party?"

"Have a prosecco, Tony," Sarah suggested.

"I don't want a prosecco. I want to know what Vivienne was doing here with you?" he asked Roland.

"Having a pre-dinner drink, at least that was the plan." Roland sipped his second glass. "Damn expensive, this hotel of yours," he said.

"So, you are dating my wife now?" Tony said.

"Your ex-wife, I think. Yeah, the chance would be nice," Roland laughed.

Tony was not amused. "First you try to seduce my girlfriend, now you start on my ex-wife."

"Now, hold on, right there."

"You should leave now or you will regret it," Tony said.

"I think I will finish my expensive drink before I go anywhere."

"I don't think so."

"Look, buddy, for your information I am not trying to seduce anyone," Roland said. "And if you really want to know, when your wife was your wife, I didn't even have to try."

Tony understood the implication because in a flash he lunged at Roland.

"You've broken my nose, you son of a bitch," Roland growled, shooting up, knocking his glass over.

"I'll break the rest of your face too, if you let me."

Sarah jumped up. "Tony, what do you think you are doing?"

"Something I should have done before, teaching this lousy American a lesson."

The staff of the bar crowded round Tony, the bass player Marco holding a restraining hand on his shoulder before he could do any more damage. Tony left with him and a few others. Guests of the hotel were talking in shocked but hushed voices, while the staff were talking loudly all at once. Sarah got some napkins and took ice from the champagne bucket. "Roland, here, this will help." She put the pack up to his face and he moaned in pain.

"I think I need to get to the hospital," he said.

The head waiter approached and insisted on tending to Roland, bringing him a huge shot of brandy and a towel. Then a man came forward from the small crowd of guests watching. "I am a doctor," he said. "I can assess the damage." He was English, dressed in a formal suit, white shirt and bow tie.

"Thank God," Roland said. "Someone I can at least understand."

"Let's have a look at you," the man said calmly.

"Now, Sydney, do be careful," his wife said, sounding very proper. "I don't think you are insured for this kind of thing."

He turned to her. "Don't worry, Cynthia, it's quite all right. I know what I am doing." He felt around Roland's nose and face. "Yes. It is not too bad at all. Not broken. But you will have some bruises. And probably a very bad headache."

"Great. You sure it's not broken, doc?"

"Quite sure. You would be in extreme agony."

"Feels like I am." Roland held up the towel wrapped around the ice.

"Go home, take some pain killers and get some rest," the doctor advised.

"Thanks, I will."

"Sydney, come along now, we are going to be late for dinner." Cynthia looped her arm through her husband's and nodding to the crowd in general they took their leave.

"Come on, Roland, I'll help you get home," Sarah said.

"Hey, wait, I gotta settle the bill here," Roland said, standing up, looking rather wobbly on his feet.

"No, no, *signore*, please, it is on the hotel charge. We cannot allow you to pay." The head waiter looked embarrassed and bowed his head.

"Well, that's very decent of you, thanks."

As they left she noticed the boy in the jeans, except here he was again in a smart suit, sitting at one of the tables with his mother, studying the cocktail menu. She looked away, feeling ashamed, they must have seen everything.

Outside, Sarah scanned the street for Tony but he was nowhere to be seen. "Roland, I am so sorry about all this."

"Not your fault. Now I know how you felt that night, huh?" He looked at her with pitiful eyes.

"Well, yes, I suppose so but it wasn't quite as bad as this."

"Look, Sarah, I'm okay," he said, taking the bloody towel away from his nose. "It's calmed down now, I've stopped bleeding. You don't need to see me home, I'll be fine."

"No, you will not, I'm coming with you," she said putting her arm through his.

They started up the hilly road back to his house. "Look, I feel a bit of a fool. I mean I am a big guy but he caught me off guard, you know, I just didn't know how to retaliate."

"It was such a shock to see him do that. He is so irrational."

"Me and Vivvie were just out for the night, for old times sake, kind of thing, we didn't know where it would lead, if anywhere."

"You don't have to explain to me, Roland, you don't have to explain to anyone."

"I know. But, well, you see, I guess I am still in love with her."

Sarah stumbled in her high heels on the uneven road. Of course he was, hadn't she seen it?

Roland stopped. "Sarah, this is no joke," he said. "I am so glad she got the divorce from that bastard. Something she should've done a long time ago."

"That bastard is now my fiancé," she said.

Roland didn't reply. They walked on in silence till they came to his small block of apartments.

"I shall leave you here and I think you should go straight to bed," she said.

"Sure will. And thanks again, Sarah." Roland tried to bend down to kiss her cheek but he winced with pain.

"Bye Roland, you take care." She waved to him and walked down the dark street, tottering on her high silver heels, wishing she had never worn them. She shivered despite the warmth of the night, noticing the flowers growing in bushes around the villas, scenting the balmy summer night.

"I'm going to be the laughing stock of this town. He is making a fool of me with you, and now Vivienne. What does he think he is up to, discrediting me?" Tony was fuming when he came home. It was after midnight and Sarah was sitting up in bed reading.

"I don't know what you are jabbering on about, Tony, get real will you."

"It's an outrage to my honour, I will kill him if I have to."

"Don't be so dramatic. You bloody Sicilians, it's all blood and drama isn't it, but this is the twenty-first century, not that you'd know it here in this bloody backwater, you're still in the dark ages. I'm surprised you let women vote."

Tony ignored her. "I do not want to see him around you or Vivienne or my son, I want him nowhere near any of us."

"Surely Vivienne is allowed to go out with who she likes. She is no longer your wife or had you forgotten that?"

"She can have who she wants. It's not about that, it's about me. How this reflects on me."

"Oh, of course, it would be about you, wouldn't it, because that's all that matters, really. You, you, you and your poxy image."

“So, you are defending this man, yet again?”

“But he hasn’t done anything. And hitting him like that was uncalled for. What kind of man are you, Tony?”

He lit a cigarette and sat on the edge of the bed.

“Please, don’t smoke in here, Tony, you know I don’t like it.”

He got up and left the room. She heard the front door slam. She tried to get back to her book but she reread the same paragraph over and over before she fell asleep, the book dropping from her hand.

Sarah didn’t see much of Vivienne after that night and she wondered if she was avoiding them. Tony took Roberto to the beach most afternoons and worked in the evenings. There were lunches at Carlotta’s every week but Vivienne was not always there. The month soon passed, Sarah discovered to her surprise, and it was time for mother and son to leave. Saying goodbye before they left for the airport, Roberto looked suddenly grown up with his new short hair cut, spiked with gel, in his baggy jeans and t-shirt, clutching his new gameboy, rucksack on his back. He refused to kiss Sarah, leaving her with a scowl. Vivienne did kiss Sarah but she was noticeably cool. She looked brown and well but not happy. Sarah didn’t go to the airport. She took one of her fifty Tetley teabags and boiled up some water in the small shiny saucepan. Taking the tea to the bedroom, she stood looking out at the hibiscus, feeling the breeze through the window, the dog at her feet.

Chapter Fifteen

Roland stopped Sarah on the Corso one afternoon soon after Vivienne and Roberto had left. She hadn't seen him since that night at the hotel. Coming back from the market, she was pulling her heavy *carello* packed full with fresh fruit and veg. She'd also stopped off at the supermarket which claimed in its slogan "We love to be close to you". Who were they trying to kid, she thought, as the girl at the till threw the items of shopping at her; it was a wonder the milk bottles didn't break. Walking back along the Corso she felt hot and sticky, the street was crowded, full of tourists who she seemed to resent now that she was no longer one of them.

"Sarah, I need to talk to you," Roland said. Sweat was pouring down the sides of his face into his hair.

"Look, I'm sorry, Roland, but I can't, I'm in a hurry."

"Don't give me that whitewash, Sarah. I'm going to press charges against Tony, thought you should know."

"What?"

"I'm not taking it, not from him, not from anyone."

"I see." She looked at his face, his nose was red and there were yellow and black blotches under his eyes, spreading out to his cheeks, bruises fading slowly from the blow Tony had inflicted.

"And I don't think you should either. You gonna back me up on this and also admit to your own battering?"

"Oh, come on, it was just a slap, it hardly amounts to domestic violence."

"Call it what you will but this guy is dangerous."

"He just has a bad temper at times."

"Which is why he is dangerous."

"And what do you think the police are going to do for you?" she asked.

"I don't know, but it's worth a shot."

"Good luck to you then."

"So, you disapprove, you think I had it coming to me?"

"Of course I don't, but I don't think it's worth pursuing."

"You should have reported your own case."

"Look, it wasn't a case of anything."

"What was it then?" He stood looking at her.

"Roland, I have to go."

"Yeah, right see you around. You really disappoint me, Sarah."

"What do you want from me?"

"Acceptance that you are with the wrong guy, that this guy is dangerous, and who knows what is going to happen next."

"Don't be so dramatic."

"He's a hood, Sarah."

"A what?"

"Some kind of hood, I dunno, you don't know who he is."

"I don't have to listen to this. Goodbye, Roland." She walked away, trembling. She looked back to see him still standing in the same spot on the Corso, watching her walk down the street. She carried on, pulling her heavy trolley behind her. She didn't want to admit to Roland that something might be wrong, but of course Tony was involved in something, she was sure of it, something more than just the gambling. He seemed different, harder and more distant since the scene at the hotel. He was good to her but she couldn't help feeling he was giving her things instead of giving her his time. She tried to talk to him but it was no use, his evasions were always more skilful. He would kiss away her concerns, always more amorous, knowing this would appease her.

As she continued along the street, the trolley snagged on an upturned piece of paving and suddenly there were oranges and onions rolling down the Corso. Cursing, she ran after the scattered fruits, scrambling on the street to collect them. Taking them back to the broken trolley, feeling flustered and hotter than ever, she bent down to see how the bottom had fallen out.

"Here we are, I think you've dropped these." She looked up to see the boy in the jeans carrying an armful of onions.

She stood up, her hair straggling loose from her hairband. "Bloody trolley," she said. "Thanks, I don't know how it happened."

"I'll have a look at it for you. Do you have a bag we can put these in?"

From the top of the trolley she took out one of the carrier bags the girls at the checkout were always so reluctant to give away, making you wait for the bags until all the shopping was scanned, which only held up the queue even longer.

He examined the flap at the bottom of the trolley. "It isn't broken, it's just come unstuck, probably because you have a lot of shopping stuffed into it. It should be okay now."

"Thanks very much, that's so kind of you." She looked at him, noticing he was back in his jeans and t-shirt.

"I can help you home with it, if you like," he said.

"No, really, there's no need, I don't have far to go. But thanks again."

"Okay, if you're sure." He smiled at her and walked up the Corso in the opposite direction. She looked back at him walking away and noticed Roland had gone.

She was putting away the shopping when there was a knock at the door. She hesitated, wondering if Roland had followed her home, but found instead two men in dark suits and oversized black sunglasses, typically flash Sicilians she thought, wishing she hadn't opened the door.

"Tony?" one said roughly. He was stocky and dark, squashed into his black suit.

"No, he's not here," she said.

"*Dov'è*?"

"I don't know where he is."

"You *Inglese*?"

"What if I am?"

He laughed, looking at her, though she couldn't see his eyes. "We come back, you tell him we come back, *va bene*?"

"And you are?"

"*Cosa*?"

"Name? *Cognome*?"

He waved his hand. "*Non è importante*, he know who we are." He laughed again, showing a gap between his front teeth. He spoke to his friend standing slightly behind him, incomprehensible Sicilian. They turned and walked away.

"Goodbye to you too," she said, shutting the door. At least she hadn't shown them she was intimidated.

She realised they never locked up at night. Tony always said how safe Taormina was, no crime existed, at least not the crime you could see.

There was another knock just as Sarah had made a cup of tea. She decided she wouldn't open the door just in case it was those two offensive men again. She sat down at the table and opened the box of biscuits she had treated herself to, square shortbread slabs covered in thick milk chocolate which was melting. She took out one and put the box in the fridge. It might be hot but it was never too hot for tea and biscuits. The knocking persisted.

"Sarah, I know you are in there, open up." It was Roland shouting and banging on the door.

"What on earth are you doing here, Roland?" she asked, opening the door. "Making all this noise, the neighbours will wonder what's happening here."

"I don't give a fuck what the neighbours think, I saw them, I saw those two hoodlums."

"What?"

"I followed you home cos I saw you were being followed by those two roughnecks who were here at your door."

"And?" She felt alarmed but was trying not to let it show.

"Well, you see, it's like I am telling you, something is going on around here."

"Look, it's really none of your business, Roland."

"Sarah, listen to me, I am worried about you, that is why I am on to you like this. I want to help."

"I don't need your help." She was about to shut the door on his face.

"Aren't you even going to let me?" He stood on the doorstep looking pathetic. He dabbed at his forehead with a grubby handkerchief.

"I certainly am not," she said.

"Tony wouldn't like it, I guess."

"No, and neither would I."

"Sarah, I am your friend, what has gotten into you?"

"You are frightening me, Roland, now please, just go away." She closed the door. Poor Roland, she knew she was being unreasonable, but she did feel afraid, and even more afraid that Tony might return to find him in the house. She went back to her tea, sitting at the table with her hands around the hot mug for comfort, feeling the coolness of the house enfolding her.

"Tony, there were two men here for you today," she said when he came home in the late afternoon. He had been to the beach. He was looking darker than ever, she thought. She had tried to tell him it wasn't good for the skin as one got older but he didn't listen. Sometimes she went with him but got too bored. Tony would swim and sunbathe and stand around smoking, always seeing someone he knew, talking to them for hours. Sicilian men can talk for Sicily, she noticed.

"What?" he said, taking off his shirt.

"Two men, they were here wanting to see you."

"You opened the door?"

"Well, of course I did."

"You must never open the door, Sarah, promise me that."

"Why? If there is a knock it is usual to open the door to see who it is." She looked at him.

"Please, Sarah, I am serious, I tell you, never again, it doesn't matter who it is."

"But how will I know who it is if I don't open the door? Anyway, who are they these men, do you know them?" she asked.

"How should I know who they are? What were their names?"

"They wouldn't say, not that I could really understand them. Sicilian is gibberish."

"They probably came to the wrong house."

"They asked for you by name. They looked like gangsters."

He shrugged. "Don't worry, just don't answer the door if they come back."

"How will I know if I don't answer the door?" She shook her head, exasperated, as Tony disappeared to the bathroom.

"Let's go for a walk, shall we?" he said, emerging fresh from the shower.

"That would be lovely," she replied, pleased he wanted to spend some time with her.

He bought her an ice cream and they sat on a bench in the public gardens looking out at Etna. Sarah licked her ice cream. "You are so busy, Tony, I hardly ever seem to see you these days."

"I know." He took her hand.

"What are you doing, then?" she asked.

"I have some extra business, I told you"

"No, you didn't. What kind of extra business?"

"Various things."

"Doing what?"

"Nothing you have to worry about, Sarah." He laughed and messed her hair, kissing her hot cheek and sticky ice cream lips.

At the end of the week she called Roland.

"I want to see you, Roland, but don't come to the house. I will meet you somewhere. Somewhere quiet, discreet."

"Nowhere is discreet in this town." Roland sounded disgruntled.

"Where do you suggest then?" she asked. "Anywhere we go people will see us and talk and Tony will find out."

"God and ain't that a crime?"

"In the circumstances, yes."

"What godamn circumstances?" asked Roland.

"Look, I will meet you in that café at the end of your road, in half an hour." She hung up before he could reply.

"This all feels very clandestine," he said. "What is this meeting for anyway? Thought you never wanted to see me again."

Having arrived early, she'd already ordered an espresso and a glass of water. "Sit down, Roland. I am worried and you've made me even more worried. Do you know what Tony is involved in?"

He sat down heavily on the plastic chair opposite her. "Haven't got a clue, why should I?"

"Well, you seem to be the detective around town."

"I am only concerned for you."

"So did you go to the police?"

"Yes."

"And?"

"They laughed at me."

"There you are then. What a waste of time."

"Gave them a laugh, I guess. They shrugged and told me to be more of a man. I got quite angry and told them all to piss off. I was drunk though so it didn't help my case."

"Really, Roland, how could you turn up drunk, at the police station of all places?"

"Needed dutch courage to go there, didn't I?"

"What were you trying to prove, anyway?"

"I don't know, but Tony is into something."

"Yes, but what? You've got me scared."

"You should be scared."

"You're exaggerating."

"I saw those two guys he is mixed up with."

"He is not mixed up with them, they were looking for him, for some reason."

"And what reason was that?"

"I don't know. Tony said he didn't know them."

"And you believe him, of course."

"No, I don't, that is what's worrying me. They were horrible men. And I have had this sensation that he hasn't been truthful with me. I just feel uneasy."

"Yeah, I'm not surprised." He looked at her, his eyes were bloodshot, she noticed.

"Roland, you shouldn't keep drinking like this," she said.

"What do you care," he said, glass of whisky in his hand.

"Of course I do."

"Look, Sarah, I know I made a fool of myself about Vivvie." He rolled the whisky round in the glass and looked up at her, despair in his eyes. He downed his whisky, silent for a moment. "I think maybe I gave you the wrong idea."

"About what?"

"Well, I think I led you on. I played a joke on you too."

"What joke, what are you talking about?"

"I sent you the thong, did you ever get it?"

Sarah looked at him horrified. "What?"

"At Christmas, remember?"

“It was you?” She could feel her cheeks burning.

“You didn’t guess?”

“How could you have done such a thing?”

“Come on, don’t be a prude.”

“If Tony knew you’d sent that to me he would give you more than a bloody nose, I can tell you. And maybe you would deserve it.”

“I’m sorry, Sarah. It was just a game. To get at Tony.”

Sarah shook her head. “I don't understand.”

He sighed. “I must seem like an old perv to you, huh?”

“A drunken old perv.”

“I am sorry. I didn't mean to offend you.”

“Well, you did. It was too big for one thing.”

He looked at her, not knowing whether to laugh or cry, so he did both.

“Come on, Roland, stop that. I wish I had never suggested this meeting.”

He rubbed his hands under his eyes, across his cheeks. “I’m in a bad way, Sarah.”

“So I can see.”

Taking a handkerchief from his pocket he blew his nose loudly and stuffed it back in the pocket of his jeans. “I was over the moon that Viv wanted to see me again. I couldn’t believe it when she suggested it. After all this time. And then we were in the wrong hotel.”

“Yes, I know.”

“Or were we?” Roland paused.

“What do you mean?”

“I got thinking, maybe she did it on purpose.”

“But why?”

“To get at Tony, make him jealous, I don’t know.”

“But why would she want to make him jealous?”

"To see what he has lost."

"Oh, come on, it's all over between them, they are divorced, remember, and he wants to marry me." Though as she said this she wasn't so sure if he did. Or if she did, for that matter. She sipped her coffee and grimaced, she had left it to go cold and the strong bitter taste stuck in her mouth. She gulped the water.

"Yeah, well, you'd be crazy to marry him. But anyway, I just felt used. And I realised I still love her, damn it."

"It's the drink, Roland, that is what it is, too much booze."

"It's true. Drinking distorts my thinking," Roland said, raising his glass of whisky.

"But we need to think straight, Roland. About this other matter. I want you to help me find out what Tony is up to."

"Nah, you're on your own, why should I help you?"

"You were willing to help the other day."

"Yeah, and you didn't want to know the other day."

"But I've thought about it now, I cannot do it alone, I don't know where to start."

"What the hell do you want me to do, follow him around town so I can get slugged again?"

"Oh, I don't know, I thought you might have some ideas."

"Forget it."

He got up and ordered a bottle of wine from the bar. He brought it over to the table with two glasses. "You look like you could do with a glass, despite the lecture and the water."

She shook her head.

"If you can't beat 'em, might as well join 'em, huh?" He poured the chilled white wine into their glasses.

"Roland, we shouldn't. Drink rots the brain," she said

"Ah, but it numbs the pain." He raised his glass and gulped a mouthful. "Not a bad chardonnay, hmm?"

They drank in silence for a while.

"So, at least tell me you are not going to stay with this creep, let alone marry him," he said.

"It's not really any of your business."

"But maybe he isn't the guy you think he is."

"It's true he has changed, but I am sure he feels the same about me."

"Are you for real, here you are still defending this guy." He shook his head. "Your brother would come here and sort him out, but then again, what would he be up against, it's a whole bigger network over here."

"Those two who came visiting looked typical mafioso," she said.

"Have they been back?"

"No, thank goodness, but I'm worried in case they do."

"Look, let's not talk about it, not here."

"What do you mean?" She looked around her, sipping her wine, feeling better.

"Places here have eyes and ears."

"It's a bit late to say that now."

"I get sucked into this place, thinking it's normal, then as I walk down the Corso I remember we are in Disneyland. Nothing is real, everything is fake in this fantasy fairy tale wonderland."

"It's sinister beneath the surface, you mean?"

"Exactly."

The cloud of the unmentionable mafia was constantly hovering. Invisible, the shadow was always lurking, always present, endemic in everything and everywhere. They live with that, these people, she thought. It's just a part of everyday life, part of their social and cultural make-up, part of their past and their present. They do not know life without this force binding them together.

The hours passed in the bar and they sat talking, Roland forgetting everything he said after the second bottle of wine, Sarah forgetting what she was listening to. It was pleasant to forget, she thought.

When she got home Tony had already left for the hotel, if had even come home, she thought. She noticed the nights out mixing with high class gangsters with beautiful women on their arms were becoming less frequent, or maybe he just wasn't taking her with him any more. She could picture her tall handsome Tony fending off the advances of these predatory women. Or not. Maybe he was leading the glamorous life without her. While the highlight of her Saturday night was queuing up at the butchers with the locals who also had nothing better to do than buy fillets of steak, Tony was crooning and swooning around his swanky hotel, making deals with disreputable men. She pushed away such thoughts as she fed Sammy and stroked his soft ears, realising she was neglecting him. She ate some bread and cheese to soak up the alcohol and took him out for a walk. It was a warm night and walking the darkening narrow streets, she didn't feel afraid, she never felt afraid here, but maybe she should. The cats were clustering round the food left out by the old women, cheap tins of cat food and spaghetti. The big bins standing on the corner were over-spilling with the rubbish, clouds of mosquitoes having replaced the day shift of flies. The smells of fish and meat wafting from open windows mingled with the jasmine growing up the old stone walls. The decayed and dirty streets were no longer quaint and charming when you lived on them. Third world conditions existed for the people living here who were not inhabiting the paradise the tourists were visiting; residents were on the edges, the idea of the idyll existing only in the postcards. But they didn't seem to mind.

Back at home, she got ready for bed and felt sick as she cleaned her teeth. It was the wine. Before she knew it, she was shitting in the toilet and puking in the bidet, sweating on the bathroom floor, self-inflicted sufferance, she thought to herself.

The phone rang and she staggered to the bedroom to answer it, thinking it might be Tony. It was her mother. She hadn't called her mother for weeks. "I don't feel well, Mum," she groaned, crawling back to the bathroom on all fours.

"Poor Sarah, my love, I hate to think of you being ill, especially in a foreign country," her mother said.

"I'll be okay, Mum, don't worry. How are you doing, sorry I didn't call, just had a lot on, what with Tony's ex and the kid coming."

"I understand, how did it go?"

"It was fine." Sarah felt the gap had closed up around their departure, Tony hardly mentioning them since they had left, except to say he was applying to the court to adjust the money he was paying to Vivienne.

"You sound terrible, Sarah, have you got a bug, those foreign places are rife with bugs you know."

"Probably just something I ate."

"Or flu, more likely."

"What about you, are you feeling better?"

"Course I am, I soldier on, you know me."

"Stop kidding me, Mum."

"Well, you could come home and see me some time."

"Yes, I'll come soon, I promise."

"We never see you, Sarah," her mother stifled a sob.

"Look, Mum, I'll call you soon, when I feel better and we'll have a proper chat.

She rang off feeling sick and guilty, remaining on the floor of the bathroom, the phone in her hand, crying.

Tony watched her as she drank her coffee the next morning. He looked fresh and handsome as usual, though it must have been late when he came home. She had gone to bed, cold and shaky after the sickness. This morning her hands were shaking, she was feeling nervous, a state produced by the strong morning coffee and late night drinking. She thought of Etna, brewing away in the background like coffee exploding on the hob, spouting out of the top.

"Are you okay, Sarah, you look strange this morning. I hope you haven't been out drinking?" He lit a cigarette and looked at her through the haze.

"Don't be daft, I had a headache last night, felt sick. Must be a migraine."

"But you don't get migraine. Don't tell me you are pregnant, please."

"No, I am not," she flared suddenly. "But what if I wanted to be?"

He got up from the table. "Please, Sarah, don't start that. You know how I feel." He downed the rest of his coffee standing up, putting his empty cup into the sink. Sarah sipped hers, wondering if she would bring it up. "I'll see you later, I have to go out," he said.

"Yes, urgent business, I'm sure."

"What?" he looked at her.

"Nothing. You run along. I will vacuum today, this place is dusty." It wasn't, Sarah hardly ever allowed it to be.

He looked around and shrugged. Walking away from her, he didn't even kiss her goodbye. She went back to bed. Sod the vacuuming, she thought.

Chapter Sixteen

One afternoon, a few days later, Sarah found herself following Tony.

He was visiting his mother after lunch and then meeting some friends, so he said, but he seemed edgy and played with his salad, when usually he ate with such gusto.

"What's wrong, Tony?" she ventured to ask as she sipped her water. "Are you not hungry or have I over-grilled the *involtini* again?"

"No. It's fine. I am not so hungry, it is true." He put his fork down on the plate.

"Leave it, then. No sense in giving yourself indigestion."

He stood up, with some relief, she thought. "I must go, I will see you later, Sarah." He kissed her forehead and left quickly.

There was something odd about his manner and his eagerness to be gone. That's when she decided to follow him.

I must be mad, she thought to herself as she dressed in jeans and a plain t-shirt. She tied back her hair and wore a pair of dark glasses, wondering if she looked too obvious rather than inconspicuous, but then everyone wore those big black glasses so she wouldn't be sticking out from the crowd. Trembling as she dressed, feeling stupid and nervous, she grabbed her keys and left the house.

Tony would be at his mother's already so she waited down a side street opposite her house, having come up through a parallel back street. She knew he wouldn't be there long, though it occurred to her he may not have gone there at all. Perhaps you are just being too paranoid, she told herself, biting her thumbnail anxiously as she waited in the shadows, thinking she had better just turn around and go home.

Suddenly he was there, running down the steps from his mother's door. He turned right onto the Corso and she emerged into the sunlight behind him, walking slowly. He seemed in a hurry, running up the steps from the piazza to the street at the next level. She decided to remain on the Corso below and follow until the next set of steps. This was a risk but she hurried and took the steps up beside the travel agency. She came to the small square she loved, old stone paving and walls, restored houses, all from the time of the Middle Ages, Tony once told her, with trees and plants, everything well kept, just how all of Taormina should look, she thought.

He was nowhere to be seen, which was just as well as he would see her. Then she caught sight of him sprinting up to the next level, higher still. She followed him, keeping well behind. He was certainly fit, much more than her, she thought, as she took the steep steps upwards, huffing and puffing in the heat of the afternoon. When she reached the top she could see he had crossed the road and was taking the long winding scenic steps up to the church of the Madonna della Rocca. What's he going up there for, she wondered. It wouldn't be so easy to follow him without being seen, though there was only one way up so she could lag behind, being sure of his destination. She took the zigzag steps, stopping at intervals to catch her breath and look at the small weatherbeaten bronze mouldings of Jesus, with inscriptions in Latin, leading all the way up to the church. Looking out over the rising views of the bay, over the whole town, she finally reached the church of the rocks, as it was known; inside the church the ceiling was partly made of exposed rock. Tony had said they would marry there one day.

She arrived out of breath, scanning the terrace with its perfect bird's eye view of the town, but there was no sign of him. Looking up at the castle, the castle that was always closed, she could see him striding up the uneven, broken stone steps. She was even more puzzled. She scrambled up part of the way and stopped when she saw him at the top, at the padlocked entrance, talking to another man. Where this man had come from she couldn't tell. Then the stranger opened the padlock and they went inside the castle grounds, locking themselves in. She crept up further to get a better view. On the ground, beside the stranger, there was a big black leather bag. After some discussion he handed the bag to Tony, slapping him on the shoulder. They hugged and kissed, then he let Tony out of the huge iron gate, while he remained within the abandoned castle grounds and ruins.

She ran down the rest of the steps as fast as she could, thankful she had worn trainers as she skidded and skipped down the crumbling slippery steps. She hid behind the shuttered kiosk, the stall where the funny little man sold tatty postcards and sweet Sicilian wine. She watched for Tony to come down. He was in less of a hurry now. He had stopped to light a cigarette, carrying the bag over his shoulder. Maybe he was going somewhere, she thought. Without her. But where? As she watched him walk down to the road the other side of the castle, she couldn't help thinking how striking he always looked, tall and thin in his black jeans and white shirt, cool, tanned and handsome. But looking at him now, she felt as if he was someone she didn't know any more. Following him and hiding like this was surreal. She wanted to jump out at him as if it was all a joke and they would laugh at her fears when he explained everything. But she couldn't move. She was fixed to the spot, sweating, her heart beating fast.

She watched him as he stood to look out at the view of Etna and up at Castelmola, the town higher than Taormina. A car approached and as he turned, it stopped. Throwing his cigarette away, he got into the passenger seat and they drove off, taking the road up to Castelmola. She hadn't seen who was driving. She emerged from her crouched hiding position, stiff and shaky, and slowly walked back down to the town via the other side, following the road first, then the hidden steps down at each winding level. Houses and hotels were built up the side of the hill, cobbled together, construction going on everywhere. She was trying to make sense of what she had seen but nothing pieced together.

She went home and cleaned the kitchen floor, needing something to do. When Tony returned she was hanging out the washing on the line strung across the yard, trying to pretend everything was normal.

"There you are, Sarah," he came out to kiss her cheek.

"Yes, here I am," she said brightly. "How was your mother?"

"Fine," he said absently. He lit a cigarette. He seemed to be smoking even more these days.

She noticed he didn't have the black bag with him. "You were there a long time," she said, continuing to peg the clothes onto the line.

"I told you I was meeting Mario after."

"Oh, yes, I forgot. Where did you end up? At the beach?"

"No. We went for a walk. Up to Castelmola."

"How lovely, I wish you would do that with me sometimes, Tony."

"Mario is looking for a house up there."

"Is there much for sale?"

"Some, if you want a house to restore. Also it is much cheaper than down here."

"Maybe we could go and live up there too?" she said.

"No, it's too far. There is nothing up there."

"I'm glad you had a nice afternoon, anyway," she said, looking at him over the line of washing.

He looked back at her, meeting her eyes and shrugged. "It was okay. Nothing special."

He is a perfect liar, she thought. Do I let him get away with it or do I say something? Just then his mobile phone rang and pulling it from his pocket, he answered it, walking away from her, back into the house.

"I have to go, Sarah, I need to be at the hotel earlier tonight." He was showered and ready to go. She was dusting the sitting room, cloth and spray in her hands, having been waiting for him to emerge, wondering how she could challenge him about his afternoon jaunt.

"Oh, Tony, we seem to be spending less and less time together. We haven't even had a chance to talk since you got back," she said.

"Talk about what?" He put his arms around her. "Anyway, what is that saying you have? Quality not quantity." He kissed her lips softly.

"And when is our quality time, these days?" she asked.

"You will see when I come home tonight, I promise." He kissed her ear. "Wait for me in bed," he whispered.

"Where else."

The next day at breakfast there was a knock at the door. Last night in bed had been so blissful she had almost forgotten the afternoon of unresolved detective work. The knock alarmed her, waking her from the dream.

"Who can that be? I hope it's not those two awful men, but no one else ever comes here," she said, the knife dripping with honey in her hand. "You've got to tell me what's going on."

He swallowed a mouthful of coffee and got up from the table. "Don't worry, Sarah."

He opened the door. As she feared, it was the two heavies, dark glasses, dark suits. She stood up and watched them from the kitchen. She couldn't understand a word they were saying to Tony. The small stocky man smiled widely, showing all his teeth, the taller man standing behind him as before. Tony looked serious. And he wasn't letting them in. When he was about to close the door the man put his foot up to stop the closure but as he did so Tony gave him a shove in the chest, strong enough to push him back, and shut the door with a slam.

Sarah was scared. "What on earth was all that about and why were they trying to come in?

"It's okay, Sarah, drink your coffee, it's getting cold, come on." He sat down and drank the coffee she had forgotten about.

"I want an explanation, Tony, not coffee."

"They are just small time crooks, don't worry about it."

"But what do they want from you?"

"Nothing. They think I have something that belongs to them, when in fact I don't."

"What? What could you have that belongs to them?"

"Nothing, I told you."

She drank the tepid coffee. "But what do they think you have?"

"Money."

There was another knock, louder than before. She jumped, clattering the cup onto the saucer. "It's them, they've come back," she said, her heart thumping in her chest. "Don't answer, Tony, don't let them in."

"Stay calm, Sarah, please, let me deal with this." Tony got up and went to the door, pausing for a second before opening it.

There stood at the door two *carabinieri* policemen in uniform, the red stripe down the side of their trouser legs, caps in hand; one was very handsome, short grey hair, smooth dark skin, even white teeth, light brown eyes. He smiled kindly at Tony, shaking his hand. They obviously knew each other.

Sarah stood at the table, clutching at her flimsy dressing gown, thinking they had come to take Tony away.

The two men came in, nodding at Sarah. "*Cattive notizie…*" She caught the words *figlio… morto…* she was trying to fit the words together but they didn't make sense. Tony slumped onto the sofa, in tears, his brown skin blanched, head in his hands.

"Tony, what's happened?" she ran to his side, no longer caring how immodest she looked.

He looked up at her through his tears. "My son. He's dead."

Chapter Seventeen

"What do you mean, he's dead?" She knelt on the floor in front of him, clutching his hands. The policemen had gone.

"Killed in the car. She crashed the car." Tony looked at her as if he couldn't really see, blinking as the tears fell.

"Vivienne?" she asked.

"She is fine."

"But how did it happen? I don't understand."

"They were coming home from a visit to friends. She was driving on the highway. She fell asleep. The car crashed into the car in front."

"Oh my God."

"She killed my son."

"No."

"She had been drinking. She is always drinking."

Sarah didn't know what to say, what to do. She sat up on the sofa beside him, holding his hands.

"I have go to the police station. Then I must go to Paris. I will bring him back here, he must come back here. To me. To the family grave." Tony broke down.

She clung to him, crying with him. "I will come with you," she said.

"No, no, I must go alone, Sarah. You stay here."

"But I want to be with you."

"No." He stood up, pulling away from her. "I have to tell my mother," he said. "I will go now to tell her. This will destroy her. What will I do." He was crying, walking up and down the sitting room.

"I'll get dressed and come with you."

"No, I go now, alone."

"Why? Let me come, please."

He shook his head. “It cannot be true. My son has gone.”

She held onto him as he cried into her hair.

“Why did I let him leave? Why did I let her take him away? This would never have happened. It’s my fault.”

“Don’t say such things. It’s not true.”

“Yes, it is. He was safe here with me, he was happy. How could I have let him go. Now all our lives are ruined.”

“Hush.”

“I must go to my mother.” He pulled away from her and left.

Sarah sat at the table, still in her dressing gown, the breakfast remains in front of her, stunned silence after all the commotion. Sammy sat at her feet under the table. Feeling numb, she got up and went to the bedroom, opening the cupboard where Roberto’s clothes were kept. There were also his teddy bears and cars in a box on the shelf below. She felt guilty. She hadn't tried hard enough with him and now it was too late. He wouldn’t be coming back.

She showered and dressed, taking Sammy out for a walk around the public gardens. She didn’t know how long Tony would be with his mother. A long time, she suspected.

She returned to the empty house, stacked the dishwasher and looked around for something to do while she was waiting. The phone rang. Perhaps it was Tony.

“Hello,” Sarah said.

“It’s Vivienne.” Her voice was flat, without feeling.

"Oh, Vivienne, I am so sorry, I cannot believe what's happened. We just heard this morning."

"Is Tony there?"

"No, he's at his mother's."

"I must talk to Tony." She sounded all cried out, as if there couldn't be any more tears left.

"Vivienne…"

"I cannot talk to you now, Sarah."

"Of course, I understand," she said, hearing how inadequate her words sounded.

Vivienne hung up.

Tony returned in the afternoon. "I have my ticket, I go to Paris tomorrow morning."

"One ticket?"

"Yes, it is nonsense for you to come. I go for my son. To bring him back. Understand?"

"Yes, of course."

"Wait here for me, Sarah." He took her hand and kissed it.

"Of course I will."

He left early the next morning and Sarah decided to go and see his mother. Carlotta was surprised to see her when she opened the door, just a fraction at first. She was shaking her head, tears ready to spill. Sarah stepped through the door and took the frail old woman into her arms. Carlotta stood still for a moment then stiffened, pulling back from Sarah. "*Vado in chiesa*," she said, dabbing her eyes with a soggy handkerchief.

"You are going to church now?" Sarah asked.

"*Certo*. I go church."

"I shall walk you there."

Carlotta put on her cardigan even though it was sweltering hot outside. The August heat felt like fire to Sarah who slapped on her factor 30 just to walk down the Corso.

"*Pregare*. We pray. You come."

Unable to say no, she walked with Carlotta to the church in the piazza, the façade newly restored, having been under scaffolding and hoardings for months. Sarah sat beside Carlotta and prayed. She prayed that Tony would not suffer too much.

Tony called her when he arrived in Paris. She was sitting at the table alone eating toast and a boiled egg for her supper. It broke her heart to hear the pain in his voice. He was going to see his son, he said. He would make all the arrangements necessary to bring him home, and there were so many to be made, arrangements between countries, between authorities, as well as emotions to negotiate, she wondered how he would do it. She felt afraid in the house alone, irrationally afraid, hearing noises from the sitting room as she watched the tv in bed, zapping the Italian channels full of silly screeching seductive women on talk shows; she would catch a few words, then flick back to the more comforting and serious BBC World. What if those two monsters returned and tried to break down the door, she thought, wishing Tony had told the police about them, not that it would have been any use, she knew.

She called her sister Lily to tell her the news. "You must be dreadfully upset, Sarah, do you want me to come out and see you, I will you know."

"No, really, don't do that, Lily, thanks all the same. I'm fine. I must stay here with Tony, I cannot leave him, but I think Mum was talking about me coming home soon, to see her."

"I'll explain to Mum, don't worry, course you must be there for Tony. Mum's probably concerned as we never hear from you."

"If you're all so worried you could call me."

"Fair enough, Sarah, you've had a shock. I can't imagine anything worse, when you've got kids that's all you really care about, everything else takes second place."

"Which is great for anybody else in your life," she snapped.

"Well, you know what I mean, except you don't, do you?"

"No, because I haven't got any." She put down the phone, suddenly in tears, staring blindly at the tv news.

Tony came back from Paris a few days later with the body of his dead son. He came back with Vivienne and their grief, an unbearable burden that they would continue to carry. Carlotta had prepared a simple supper for them all.

As they sat at the table an argument broke out between the three of them that Sarah couldn't understand or participate in.

"What is it, Tony?" she asked, at the last round of shouting, after which Carlotta had waved her handkerchief at him and marched to the kitchen, while Vivienne retreated to the bedroom crying.

"My mother. She wants Roberto at home, laid out in his coffin."

"Oh no, surely not."

"No, I forbid it. She did this with my father but I say no, not for my son."

"I totally agree. What a ghastly idea."

"Like a stuffed animal on display," he continued, beginning to cry. "It was terrible to see him, to see my son dead like that, so cold but as if life could still be within him, if only he would wake up. I will not have him made into a dummy, prodded and padded and all made up, no, it will not happen." He shook his head, the tears spilling.

The funeral procession advanced through the street on foot, only the small wooden coffin in the black hearse slowly leading the way up to the church of San Antonio. Carlotta was wailing, falling onto the steps. Tony half carried her into the church where she fainted. Vivienne was like an empty shell, as if there was nothing left inside her. She stood beside Tony like stone. Her hair was scrapped back in a black bow and she wore the same black suit Sarah had first seen her in when she arrived in Taormina last Christmas. She wore the same black sunglasses and high black shoes. Sarah wore a plain silk black dress making her look far more sophisticated than she felt. She realised how glamorous everyone looked, Tony dashing in his black suit and white shirt, yet in what tragic circumstances were they glamorous, she thought. She noticed Roland standing in the crowd outside, he nodded but she didn't think Vivienne or Tony had seen him. He looked like he was crying.

There would be photos of Roberto displayed on the grave, the grave he would share with his grandfather. A strange custom, Sarah thought, as they walked through the cemetery, the faces of the dead looking out from their frames, captured in that moment of life. The cemetery was all marble, stone and concrete: cold, hard and lifeless.

After the funeral everyone went home. Vivienne and Sarah walked back to Carlotta's house. Carlotta was leaning on Tony, her sobbing continued.

"You never liked my son, I could see," Vivienne said to Sarah as they walked slowly up the Corso.

"Vivienne, what a dreadful thing to say. I tried, really, I did." She could feel herself flushing, feeling guilty.

"It doesn't matter now," Vivienne said, lighting a cigarette.

They continued to walk in silence.

"I didn't fall asleep, you know," Vivienne said.

"What do you mean?"

"The accident. I don't know how it happened, one minute we were driving fast on the highway, the next I lost control, I don't know how. Maybe I fainted."

"Tony said you were drinking."

"I drank just a few glasses of wine that night."

"Surely that wasn't a good idea?"

"No. But I wasn't drunk."

Sarah didn't reply.

"I wish it had been me who had died." Vivienne looked frozen in her grief. Although the afternoon was hot it had been chilling in the cemetery and the chill remained.

"What are you going to do?" Sarah asked.

"Do? Nothing. I am going to stay here with Carlotta for a while, I cannot face going back to Paris to be there alone without him."

"I see."

"This is ironic, no, to stay here now, when I should have stayed here with Roberto when he was alive."

Sarah shook her head. "I make no judgements on you, Vivienne."

"Ah, but I think Antonio does. Strong judgements. Maybe he is right to." Vivienne turned and looked at Tony walking behind them with his mother.

Tony poured himself a glass of whisky as soon as they arrived at Carlotta's house.

"I want one too," Vivienne said lighting another cigarette. Sarah noticed she was chain-smoking. He didn't ask her if she wanted whisky so she went to the kitchen to pour herself a glass of Carlotta's red wine. Carlotta had gone to bed, her intermittent sobs could be heard in the small sitting room where they sat around the table.

"Are you still angry with me, Antonio?" Vivienne asked him.

"No, there is no point now." He gulped his drink.

"But you blame me, of course, you always will."

"I don't want to talk about this again."

"But we have to talk about it."

He looked at her across the table. "I just don't understand how you could fall asleep."

"I didn't, I keep telling you."

"You say you fainted, so that is the same thing." He poured himself another whisky. Vivienne pushed her glass across the table for him to refill it.

"But I just cannot be sure. I lost control but I don't know how it happened. Maybe I didn't faint at all."

"You don't remember?" Sarah asked.

"It happened so quickly. A car came from nowhere."

"But you hit the car in front?" Sarah said.

"Yes, but behind, there was someone behind me."

Tony shook his head. "We have gone over this so many times, I don't want to hear it again, not today, Vivienne."

"But I think someone was following us, someone was driving very close behind me. Don't you see what I am trying to say?"

"No, I don't, you don't even remember the full story." Tony finished his drink and stood up. "Come on, Sarah, let's go."

Sarah rose from the table. Vivienne looked up at Tony. "Don't leave me here like this," she said.

"Try to sleep," he said, putting his hand on her shoulder. "Take the pills the doctor gave you. You must sleep, Viv."

"And you? Can you sleep?"

He shrugged. "I'll come back later. We can eat together tonight, if Mamma cannot cook I shall make us something here, okay?"

Vivienne nodded and they left.

"I am tired, Sarah, tired of this," he said, as they walked down the steps from his mother's house.

"Today was the hardest bit," she said, squeezing his hand.

"You think so? I fear it is yet to come."

As the days passed she thought Tony was right, perhaps it would get harder, living with the grief. She could see he was withdrawing from her more and more, but wondered if he was confiding in Vivienne, visiting his mother as he did every day. Sarah gave up going with him, she couldn't face those sessions. She wasn't part of the grieving family, no matter how hard she tried to be. She felt guilty and excluded. Guilty that she couldn't feel the grief as they did and excluded because she didn't. She felt selfish because she wanted it all to go away and life to be lighter again. Not that it had been all lightness before; she hadn't forgotten that Tony was involved in a mystery that remained unsolved. But she couldn't ask him about it, not now, not after the death. But she felt as if she was waiting, waiting for everything to be better, waiting to breath again.

She ran into Roland on the Corso one afternoon, a week after the funeral.

"Will you come for a drink?" he asked her.

"Only if that drink is a coffee," Sarah said. "No alcohol."

He hesitated. "Okay. Though you may be in need of it, I should think."

She looked at her watch. "It's too early."

"Never too early for a drink, but anyway, I have been cutting back on the booze, as it happens. I've even lost a few pounds." He managed a smile.

He was looking better, she noticed, not quite so bloated and red. His bruises had healed and his skin was slightly tanned. They went to the small café near Tony's house, the Condorelli. Sarah hadn't been there since that day of shock when she first met Vivienne, even though it was once her favourite café. They sat outside on the pavement, the cars and scooters heedless of the pedestrians strolling across the narrow streets to the ceramic and wine shops.

"Are you proud of me?" he asked Sarah. "Here I am with a cappuccino, caffeine being the only substance to abuse around here." He took a sip.

Sarah nodded.

"I'm sorry about what's happened, Sarah, it's just terrible. I know it must be tough on you."

"Tougher on Tony, of course."

"Sure. God, I still can't believe it, he was just a kid." He shook his head, tears in his eyes. "I've seen Vivvie a few times, she knows I am here for her, when she needs me."

"I'm sure she will. She blames herself."

"I've heard the story, you know this town can't keep anything down. Gossip is for everyone here. No discrimination."

Sarah sighed. "Everything gets exaggerated, I actually think they thrive on the drama."

"And it sure is that. It's a tragedy, a terrible tragedy." Roland sighed, stirring his coffee, the tears still sitting in his eyes.

Chapter Eighteen

"Can't we get away, Tony?" Sarah asked. "It's too hot and it's too crowded here."

They stood in the yard, Tony was washing the fall-out of dust and debris from the building work on the house towering opposite them, three floors high while they remained at ground level. The brick walls of this house had been painted a mustard yellow and the empty shells of the windows gaped down at them. The drilling and banging and shouts of the workmen woke them early every morning.

"I cannot leave now, I am too busy. We get lots of tips at the hotel and play extra sets sometimes, afternoon teas and early evening *aperitivo*, you know, for all those fat, rich tourists."

"So we cannot get away, then, not even for a few days?" She looked at him, hesitating. "I just thought it might make you feel better."

He sighed. "Nothing can make me feel better. But at least if I am working I have less time to think."

"And Vivienne, is she staying?"

"Looks like it, for now."

"I am sure you like having her around."

"So we can remind each other of what we have lost?"

"Your mother needs her, I imagine."

"Of course, but she cannot stay here forever."

But she could if she wanted to, Sarah thought. She watched Tony as he watered the plants, the large earthenware pot with the jasmine tree, the hibiscus and small pots of mint and basil.

"Look, if you want to get out of Taormina, why don't you take a day trip?" he said.

"But I thought it might be nice for us to go somewhere together," she replied.

"It's impossible for me to leave, you know that. But you can do an excursion, why not. Go to Agrigento or Syracusa or up to Etna, or…"

"Catania."

"What?"

"Well, it would be good to go to a city, Catania is a city after all."

"Huh, pig of a place. I wouldn't go there."

"We've been there once, together, remember?"

"So why do you want to go again?"

"We didn't see much of it. I can get the bus."

"On your own?"

"Yes, why not?"

"I suppose so." He looked at her. "Are you planning to escape without me, go to the airport and fly away from me?"

"Don't be daft. Why would I want to do that?" She thought he was joking but he looked serious.

"I know I am not easy to live with. I know it is hard for you."

"Don't say that. You're grieving, I do understand, Tony," she said, though she did feel the grief was pushing them further apart.

"You cannot understand how terrible I feel." He threw down the hose.

She was silent.

"Look, if you really want to go to Catania, then go. But don't go looking too beautiful or you will never come back." He smiled.

She walked to the bus terminal, the curving road almost pavement-less, though she was used to car dodging. At the terminal, the small café had set out plastic chairs and tables outside on the broken road. Sarah sat with an espresso, breathing the fumes of the buses and delivery lorries parked to offload their goods. Packs of tourists were waiting for various buses, it was always unclear as to where each bus was heading and the announcements were incomprehensible. This often led to bus hopping as people discovered they were on the wrong bus, which the drivers seemed to take delight in. Sarah made sure she was on the right bus, asking the driver as he clipped her ticket. He was smiling at her suggestively, laughing at her stuttered Italian. She snatched back her ticket with a *grazie*. They gave her the creeps these men, so full of themselves, trying it on with every female in sight but it was unimaginable that anyone could ever fall for them, at least it was to her, though she knew in reality there were plenty of lonely women who did.

Finally they set off, the big blue bus steering out of the terminal onto the road with some difficulty, slowly manoeuvring on its way, holding up the traffic and beeping as it turned the treacherous corners, almost colliding with cars coming up as they drove down the mountain curves over the coast from the town. She looked out of the window, the coffee burning in her stomach. She felt the thrill of going alone, now they were on the way. This was an adventure, she thought to herself, feeling faintly excited as well as apprehensive. She needed to get away for the day, be by herself, away from the grief, she felt exhausted by it, as well as guilty. Reassurance had always came in the bedroom, Tony was an expert at that, but since Roberto's death all that had changed. She understood why, of course she did, but still she missed the intimacy. He called to check she was safely on the bus, telling her to let him know when she arrived, making it sound as if she was going on a dangerous expedition.

Through Giardini-Naxos they drove, the Blackpool of Sicily, she called it, with its *lungomare*, the long beach walk of tacky shops, cafés and bars and penny arcades; filled with an assortment of fat families and prancing, posing beach bodies, shuffling in flip-flops; noisy, polluting scooters on the road beside them. Then they were speeding on the highway, past the lemon and orange groves, the ruins of old villas, Etna steaming in the distance, hidden behind the haze of heat.

Finally, there was the old charm of Catania, the run down outskirts with graffiti on the walls, she read the scrawl 'John Travolta' as the bus passed, which made her smile. There were also the Catanesi slums like ghettos, blocks of shabby apartments, overgrown wastelands and rubbish everywhere. Tony had warned her about the packs of wild dogs roaming the streets at night. But she didn't intend to be walking the streets at night.

She stepped off the bus, a city at last, she breathed more easily even though it was very hot. She clocked in with Tony, telling him she had arrived and all was well. He told her to be careful. She promised she would. As she walked through the insalubrious outer area to reach the centre, past the corner bar full of men inside drinking coffee standing up, others loitering outside on their mobile phones, she hurried, clutching the map Tony had drawn for her, and continued until she came to the long avenues of shops off the huge main square paved in lava, its fountain and Baroque cathedral recently restored. There were the same designer shops as Taormina: Calzedonia, Intimissimi, Yamamay, but exclusive to the city was The Hard Rock Café and Macdonalds. There were many traditional cafés and bars, and two department stores Coin and Rinascente. Off one of the main roads was a small international shop selling sacks of basmati rice, frozen spring rolls, curry pastes and chocolate covered pretzel sticks. Next door there was a tea shop selling all types of tins of tea and other English fare, like Walkers shortbread. She bought a packet and ate two fingers while walking the strange lava-paved streets.

She encountered one of the small round kiosks famous for their juice: green, orange or red coloured syrup with half a lime squeezed in a small hand press and mixed with water. She handed over her euro and sipped the sweet livid green liquid in the plastic cup, not sure if she really liked it. Lonely men loitered at empty bus stops, looking at her. She wandered back through the maze of the market, stalls of veggies and fruits, kilos of oranges and tons of fish, hanging pigs and piles of potatoes. Bewildering rows of endless gear, cds and dvds, make-up and toiletries, cakes and biscuits, sweets and chocolate, the Chinese selling lycra underwear, vests and toe socks, pjs and sexy nylon nighties, shoes and slippers, woollen jumpers and cardis. All alone was a tiny Indian stall set up with onion bahijs and pakoras and sticky gulab jaman. Feeling as if she was back in Ilford Lane, she bought a small mixed bag for two euros and ate one of the cold cauliflower pakoras as she walked slowly past the boys shouting from their stalls, hoping to entice the passers by.

There was the Villa Umberto, cultivated gardens where it was said an elephant was once kept, though she was not sure if that story was true. She was walking up the slope to explore the gardens, an ice cream in her hand, when she was suddenly accosted by an old man wanting to take her for coffee, that much she understood. Shaking her head she walked away from him and left the gardens, afraid he might follow her. Crossing the road, she dodged the traffic and found herself outside a glass fronted café called Savia, shelves inside stacked with freshly baked *arancini*, rice balls or cones full of *ragu* sauce and peas, baked to a crisp.

She walked on up the wide avenue of Via Etnea, feeling free and uninhibited. No one here seemed to look at her, no one seemed to care and this is what she savoured. Finally, feeling hot and tired, she stopped in one of the many bars and cafés, unassuming exteriors hiding surprising depths, small tables and chairs crammed inside, where with a glass of wine you were presented with a feast: plates of *bruschetta*, pastry bites filled with spinach, mini pizzas, bowls of olives, peanuts, pistachios and other savoury snacks. She sipped her chilled *vino bianco* and nibbled on the dishes, feeling very sophisticated. Men standing at the bar eyed her, would-be playboys with their mobile phones stacked on top of their pack of cigarettes, shirts open revealing too-brown chests and flashy chains, pony tails or gelled up hair-dos. She ignored them but smiled at the waiter as he brought her another glass of wine, until she realised she hadn't ordered it. He pointed to the man standing at the bar drinking a beer, his back to her. She wasn't sure if she should accept it. As he turned around and walked over to her table she realised who he was. The boy in the jeans. "I didn't realise it was you," she said, standing up.

"We've seen each other so many times before how could you not? I am most offended," he laughed.

"I'm so sorry."

"That's okay, I guess you think we Sicilians all look alike."

"But I didn't think you were Sicilian," she said, looking at him as if for the first time, suddenly realising how handsome he was. Not a boy at all, of course. "Thanks for the wine."

"My pleasure. May I sit down?"

"Yes, of course, though I was warned about being accosted by strange men in this dangerous city."

"But I am not really so strange, am I?"

"No, not really."

"Who were you warned by, your mother?"

She hesitated. "No, my boyfriend."

"Ah yes, of course, your boyfriend. Your very jealous boyfriend." He laughed.

"How do you know he is jealous?"

"All Sicilian men are jealous, it's genetic."

She looked at him, wondering. "So, are you going to tell me, are you from here or not?"

"From here, meaning Catania, or Sicily in general, which do you mean?"

"Both."

"No, I'm not from Catania, but yes, half of me is from Sicily."

"At last, you've admitted it. Where in Sicily?"

"Piazza Armerina, maybe you've heard of it?"

"I have. It's famous for the mosaics, right?"

"Yes, but I think you have not yet visited, don't tell me, you got as far as Taormina and stayed there, like many others before you."

She laughed. "Yes, that's true. And the other half of you is?"

"German. My father is German, my mother is Sicilian."

"Quite a combination."

"He came here on holiday and fell in love. It's very common." He smiled at her. "Germans love Sicily. At least they used to, now there are maybe not so many coming here."

"Why is that?"

He shrugged. "I guess it's too expensive here. They go to other places in Europe that are much cheaper, Spain or Portugal, for example."

"I don't blame them. Overpriced and overrated, that's Sicily."

"You sound quite vehement," he said.

She caught herself. "Sorry, yes I suppose I do, I am becoming aggressively negative these days," she laughed. "Better not drink to that, not that you've got a drink." She smiled at him, feeling herself caught for a moment as she looked into his eyes, melting brown eyes, she noticed, feeling herself quite intoxicated, though she knew that was just the wine.

"I will have another beer then." He got up and ordered his drink at the bar. "There, are you happier now?" he said, coming back with a bottle of Messina.

"Yes. So that's why you speak such good English," she said.

"Because I drink beer?"

"No, because you are half German."

He laughed. "Does that follow?"

"Well, no, I suppose not. But England is not so far from Germany." She knew she sounded stupid.

He looked amused. "Well, I did learn English at school. I was raised in Germany." He smiled at her.

"So, why are you here alone then in this city of delinquency?"

"Just to look around, I've only been here once before."

"And your boyfriend allowed this?"

She laughed. "Yes, of course."

"Shame on him, any good Sicilian man would not have permitted you to come here alone."

"Well, he wouldn't like me talking to you, that's for sure."

"Should I leave then?"

"No, no, please stay," she said quickly. "It's so nice to have someone to talk to. I mean, well, it's just nice to forget, that's all."

"Forget what?"

She sighed. "My boyfriend's son was just killed in a car crash, eight years old." The words spilled out of her before she could stop them.

"Good God. That is terrible."

"Yes," she said, gulping back a large mouthful of wine.

"But, he is not your son?"

"Oh no, by his first wife."

"But you are not his second?"

"No."

"Not yet?"

"No."

"But you will be?"

"Yes." She looked down at her ring.

"I'm very sorry," he said. "It must be a dreadful time for both of you."

"Yes, it is, but I must admit rather selfishly that it has been good to get away for a few hours." There was an awkward silence. She sipped her wine again. "So, you don't live here in Sicily, do you?" she asked.

"No, I live in Germany. My parents married here in Sicily and then my father took my mother back to Germany with him where they lived all their married life. My mother only moved back to her home town of Piazza Armerina when my father died some years ago. I come here to visit her and this time we stayed in Taormina for a while."

"Yes, of course, I remember her. That's where Tony works."

"Tony?"

"My boyfriend, he's a musician at the hotel."

"Ah yes, my mother and I sat there in the bar one or two nights, she wanted to hear the sad songs of Sicily. Made her cry. She thinks of my father still."

She wondered if he had witnessed the scene there with Tony that night. "It's a beautiful hotel, one of the best in Taormina."

"My mother deserves the best, of course."

"But you're not staying there now?"

"No, I am here in Catania for a few days staying with friends."

"You don't want to live here in Sicily, then?"

"I love Sicily, I have been coming here since I was born, of course, but I prefer to live in Germany, it's green and clean, it's a good place to live."

"I can imagine. So, you work there, of course."

"Yes, I have a business. I take some of Sicily to Germany, the famous ceramics of Caltagirone, you know them?"

"Yes, of course I do." She had often thought about taking some of the pretty plates and candle holders home for Lily and her mother.

"So, I import them to my shop there."

"Where?"

"Berlin."

"How lovely."

"My father started the business and I took over. It seems to work well."

"So, you're not married, I take it?"

"Is it so obvious?" he asked, laughing.

"No, sorry, I'm just being nosy and asking too many questions."

"My mother would have me wedded to a good Sicilian girl from her town."

"Are there any of those left?"

He laughed again. "I doubt it. I'm not so sure I would want one anyway."

They talked for hours, she drank more wine and he drank more beer, and when she looked at her watch it was after eight o'clock. "Oh no, it's late, I have to get my bus!" She stood up, in a panic.

"You do?"

"Yes, I have half an hour to get to the bus station."

"Okay, I can walk there with you."

"No, really you don't have to do that. I lost track of time."

"Me too." He looked at her. "It was about time we really talked, all that running into each other around town."

"Yes, I'm sure I shall see you again there."

"No. From here I am going back to see my mother in PA, as I call it."

"Oh, that's nice."

"But I can give you my number, maybe you can visit us there, it's a beautiful place."

"Perhaps," she hesitated.

"I don't even know your name. I'm William." He held out his hand, rather formally.

"Sarah." They shook hands and exchanged numbers. "I must dash," she said, bending to retrieve her bag from under the table, feeling flustered. "I need to pay my bill."

"No, please, allow me."

She could feel her face flushing as she stood up. "Thank you, it was lovely to meet you, I mean it was good to talk to you, finally."

He stood in front of her and kissed her on both cheeks. "*Ciao, bella*," he laughed.

"*Ciao*," she looked into his eyes and felt dizzy for a moment. Definitely too much wine, she told herself.

She ran out of the café and up the road, past all the shops and stores which would be open till late in the evening. As she ran, stopping every now and then to catch her breath, she wondered if William would follow her, but he didn't. She walked back up the broken old street leading to the bus station, passing Chinese gadget shops and motorbike repair shops, the pavement full of rubble and holes. Opposite was a fair ground and looking up she could see the full moon in the darkening sky behind the big wheel. Reaching the large bus station, she had to check the stops for the right one. At least it was more organised here, but then it had to be, the buses went all over the island. She looked up and read the names of towns she hadn't even heard of. She wondered if there was a bus going to Piazza Armerina. Of course there would be. Sitting down, feeling hot and dusty after the run, she looked at her reflection in the glass of the bus stop. In her floral skirt and strappy top she looked girlish, not the sophisticated woman she had felt herself to be while talking to William. She sat on the bench and waited with the crowd for the bus back to Taormina.

Suddenly he was there beside her.

"What are you doing here?" she said, standing up.

"You forgot this." He held out her silver hoop ear-ring.

"Oh..." she reached up to her ears not realising she had lost one. "It must have fallen off, how odd I didn't hear it."

"No, but it was under your chair."

"And you came all this way, how kind."

"It was my pleasure." He smiled.

She slipped the ear-ring back on. The bus pulled up and everyone started to push on to it. "Well, I must try to get on, thank you so much and thanks again for a lovely afternoon."

He kissed her again, this time a soft kiss on her lips. "Goodbye," he said, looking into her eyes.

Momentarily stunned, she stepped up onto the bus, looking back at him. He waved to her as the bus pulled away.

It was dark as the bus weaved its way back up to Taormina. She could see the red lava running down the mountain in the darkness, the moon above, glowing and golden in the dark sky. She shivered as she thought of William and his unexpected kiss. She checked her phone, strange that Tony hadn't called. He would be at the hotel now so there was no point calling him. As the bus drove up the winding roads, the sea shimmering in the darkness, she could feel her head beginning to ache. Perhaps she had drunk too much wine.

She got home just before ten. The house was in darkness. Sammy needed feeding. She mashed up his tinned sloppy stuff with the hard nuggets of food. Her head was throbbing. She lay down on the sofa in the darkness. She started to feel sick, then waves of cramps contracted in her stomach and she sat on the toilet, vomiting into the bidet, freezing and shivering, feeling it would never end. Was it the wine, she wondered, or the Indian stuff that her stomach was unaccustomed to. She finally crawled into bed feeling cold and empty. She wrapped a blanket around her shivering body and slept.

In the morning she was sick again, she couldn't keep down the coffee Tony made for her.

"See, this is what happens when I let you go to Catania," he moaned. "What on earth did you do there? Spend all day drinking?"

"No, course not," she said, emerging from the bathroom again, feeling guilty that she had indeed spent the afternoon drinking with another man. "Maybe it was those spicy things, I brought you some home to try."

"No thanks."

"I also bought you some jazz cds." She took them out of her bag and put them on the table in front of him.

He looked at them and softened. "Thank you, these I do not have. Miles Davis and Oscar Peterson."

"I know, that's why I bought them."

"Are you feeling better now?" he asked.

"Not really."

He looked at her, shaking his head.

She was due to start a new month of her pills and as she took out the old packet from the bottom drawer of her bedside cabinet, she noticed something: there was one tiny pill still in the pop-out. Her stomach lurched. How could there be, how could she have forgotten to take the pill and not see it still there in the packet? It was impossible, she never forgot her pill, never. She sat on the bed, still holding the packet.

Chapter Nineteen

Tony had gone to see his mother after breakfast, as usual. Sweating and shaking she pulled on her sundress and not even bothering to wash her face, she ran to the pharmacy, the green cross outside flickering on and off. Wrapping up the box in the green and white paper stamped with *'La Farmacia al tuo servizio'*, 'at your service', as if it were gift wrapping, the heavily made-up woman behind the counter didn't say a word as Sarah handed over the money. Of course she wouldn't, but the expression of disdain was evident on her face. Sarah thanked her and took the box.

She ran back home and did the test. One blue line. It was one blue line.

She sat on the edge of the bath, holding the white stick in her hand. It couldn't be right, it wasn't possible, one missed pill and she was pregnant, how could she be, since Roberto's death they had hardly made love. Then she remembered the night Tony returned from Paris, he had been almost desperately passionate, as if to forget for a moment the tragedy. Maybe that's when it happened. She bit her thumbnail, wondering how she could tell Tony. Having just lost a child how could she tell him he was going to have another. She didn't know what to do. Go to a doctor. But not here. But she couldn't go home, she couldn't tell her family what had happened. What was she going to do? She put the stick back into the box, wrapped it back up in the chemist paper and stuffing it into a carrier bag, took it out to the big bins on the corner of the street. The lid crashed down with a thump, dust and flies scattering. She walked alone to the public gardens, not even taking

Sammy. She had to think. She sat on a hot wrought iron bench, dazzled by the sun full in her face, flickering on the sea below.

Her phone rang and she looked down at it in her hand, fearing it might be Tony, probably the only time she hadn't wanted to hear from him. She didn't know the number. "Hello," she said, noticing her hand was shaking.

"It's me, remember me?"

"William?"

"Yes. You don't remember?"

"Of course I do. How could I forget you?"

"How are you?"

"I'm okay."

"Only okay?"

She burst into tears.

"Sarah? Are you there?"

"Look, I'm sorry, I must go. It's not a good time at the moment."

"You are crying, I can hear you, what's happened, what's wrong?"

"Nothing, really. I must go."

"Please, don't hang up, I have to tell you something."

"What?" she sniffed.

"I am going to PA to stay with my mother before I go back to Germany."

"Oh yes, how nice for you."

"But I am coming to Taormina first, for the day, at the end of the week, on Friday, in fact."

"Oh, are you?"

"Can I see you?"

"I don't know."

"You don't want to see me?"

"No. Yes. I mean, I don't know."

"I understand."

"No, I would like to see you."

"You mean yes, then?"

"I mean yes." She laughed.

"We could meet about eleven in the morning, outside the gardens, does that sound convenient?" He sounded so correct.

"Yes."

"Perhaps then you can tell me what is wrong?" he said.

"Perhaps."

She sat looking out at the view, wondering if the test could be wrong, sometimes these things were wrong.

"Sarah, are you okay, you haven't been well the last few days," Tony said, putting down her cup of coffee on the table.

"It's just a bug or something I ate from that dodgy Indian stall." She looked up at him. She couldn't bring herself to tell him, not yet. They were more like strangers these days, how could she tell him she was expecting his baby?

"I never trust food like that."

"Not unless it's covered in pasta, right?"

"What?"

"Never mind, it was just a joke."

It was almost a month since Roberto had died and it showed on Tony's face, the grief had aged him, he looked sad and tired. He was working hard of course but was that really all he was doing, she wondered. She hadn't forgotten that afternoon she had followed him.

"What do you think happened to those two men, Tony, do you remember them?" she asked.

"What two men?"

"The heavies as I called them. The men in black. You remember them."

"Oh, those two." He shrugged. "I don't know."

"Maybe they got arrested," she said.

Tony laughed. "I doubt it."

"But what was it all about?"

"Nothing that concerns us."

"Maybe not." She hesitated. "I followed you one afternoon."

"What? You did what?" He choked on a mouthful of coffee.

"I followed you." She could see the shock on his face.

"You followed me? Why?"

"I just wondered what was going on," she said.

"Going on? What are you talking about?"

"You met some man."

"What man?"

"I don't know who he was. He gave you a bag."

"A bag?"

"Up at the castle."

"The castle?"

"The *castello* at Madonna della Rocca."

"I don't know what you are talking about, Sarah." His face was reddening, she could see it beneath the brown.

"What was in that bag, Tony?

"You must mean Mario and his tennis gear, he is always leaving it with me."

"No, I do not mean Mario and his tennis gear."

"I don't know what you mean then," he said, looking angry. "It wasn't me, Sarah, you must be imagining things."

"It was you, Tony."

"I think you've gone mad. You haven't been the same since that trip to Catania. I should never have let you go."

She shook her head, realising he wasn't going to tell her the truth. "Maybe it was someone who looked like you. All Sicilians look alike after all." She got up from the table and cleared away the breakfast plates, unable to eat her toast again this morning. "I should come and see your mother and Vivienne with you," she said, changing the subject.

"You don't have to." She could see he was trying to recover from their conversation, lighting a cigarette and getting ready to leave.

"But I never do. I haven't seen them for ages."

"Come, then," he shrugged, "if you want. I'm going now, I shall see you there."

She arrived at Carlotta's, the sun streaming in through the open balcony doors. Vivienne already had a gin and tonic in her hand, Sarah noticed and it wasn't even midday. Carlotta was sitting in her comfy chair knitting, Tony on a stool beside her, talking to her quietly, stroking the thin skin of her arm. He ignored Sarah.

"I don't see you these days, Sarah, where do you run off to all the time?" Vivienne took sips of her drink in between puffs of her cigarette.

"I don't run off anywhere," she said.

"Antonio told me all about your day in Catania, what a brave girl you are," she mocked.

"It was nice." She thought about William, feeling guilty.

"You could have taken me with you, but maybe you prefer to be alone?"

"We could go together, next time."

"Oh, so there is going to be a next time, Antonio did not forbid you to go ever again?"

"Course not, why should he?"

Vivienne shrugged. "You know Antonio. He can be very possessive. But I think you are like me, you feel stuck here, so did I, believe me."

"But you are here now."

"Ah yes, here I am, a voluntary prisoner. This is true."

"But what about your job in Paris?"

"I gave it up."

"Just like that?"

"Yes."

"But how will you live?"

Vivienne started to cry. "I don't know, I don't want to live. Not without Roberto."

"Oh Vivienne, I'm so sorry." Sarah felt mean.

"It's the pain, you know, it will not go away. I don't know what to do. I know I must go back to Paris, you are all sick of me here."

"I imagine you are great comfort to Carlotta."

"She needs me, yes, maybe, but as for you and Antonio..."

"But what do you need?"

"I need my son back. I need my son." She got up and refilled her glass. "This helps, by the way, so don't judge me," Vivienne looked at her as she sat back down at the table.

"I'm not judging you."

"Rollie helps too. He was good to me once. Years ago." She looked far away as if into her past. "He is a good man, in fact. Drinks too much but we can all do that, even you, little perfect Sarah."

"Yes, of course I do."

"I have heard."

"Really?"

Vivienne laughed. "Don't worry, don't look so shocked. Would you like a gin?"

"No, thanks." She sighed, thinking of the baby and wondering what on earth she was going to do.

She felt nervous and guilty as she got ready Friday morning. How could she see William again, what did she think she was doing, what about Tony? But she was trying not to think about Tony. He had gone out early, he was dealing with some business, he said, and would be gone most of the day. She brushed her soft shiny hair and slipped on the pretty red dress Tony had bought for her from the ultra snooty Deborah of Fifth Avenue, red wedges on her slender feet and a small red bag completing the outfit. She looked down at her flat tummy, no signs of anything. If she didn't think about it maybe it would go away.

They met by the entrance of the public gardens. Sarah could see the tourists sitting outside the café, looking out at the view of Etna, sitting on plastic chairs eating frozen pizza, thinking this was the real Sicily. Unfortunately it was, she thought.

He was there already, waiting for her outside the gates to the gardens, leaning against the wall.

"This is where I first met you," he said. "Do you remember? You were eating your ice cream."

"Yes, of course I do."

"But we shouldn't be seen together here, all eyes are watching," he said.

"This is sinister Sicily and now you are in twilight Taormina, I warn you," she laughed.

"I am not joking, I know this town, *mamma mia*."

"But you stayed here for a while, it was okay then, wasn't it?"

"Yes, but that was different, I was with my mother. You are not my mother." He looked at her and she blushed.

"Shall we go somewhere else then?" she said.

"I think we should, I can drive us out of town."

His car was parked on the long road stretching over the bay down at Giardini Naxos. "Look, all of the town is falling down the mountain," he said, as they walked, looking over the low wall at the rivers of rubble the rocks had made, gouging out the earth.

"Good riddance," she said. "Let it fall."

"I have a feeling you do not like it here very much," he said.

"It's beautiful, of course it is, but the beauty is not maintained. Look down there, at the masses of concrete eating up the countryside, the hotels are building higher and higher without restriction. There is no conservation or preservation, the authorities are allowing the town to go to ruin. It's scandalous."

"That is called corruption, I think."

"Exactly, and that is what I hate." She sighed. "It isn't just that. This town is claustrophobic and oppressive. It's all so inevitable here."

"Inevitable, how?"

"Nothing ever changes."

"But that can be charming."

"In the summer it's the same old show, the stereotypical sun, sea and sex, the bars, the beach parties, the looks, the leers, the gossip. It's a town for tourists but they hate tourists. Everything is for the locals who act like they are on a permanent holiday."

"Is that so bad?"

"Just you try living here."

"Yeah, on a permanent holiday, that sounds really bad, I feel sorry for you." William laughed.

"But I'm not a local, I'm an outsider."

"But you are living with a local."

"You just don't understand, do you?"

"I think you are exaggerating."

"But can't you see the differences between here and your own country? For example, in Germany there is a sense of equality between men and women, like in England. Here there is nothing like that. Women are tolerated or idolized but never seen as equal. Women might rule at home but this is definitely a male-dominated society and nothing changes with the younger generation."

"Sexism in Sicily is inevitable, I'm afraid."

"Sexism and sex in Sicily is inevitable."

"I'm laughing but you sound serious, I guess because you have experience of the Sicilian man."

She looked at him. "Do you feel more German or more Sicilian?" she asked, as they got into the car.

"You have scared me so much I have to say German."

She laughed. "You don't have to say that if it isn't true."

"Actually, I suppose it is. But then I have lived in Germany more than in Sicily. Have I given you the right answer?"

"Yes, you have. Genetics and environment have combined to give the best answer. What a relief."

He laughed. "Dear Sarah, I think I might be in love with you already." He looked at her and suddenly stopped laughing.

She looked back at him, too shocked to reply. Abruptly, she turned her head away from him, winding down the window. "Where are we going?" she asked.

"Forza d'Agro."

She remembered Tony promising to take her there but it had never happened, somehow he had never found the time. They drove up along the coast line until it was far below them as they climbed higher up the winding roads. "I always feel sick on these curves," she said, trying to restore a normal conversation. "Sicily is made up of them, never a flat piece of land to be found. That's what I miss. The flatlands, green open spaces." She could hear herself gabbling on inanely.

"Ah, but the centre of the island has fields, like those surrounding Enna, for example."

"Really? I thought they were all crop fields but I haven't been there, so I wouldn't know."

"You have seen very little of Sicily, I think."

They reached the tiny semi-abandoned town high up on the hill, parking in a nondescript square. The town was built uphill, *vendesi*, for sale, signs in every broken home, the wind whistling through all the cavities empty of life but for the Barcardi Breezer bottles and condoms, debris discarded into heaps, though this was once a home to someone. They climbed up broken steps, scraggy cats fled as they passed and a man sat on a chair outside his house fanning himself with a fly swatter. They came to the old church made of sandstone.

"This was where the Godfather was filmed, I think," Sarah said in low voice as they entered.

"They robbed the marble everywhere in Sicily, did you know, the original stone from these churches has all gone?" William said.

"Tony says it was sold to rich Americans for their villas."

Looking at the columns of stone and the two women sitting on plastic chairs near the altar uttering prayers, rosaries between their fingers, she felt like an intruder; in her short dress with her bare legs and high wedges she felt she would be deemed inappropriate. William walked over to the glass topped crypt covers. "See, they were buried down there," he said, beckoning to her. "The tombs are here beneath our feet."

"That's creepy," she said, walking over to him.

They looked at the old wooden confessional box and she sat on the white crochet cushion where the priest would sit. "Tell me your sins," she whispered to William sitting the other side.

"I have fallen in love with a woman who belongs to another man," he said, getting up suddenly and leaving the box. She remained seated for a while, unable to move. How could he love her, he didn't even know her.

At the top of hill, they walked through the crumbling cemetery, stone walls and dry plants, flies buzzing, flowers decaying and scattered in the wind. It was eerie and strange and back in another time.

"It's like another world here, isn't it?" she said.

"Let's go," he said, taking her hand. "It's cold up here, let's go down."

They walked down the treacherous uneven steps back to the relative flatness. There was a small café selling *gelati* and *granita*. "Shall we have something?" he asked.

He was so polite, she thought. Not like Tony who would tell her what she should have. She smiled at him. "Yes, let's have a lemon *granita*," she said.

Into small glass bowls the woman scooped the iced mixture, made from fresh lemons and sugar. They sat outside in the sunshine on wooden chairs at a wooden table, all rather rickety and ancient. She remembered eating lemon *granita* with Tony once, but that seemed a lifetime ago.

"I am sorry about what I said before," William said.

She shook her head, embarrassed.

"I know you think I am like the others, you have just met me and all I want to do is get you into bed, but remember my German half is reserved and correct." He laughed.

"I can believe that." She sighed. "But life is rather complicated at the moment."

"I understand."

"You cannot understand everything."

"What do you mean?"

She shook her head again. "You don't know me. You don't know anything about my life."

"But I want to know."

"No. You can't. Look, I shouldn't have come, I shouldn't have agreed to see you again, it was wrong of me. I'm sorry. Please take me home now."

They drove back in silence, an awkward, tense silence. He stopped the car at the gates of the gardens. Turning to look at her, he kissed her, a brief chaste kiss.

"Goodbye, Sarah." He pulled out a business card from the back pocket of his jeans. "Just in case," he said, handing it to her.

"Goodbye, William." She got out of the car feeling foolish, feeling sad. She watched him as he drove away, the card in her hand. William Glockner, black bold print on thick cream card.

It was early evening and she couldn't bear to go home yet. She walked through the streets but felt the limitations, no space to walk, no space to breathe, only the view of the bay and Etna, but even that was beginning to tire her. She remembered the day she had arrived, the fantastic view dazzling her, while Ruth waved away her rapture. Now she understood how Ruth could feel like that.

She saw Roland sitting at the new bar opened up for the summer, the terrace facing the famous view. He waved to her. "Hey, Sarah, where you going, come and sit down, it's a lovely evening, don't tell me you are going home to your hovel? Come and join me."

"I'm tempted to have a cocktail," she said, pulling out a chair and sitting down. She felt like she needed a strong drink.

"Hey, you sound serious," he said, "like you're about to do something really naughty."

"Well, maybe I already have."

"Done something naughty, you?"

"Almost."

"But not with me."

"Not with anyone. But I heard you've been seeing your Vivvie."

"Yes, as a matter of fact, I have. I am some comfort to her, which is rewarding. I love her, I can't help it."

"She needs comforting, that's for sure."

"Don't we all." He looked at her. "Are you okay, Sarah, you look flushed, though maybe it's just the heat, the temperature is rising around here."

She looked back at him, hesitating. "Can I tell you something, Roland, in confidence?"

"Course you can, you can tell me anything, you know that."

"Yes, but I have to be able to trust you."

"Well, go ahead, trust me. You can."

She took a deep breath. "I'm pregnant."

"Wow, that's great, congratulations!"

She shook her head. "No, it isn't great."

"Why? Isn't Tony happy?"

"He doesn't know."

"You haven't told him?"

"No."

"But, why? I presume it is Tony's?"

"Of course it is. But I can't tell him, not yet. It just seems so inappropriate after the death of Roberto."

"So, it was an accident, I take it?"

"Yes. I made a stupid mistake, I don't know how."

"A real mistake or a deliberate mistake?" He looked at her.

She sipped her margarita, knowing she shouldn't be drinking alcohol. "Genuine, believe me, this only complicates life even more."

"What the hell will you do?"

"I don't know."

"You must tell Tony."

"No, I can't. Maybe I just need to get rid of it and he will never know."

"Can you do that, do you want to do that?"

"I don't know what I want."

"Maybe having a child could be a kind of compensation for having lost one?"

"I am not sure if he will see it that way."

"Do you want a child with him?"

"I did."

"And now?"

"I'm not so sure. I think we're growing apart. Sometimes I feel like we are strangers. That day I followed him, well, it was like watching a stranger, he wasn't the Tony I know. And now, since his son died, it's been a strain. I don't think he needs me any more."

"Hang on a minute, what do you mean you followed him?" Roland put down his glass of wine.

"I didn't tell you? Oh no, course I didn't, it happened just before the accident."

"Where did you follow him?"

"He had a rendezvous up at the *castello* but I don't know what it was all about."

Roland raised his eyebrows. "You mean you didn't confront him?"

"I tried to but it got me nowhere."

"He's not going to tell you the truth anyway." He sighed. "Look, you don't have to stick with this guy but maybe having a kid will make you stick with him. Not that Vivvie did, she up and left, eventually, but you know once you have a kid it's no joke. I should know."

She nodded, wiping her eyes.

"You know, this is *déjà vu*, hell it is." Roland drank back his wine.

"What is? What do you mean?"

"Well… I shouldn't really say, but…"

"Tell me, what is it?"

"It happened with Viv, she came to me too, like this, when she got pregnant with Roberto."

"Did she?"

"Yes, but anyway, it was a different case entirely with her."

"How?"

He hesitated. "Look, I may as well tell you, all these secrets and lies all over the show, I hate it."

"Tell me what?"

"Vivvie didn't know if the child she was pregnant with was Tony's."

"What? But who else's could it be, mind you she had so many affairs, didn't she?"

"Yes, she did, but this was more than an affair."

"Who with?"

"Me."

"You had a fling, I know that."

"Yes, but something else happened."

"What?"

"Look, Sarah... Roberto is my son, he isn't Tony's."

Sarah dropped the glass from her hand, she watched it fall in slow motion, the contents spilling onto her sandal, the glass shattering onto the ground. She shot up out of her seat and started flapping a napkin.

A waiter rushed up and hushed her, bringing a mop and bucket. "Don't worry, *signora*, we bring you another drink, no problem," the waiter smiled.

She sat down rubbing her sandal and leg with the napkin. "I can't believe it, Roland."

"Well, you had better believe it because it's the truth."

"You are Uncle Rollie, of course!"

He nodded.

"Oh Roland, and now he's dead."

Roland continued to nod, tears in his eyes.

"But how did you get away with it?"

"Vivvie and I agreed that the boy should be brought up as Tony's and Tony would never know. As it turned out the kid didn't exactly look like me and he didn't exactly look like Tony, he looked just like Vivvie, blond and beautiful, so that's why we were getting away with it."

She thought of the boy, fat and fair like his real father, though that was the only likeness.

"But didn't Tony ever suspect?"

"Not that I know of. Vivienne had to have a test in order to be sure. She knows and I know but Tony definitely does not know."

The waiter brought her a fresh margarita and she knocked back a large mouthful.

"Hey, steady on, Sarah, you shouldn't even be drinking in your condition," Roland said.

"Right now I don't care." She took another mouthful and set the glass down carefully. "But why did she leave him, why did she leave her son here with Tony? Your son. I don't understand."

"She had a breakdown. She wanted to leave Tony and take the kid. But he stopped her. It got ugly and she left, planning to come back and get him when she could."

"What a dreadful mess."

"Well, all I can say is, at least this kid is Tony's, it is, right?"

"Yes, I told you that. I have not been unfaithful to Tony." She blushed, realising how close she had come.

"So, this would be his real son, if it's a boy, only he doesn't know Roberto wasn't his, and he never will know. Not unless you tell him, and you'd better not go and do that, Sarah, I'm warning you." He put his hand on her arm.

She looked at him. “Of course I won’t, I promise.”

Chapter Twenty

"Sarah, what is going on, are you going to tell me?" She could feel Tony studying her face.

"What do you mean?"

"You have changed, something isn't right, you look different, you are acting differently."

"I am not."

"Yes, you are, I can see it."

"You're imagining things."

"No, I am not, you have not been the same since you went to Catania."

"What?"

"I want to know what happened there. Are you going to tell me?"

"Nothing happened, don't be daft."

"Don't lie to me, Sarah."

"Why would I lie?"

"What are you keeping from me?"

"Nothing." She gulped a mouthful of her morning coffee, swallowing back the lies with her scalding coffee didn't come easy.

"Sarah, look at me, will you?"

"What?" She looked up at him, almost afraid.

"You cannot lie to me, tell me what is going on."

"Nothing is going on."

"You have met someone. That is it, isn't it?"

"No!" Her face flushed, betraying her, she could feel it.

"You have, I knew it," he shouted now, slamming down his cup on the table, spilling the remains of his coffee. "Who is he? Tell me, now!"

"Tony, stop it, you're frightening me."

She stood up, took her cup to the sink, afraid to turn and face him.

"I will not be made a fool of," he hissed, suddenly beside her, grabbing her wrist. "Look at me and tell me the truth." He took hold of her face with his other hand twisting it to make her look at him.

"Tony," she cried through gritted teeth.

He squeezed her chin harder, tears catching in her eyes, a thin wail escaping her mouth. "Tell me," he shouted.

"I'm pregnant," she managed to slur out the words.

"What?" he dropped his hands, deflated, and looked at her as if she had just slapped him in the face.

Her own face felt dislocated, like something from a Picasso painting.

"You can't be," he said. He looked horrified.

"But I am." The tears were rolling down her cheeks, she could barely feel them, tasting the salt as the tears ran into her mouth, surprising her.

"How?" he shook his head. "Are you sure?"

"Yes, I did a test."

"Your pills. You always take your pills."

"Yes, but something happened." She rubbed her face.

"Something happened, what happened? You had sex with somebody else? You did, didn't you?" His anger was flaring again.

"Don't be so stupid, of course I didn't."

"What then, tell me?"

"I missed a pill."

"What? How could you?"

"I don't know, I was trying to work it out. It must have been when you went away to Paris, I missed a day. I was so distraught, I think that's how I forgot."

"Forgot?"

"My routine without you, there wasn't one."

"Routine?"

She looked at him, afraid again. "I don't know how I missed one but I did."

"You did this deliberately."

"No, I didn't, I wouldn't, it was an accident."

"I don't believe you, Sarah," he said, the fury shining full in his face.

She backed away from the sink. "Look, I didn't want to tell you, considering what's just happened. But, I thought maybe you would be pleased?"

"Pleased?" he spat out the word, incredulous.

"Well, I used to think it would be nice for us to have a child and now…" she trailed off, unable to meet his eyes.

"How can you be so insensitive. Roberto can never be replaced, how can you think like that?"

"I wasn't thinking he could be replaced, but…"

"But what? How could you do this?"

"I didn't mean to."

"That's why you've been so sick, of course, how stupid of me not to realise. You have to get rid of it, and quickly."

"Do I?"

"Yes, of course you must."

"Why must I? Can't this in some way redeem your loss, Tony, isn't it a sign?"

"A sign? It's a disaster. I don't need this."

"And me?"

"Sarah, I cannot think of having another child, I have just lost one."

"I know that, but…"

"I can fix up a doctor."

"Oh, Tony, no."

"What else do you suggest?"

"I don't know. I don't know how I feel. I'm in shock."

"Not as shocked as I am." He lit a cigarette and started to walk around the kitchen table. Watching him made her feel dizzy.

He stopped. "I shall call my doctor this afternoon, he can recommend someone. We must act quickly."

"Right, that's that, then."

"Sarah, be reasonable, I cannot deal with this. Not now." He was making an effort to be calmer, not to raise his voice.

"But..." she hesitated, afraid again. "Well, I might want to keep it."

"What?"

"It's my body, it's my decision."

"Your decision? But I don't want it, can't you understand, I don't want a child."

"You don't want a child. But I might. Why don't you want a child with me, you had one with Vivienne?"

"We were married, it was a long time ago, it was different." He sighed, looking suddenly tired and old.

"Why so different? Just because we're not married? I thought we were going to be. You said we were."

"That's got nothing to do with it, Sarah, I have a son, I mean, I had a son. You know I didn't want another."

"And now?"

"I tell you, I don't want another. Not now, not ever. *Hai capito*!"

She looked at him, hating him at that moment. "And what if I tell you, you never had one."

"What are you talking about?"

"Roberto."

"What do you mean?"

"He wasn't your son, Tony."

"What?"

"He was never your son."

"What?"

"Vivienne betrayed you. You were not Roberto's father. *Hai capito*?"

He slapped her hard in the face. The force of it knocked her sideways and she fell onto the stone floor, cold and solid. "You lying whore. How dare you say such things."

She remained on the floor, the coolness soothing. "Go and ask your precious Vivienne if you don't believe me."

He left her laying on the ground. Sammy came and licked her knees, bare in her thin nightdress. She got up slowly, rubbing her bottom, feeling a pain in her lower back. That's it, she thought, I've done it now. She knew it was a terrible, spiteful thing to have done. Cruel. But he was cruel too. And selfish. He was always selfish, didn't she know that much by now.

Slowly she got herself dressed, wincing with pain. What was she going to do now? Find Tony. Go to Vivienne. Watch the explosions. There would be war and she had caused it. She walked as fast as she could to Carlotta's house but there was no answer. She stood and waited, her finger on the buzzer. No sounds within. She rang Tony's mobile. No reply. She ran down the steps and up the Corso. She had to warn Roland. She rang his number but there was no reply. She continued running along the Corso but kept stopping, a stitch in her side, pain in her back.

Eventually she reached Roland's door, panting. Inside she could hear voices. She banged on the door. The voices stopped. "Roland, it's me, let me in," she shouted.

"You bitch," Vivienne snarled at her as Roland opened the door.

"Where is he, where's Tony?" Sarah asked.

"He was going crazy, in front of his mother, he started screaming and smashing things, I think he wants to kill me, all thanks to you, you stupid bitch. You have destroyed our lives. Are you happy now?"

"I'm sorry."

"Sorry? Is that all you can say?" Vivienne cried, turning on Roland, crying and beating his chest with her fists, thin and hard, without strength. "Why did you tell her, Rollie, why oh why did you have to do this to us?" Roland held her in his arms.

"Look, Vivienne, I had my reasons, I am pregnant," Sarah said.

"What?"

"And this time it is his child." She knew she sounded spiteful.

"*Mon Dieu.*"

"It was an accident. But Tony doesn't want it, anyway." Sarah started to cry.

"What the hell are we going to do?" Roland looked at the two women.

"Call the police," Sarah said.

There was a banging on the door.

"I think it's too late for that," Roland said. "Don't anyone open that door." He grabbed hold of Vivienne. They sat all three huddled on the sofa, Tony shouting and banging at the door.

He broke the door down, flimsy as it was, and blazing into the room, he fired the gun.

Chapter Twenty-One

That night she slept alone. The smell of jasmine outside the window was stronger than ever.

The police caught Tony, not that he had run very far, and he was taken to a prison in Messina. She couldn't believe what he had done. The shot so loud, so sudden. She remembered screaming, Tony dropping the gun, running away, Vivienne fainting, falling to the floor, Roland slumped on the sofa, blood seeping out of him.

She had wanted to blot it all out. She took the sleeping pill Vivienne had given her and slept a dreamless sleep. But the nightmare was still there when she woke up.

Vivienne came to the house early the next morning and made them coffee. Sarah realised she had never made coffee, always leaving it to Tony, something as simple as making coffee she couldn't even do. She sat at the table, pale and shivering, feeling sick.

"He wanted to kill me, not Roland," Vivienne said. "You know that, don't you?"

Roland had launched himself across Vivienne, taking the bullet meant for her. Sarah was silent for a moment, tears in her eyes. "He shouldn't have wanted to kill anyone. But it was all my fault. It is my fault Roland is dead," she said.

"I loved him. I loved Roland." A dry sob shook through Vivienne's body as she said it. She lit a cigarette and watched the coffee pot on the stove. "When I was pregnant with Roberto, I went to Rollie first because I thought it could be his, I just didn't know. I didn't love Antonio. Not really. I used him, I guess."

"I don't understand," Sarah said.

"He was besotted with me, he would do anything I asked, I could have anything I wanted, so I married him."

"And?"

"I had affairs but then I fell in love with Rollie, as unlikely as it was. He was a different man then, much more attractive."

"And after?"

"I always loved Rollie, and being the father of my son I was always drawn back to him."

"But if you loved him, why couldn't you leave Tony and have the child with Roland?"

"No, I couldn't do that to him. Antonio wanted a child and Rollie didn't, he had already left two behind. I am not so sure if he even really wanted me back then. Only now, I could see it happening." Tears fell down her cheeks as she put the coffee cups on the table. "We lived with the lie. But what I did was unforgivable. Maybe for a Sicilian man this is the worst thing you can do."

Sarah sipped her coffee, noticing Vivienne had made it far too strong. She spooned in two sugars, stirring it for ages.

"He meant to kill me," Vivienne said again, her head in her hands. "This time I wish he had."

"This time?"

"It's not the first time he wanted to kill me."

"What?"

"When I wanted to get away from here, away from him, with Roberto. That's when he threatened me. And… well, he wasn't joking. He made it clear."

"That he would kill you? But how could he?" Sarah said. "How?"

"You know his temper, what he is capable of."

"I didn't know he was capable of killing."

Vivienne looked up, wiping away her tears with the back of her hand. "Antonio was capable of many things. " She hesitated. "You know he was involved, don't you?"

"Yes, but involved in what?"

Vivienne shrugged. "Money laundering, that kind of thing, all illegal involvements, of course. But he was getting in deeper. He knew a lot of bad people."

"That explains those two nasty men knocking at the door."

"They probably wanted money."

"The black bag. Of course, the black bag was full of money. All the money I thought he won from gambling. What a fool I was."

"He got caught up. You owe money to this one, so you do something else to wipe the slate clean, only you make it more dirty."

"He was involved with the mafia, you mean, working for them? Killing people?"

Vivienne sighed. "It's complicated. Mafia is a dirty word, but it means many things. It comes in many forms. Mostly respectable ones."

"How do you know all this?" she asked.

Vivienne shrugged. "It doesn't matter now. Do you want to see him, in prison, I mean? You can if you want, I will take you."

"No, I don't want to go. I don't want to see him ever again. Surely you don't either, not after this? How could you?"

Vivienne sniffed and drank her coffee. “No, I don’t. But I feel guilty too. Like you do.”

“I drove him to it, I know I did. But he is a criminal. He was never the man I thought he was. I just didn't want to see it.”

Vivienne was silent. “There won’t be a funeral for Roland, you know, his body is being flown back to the States,” she said, finishing her coffee. “That’s what he wanted.”

“At least his name won’t be plastered on posters all over town announcing his death,” said Sarah.

“And his legacy to Roberto, that comes to me now. The money.”

“Well, that’s something.”

“It’s nothing compared to what I have lost. I have no one left. Except Carlotta. She is in hospital, she collapsed, did you know?”

“No, but I'm not surprised.”

“I will stay here to look after her, I am not going back to Paris.” Vivienne lit another cigarette. “And what will you do, Sarah, you have lost everything too?”

“Not quite everything.” She placed a hand on her still flat tummy and thought of the baby, the new life inside her. “I shall go back to England,” she said. At last she would leave, taking something good from here, leaving all the bad behind.